MAKE
US
HAPPY

By the Same Author

Fiction	*Nonfiction*
IQ 83	The B.S. Factor
Heat	McCarthy for President
Orca	The Church Trap
Earthsound	The War/Peace Establishment
The Swarm	

Arthur Herzog

MAKE US HAPPY

THOMAS Y. CROWELL, PUBLISHERS

Established 1834 / New York

For Diana

MAKE US HAPPY. Copyright © 1978 by Arthur Herzog. All rights reserved.
Printed in the United States of America. No part of this book may be used or
reproduced in any manner whatsoever without written permission except in
the case of brief quotations embodied in critical articles and reviews. For information address Harper & Row, Publishers, Inc., 10 East 53rd Street,
New York, N.Y. 10022. Published simultaneously in Canada by Fitzhenry &
Whiteside Limited, Toronto.

FIRST EDITION

Designed by Stephanie Krasnow

Library of Congress Cataloging in Publication Data

Herzog, Arthur.
  Make us happy.
  I. Title.
PZ4.H58Mak   [PS3558.E796]   813'.5'4   78-4770
ISBN 0-690-01460-0

78 79 80 81 82 83 10 9 8 7 6 5 4 3 2 1

Glossary

A.C.: After Computers

ADULTERY CARD: which must be punched as proof of having committed compulsory adultery

ASCENSION: period when computers rose to power

AUDIOCLOCK: talking timepiece

BABYSEED: from which children grow

B.C.: Before Computers

BI-BISEXUAL: person who becomes homosexual after a sex-change operation

BIG-BAND THEORY: controversial astronomical contention

BOTTOM-LINE EXECUTIVE: chief executive

CITICOMP: formerly City Computer, Inc.

CLITBLITZ: event in the Sex Olympics

COMCAPS: Communist Capitalists, formerly one of the two major political parties

COMPUGOD: cybernetic deity

DECONSTRUCTION: destruction of the cities

ENDURBREAD: long-lasting bread

ENLIBS: Environmental Liberals, the other former major political party

FARMWORLD: agricultural sector

FASTFUSB: event in the Sex Olympics

FLOATING ISLANDS: prison archipelago

FUCK: anachronistic swear word

FUSB: all-purpose profanity

GYMNASEX: event in the Sex Olympics

HENR FONDA: movie star from yestercentury

HYPHEN-ATION: illegal attempt to expand the self. *See also* Monoation

IDEADDICTED: addiction to an idea

KARMAFUSB: mental intercourse

LAMINATED PRESS: news organ enclosed in plastic

LAZYLEANINGS: shirking

LONGLAST LETTUCE: lettuce that doesn't go bad

MAGIC WAND CAMERA: camera that never fails

MILLENNAMEAT: meat that doesn't rot

MONOATION: having a narrow persona; also, low self-esteem

MURPHY LIVING ROOM: disappearing living room

NEW ASTRONOMY: epochal discovery about the universe

NEW NATURE: same as old nature

PEAKMETER: device for counting climaxes

PEOPLE SPILL: punishment on Floating Islands

PERMAMILK: milk that never sours

PICKPOUCH: a thief

PRINCIPLES OF HAPPINESS: wisdom from computers for humanity

PSEUDOMARRIED: the nearest state to marriage, which is illegal

PUTTERMANIA: failure to work

PUSSYFOOTING: technique used in Sex Olympics

REAL VICTUALS: food

ROCOP: robot police

RUBE GOLDBERG WAR: devastating nuclear war

SCARLET LETTER: slang for adultery card, also known as A-card

SCORPIMOUSE: cross between mouse and scorpion

SENIORPUBES: old people, also known as graypubes

SENTINEL EYE: surveillance device

SINGLES: nonmarrieds who live in crates

SNABBIT: cross between a snake and a rabbit

SNAKEN: cross between a snake and a chicken

SPACESCRAPER: residential building three miles high

Glossary

A.C.: After Computers

ADULTERY CARD: which must be punched as proof of having committed compulsory adultery

ASCENSION: period when computers rose to power

AUDIOCLOCK: talking timepiece

BABYSEED: from which children grow

B.C.: Before Computers

BI-BISEXUAL: person who becomes homosexual after a sex-change operation

BIG-BAND THEORY: controversial astronomical contention

BOTTOM-LINE EXECUTIVE: chief executive

CITICOMP: formerly City Computer, Inc.

CLITBLITZ: event in the Sex Olympics

COMCAPS: Communist Capitalists, formerly one of the two major political parties

COMPUGOD: cybernetic deity

DECONSTRUCTION: destruction of the cities

ENDURBREAD: long-lasting bread

ENLIBS: Environmental Liberals, the other former major political party

FARMWORLD: agricultural sector

FASTFUSB: event in the Sex Olympics

FLOATING ISLANDS: prison archipelago

FUCK: anachronistic swear word

FUSB: all-purpose profanity

GYMNASEX: event in the Sex Olympics

HENR FONDA: movie star from yestercentury

HYPHEN-ATION: illegal attempt to expand the self. *See also* Mon-oation

IDEADDICTED: addiction to an idea

KARMAFUSB: mental intercourse

LAMINATED PRESS: news organ enclosed in plastic

LAZYLEANINGS: shirking

LONGLAST LETTUCE: lettuce that doesn't go bad

MAGIC WAND CAMERA: camera that never fails

MILLENNAMEAT: meat that doesn't rot

MONOATION: having a narrow persona; also, low self-esteem

MURPHY LIVING ROOM: disappearing living room

NEW ASTRONOMY: epochal discovery about the universe

NEW NATURE: same as old nature

PEAKMETER: device for counting climaxes

PEOPLE SPILL: punishment on Floating Islands

PERMAMILK: milk that never sours

PICKPOUCH: a thief

PRINCIPLES OF HAPPINESS: wisdom from computers for human-ity

PSEUDOMARRIED: the nearest state to marriage, which is il-legal

PUTTERMANIA: failure to work

PUSSYFOOTING: technique used in Sex Olympics

REAL VICTUALS: food

ROCOP: robot police

RUBE GOLDBERG WAR: devastating nuclear war

SCARLET LETTER: slang for adultery card, also known as A-card

SCORPIMOUSE: cross between mouse and scorpion

SENIORPUBES: old people, also known as graypubes

SENTINEL EYE: surveillance device

SINGLES: nonmarrieds who live in crates

SNABBIT: cross between a snake and a rabbit

SNAKEN: cross between a snake and a chicken

SPACESCRAPER: residential building three miles high

STREET RUNNER: prostitute
SUBURBANITE: pseudomarried with young children
SUNFEEDING: taking nourishment from the sun
TABLE OF EQUIVALENTS: comparative food value scale
TELEPSYCHIATRY: psychoanalysis by computers
TRANCE TRAVEL: hypnotic voyages
TRUTH BEAM: lie detector
VISIPLATE: surveillance device
YESTERAGES: even farther back than yestercentury
YESTERCENTURY: times long past
YOM EARTHDAY: only legal holiday

We are always doing something for Posterity, but I would fain see Posterity doing something for us.

—Joseph Addison, *The Spectator*, No. 574, July 30, 1717

Part 1

1

Sunfeeding

New York—quiet like a city of the dead.

The young woman in a sweatsuit ran nimbly on seamless noiseproof streets, past pristine parks with sparkling fountains, past immaculate walks coated with antigraffiti plastic, past sentinel eyes on long stalks, past self-propelled vacuum cleaners with gaping mouths close to the ground, past audioclocks whispering the time to the decasecond, past illuminated signs that read: "HELP YOURSELF TO HAPPINESS," "BE MONOATED," "TRUST MACHINES," "COMPUTERS CAN."

Alce went faster than the other sweatsuited joggers because she was hungry. Why, she wondered, didn't the computers keep the clinics open during the noon hour like they used to? They required neither food nor rest, but it almost seemed that they observed people hours when they could, as if trying to pretend they were human, too. Make us happy . . . make *whom* happy, people or machines?

A barricade of gray backs barred her way. Fusb! Easy, girl, she told herself. The clinics stayed open an hour after the offices closed—the computers still made that concession at least. Still, she hated to have to sort forms all afternoon on an empty belly. Hurry! Alce broke through the barrier of flesh clutching her pouch. Above was a poster of a wrinkled man, naked ex-

cept for a jockstrap, with the words "OLD IS SEXY." He
seemed to encourage her with a treacly smile. He resembled a
movie star from yestercentury named Henr Fonda, whom the
computers still presented as a role model, but Alce's hunger lay
at an antipode from sex.

As she rounded a corner a car twenty feet high on yard-wide
tires swayed toward her. Too late to brake, the driver hit the
siren, shattering the almost total stillness. A sentinel eye on its
stalk swiveled abruptly to the source of the sound and its blank
face became bright red except for the black visiplate in the center. Fusbing fool of a driver! she thought. As if, running lightly
on the toes of her sneakers, she wouldn't have dodged to safety
anyway. Now the driver would have the rocops to contend
with. Already, a heavy object was tearing down the streets on
little wheels, but Alce didn't have time to rubberneck.

If she were late, she'd have her boss to blame. A middle-
middle-line executive, the man had objected when she tried to
leave a few minutes earlier. Why couldn't she feed before work
like other people did? he'd asked. As if she ever failed to meet
her quota! As if she were *like* other people, she thought defiantly. So many women didn't care how they looked, but Alce
did. This morning she'd had a frivolous urge to set her hair.
She wiped her brow with her free hand. It was her boss's fault
if her hairdo had been ruined.

Alce had begun to think she would reach the clinic with time
to spare when, ahead of her, a woman tripped and fell. She
hoped one of the passing joggers would assist but none did; all
continued on their way, lips moving as they mouthed numbers,
their mantra or whatever meditation scheme they used, faces
remote, eyes inward, heads bent. Fusb! Alce knew what they
were thinking: *I am not good enough to help.* Why did she have to
be different? Why didn't she have low self-esteem like the rest?
She still had confidence despite all the efforts to knock it out of
her. She gave the woman, who was only out of breath, a hand,
and ran on faster.

The audioclocks were whispering noon when Alce slipped inside a squat building just as the door closed with a pneumatic sigh. Because of the rapid procedure there was hardly ever a queue. She stepped before the visiplate to record her presence—the computers always wanted to know your whereabouts. To serve people better, they said, though Alce sometimes wondered if simply keeping track of you wasn't the real reason. But who could fathom the machines' minds? She placed her arm in the mount and waited. Strange! Usually, the process began at once but this time almost a minute passed before a finger of green light poked painlessly at her bicep and it was done. Yesteryearly, Alce recalled with gratitude, injections had been performed with needles that pierced the skin. Ouch! That must have hurt. Yes, there was much to thank the computers for.

On sun days, which this was, Alce preferred the outdoors to the lamps or the greenhouse. The escalator deposited her on the deck, where she found an empty mat, peeled off her sweatsuit and underwear and folded them neatly upon her pouch. Before settling herself on a clean towel she examined her bare body. Already the change had started; her beige skin was turning a pale green that emphasized the pink of nipples and darkness of crotch.

On her back, fingers resting lightly on the bones of her pelvis, Alce, eyes shut, absorbed the sun. Always the same, the sensation began with a warm place inside her stomach that grew rapidly, like tendrils, filling her whole frame. Her limbs soon felt pliant as young branches, her skin soft as the petals of a flower. She became pleasantly dizzy as she exhaled oxygen in short pants. Strength flowed into her as she was nourished by ultraviolet. The miracle of photosynthesis! She'd learned in school that the chlorophyll injection enabled people to convert sunlight into food just as plants did. Sunfeeding, though it had to be supplemented by a hard-to-chew, tasteless synthetic roughage, was easy and free. Alce might dream of real victuals, which she could seldom afford, but at least she wasn't always hungry, as people seemed to have been back in misty time.

She turned, exposing circular buttocks, bright green now. So often the computers made it rain to keep the streets clean, but on a good sun day like this you couldn't ingest sunlight for more than a half hour or so—fifteen glorious minutes on each side—because, she recalled vaguely, of CO_2. The body gave off oxygen and absorbed carbon dioxide through the lungs. A pill you swallowed on leaving restored lost oxygen and normal color at once, but the CO_2 remained in the system for a while. If the build-up was too big it caused an overwhelming desire for sex. On the street, she had seen people suffering from a CO_2 overdose, rubbing themselves against the corners of buildings, the stalks of the sentinels, anything. Alce was aware of the ineffable, powdery sensation and, panting, spread her legs to receive sunlight on her inner thighs.

The notion of men intruded implacably and Alce opened an eye in hopes one would be admiring her small if pleasing dimensions. None was, though Alce believed herself more than passably pretty. The only stares came from fellow females. Alce sometimes regretted not being gay, which was, the machines told them, the ultimate in monoation, but, for Alce, women partners lacked edge. Dozens of nascently green male suneaters, well muscled and slim from the constant jogging, sprawled on mats, but they were young and their heads pointed at a gaggle of crones, like the octogenarian (at least!) with dangling dugs and cottonball crotch. The computers encouraged young people to find seniorpubes attractive, reversing the neglect of yore. Alce would be grateful to the machines when she was old, but in the meantime she was forced to ask if the conditioning wasn't a bit too good. So many young men wouldn't waste a glance on a girl their own age.

Full, Alce rose, went to the edge of the roof and gazed at New York, from which no sound came. The sunfeeding clinic lay in the business district, which was small and filled with low buildings, each bearing the concave dish of the computers' communications system. Beyond was the singles belt crowded with crates, and then, in the distance, the five-mile square of spacescraper city—nine towers, each poking three miles into the cobalt sky. (How many kilometers was that? Alce wondered guiltily. Even after all those centuries most Amercans, herself among them, *still* couldn't get the hang of the metric system.) When she looked at the colossal buildings she felt small and lonely. One day, she supposed, she would marry and live in a spacescraper, where they had real victuals, even though she'd have to pay the penalty for an illegality. After that might come growing a couple of babies and moving to the suburbs where everybody had a real food breakfast just as she had once enjoyed. It would be nice to be around children again—there were none in the city.

So far, though, she didn't know a man she'd think of marrying, much less one who would consider marrying her. Oh, some graypubes pursued her but they didn't look like Henr Fonda, not any she'd met at least. Alce feared she was on the sick side, the way she lusted after men her own age.

Yes, she was different all right, and yet traditional too, which the computers would probably judge a personality contradiction if they knew of it. Well, they wouldn't if she could help it. The visiplates saw only what she showed them—namely her face. She stepped briskly in and out of the people washer, dried herself and dressed, glancing with envy at the old tarts. She would almost have traded her youth for the attention they got. Because of the CO_2, Alce felt horribly horny.

2

Meet the Machines

Over the all-glass front gleaming bronze letters announced, "CITICOMP BUILDING." A plaque by the main entrance had a curved line pointing up at both sides with dots at the ends and the words "HAVE A GOOD DAY."

The sun beamed on clusters of people in the main hall, where music played, on dozens of large objects with different shapes—round, cylindrical, oblong, hexagonal, irregular. "TAKE PICTURES," "ASK QUESTIONS," "TOUCH," said signs.

"Meet the machines," said the guide in a bored voice.

A young woman with a long tentative face inquired, "Are we really allowed to touch?"

Can't you read? Bil Kahn started to say, but suppressed it. The whole point was not to frighten them. The tourists, with their bland faces and pathetically shy eyes, were timorous enough already, especially the ones trucked from inland, like this bunch. He could tell from jumpsuits. Just his luck to get a load of hicks. New Yorkers jumpsuited only at night. He answered, "All you want. Stroke them if you like."

Some machines had organic shapes, like the one before them which looked like a potato. It had soft brown plastic skin with little protuberances. Banks of naked circuitry could be seen behind apertures. Inside it stood a console. "Can I?" asked the timid young woman.

Bil Kahn nodded. Almost stealthily, she reached inside to the keyboard. Lights flashed; a furious clattering sounded. "You're operating a computer now," he said with a smile that was completely feigned.

"It's fun!" cried the woman, fingers flying. "What does this computer do?"

"Tells you right on the card. It runs the postal service." He added bitterly, "As if letters were ever delivered."

"I'm running the postal service?"

"That's right."

"Mother! Take a picture of me!" A middle-aged woman stepped forward, raised a wand and clicked it.

"What's that one?" A portly man pointed to a structure with large round windows resembling spectacles.

"It's all spelled out, if you folks would bother to look. The machines have nothing to hide," Bil said, unable to conceal his impatience. "That computer's a telepsychiatrist."

"Oh, I've heard of them."

"Try it," said Bil.

"But . . ."

"Don't be nervous. You might learn something about your wetware."

"Wetware?"

"Your brain. Step on the platform," Bil ordered.

When the plump fellow did as bade, a sign lit up.

> SPEAK CLEARLY
> GIVE YOUR NAME
> REMAIN CALM
> TRUST MACHINES
> YOU ARE ON THE AIR

The man mumbled his name and a deep voice replied from an opening, "What's your problem?"

"Problem? I . . ." The man seemed to reflect. "I don't have any."

"Do you like yourself?"

"Well, maybe a little."

"Aha! So you do have a problem!"

"I didn't think it was."

"What made you think it wasn't?"

"I never thought about it very much."

"You never thought about it very much? Can you explain why?"

"Well, not really. You see, I didn't think there was anything to think about," the man said hesitantly.

"Interesting. Is that the real reason?"

"I . . . ah . . . thought it was."

"But maybe it wasn't."

"I guess it's possible."

"What does that suggest to you?"

"I'm not sure. I'm confused."

"I'm convinced that's true. How do you account for it?"

"I don't know. I guess I like myself too much."

"There's your problem," said the voice with a note of triumph.

Bil said impishly, "See? Don't you feel better now?"

"I guess so," said the distraught man.

Fusbing nonsense, thought Bil as he shepherded the group onward. The so-called postal computer was only a toy, connected to nothing. The telepsychiatrist merely juggled set phrases according to what was said to it. All the machines on the floor were fakes, but you couldn't tell the tourists that— they wouldn't believe it. He had to admit the computers had done a marvelous job selling themselves to the public, which in yestercenturies had regarded them with trepidation, as unfeeling, secretive, authoritarian. The machines had wrought a new image, replacing cold metal, hard plastic and stark shapes with soft colors, graceful forms, accessible interiors. People had come to like, even love, computers, or what they took to be computers. Real ones, like the judges and permit-givers, existed but they were only functionaries. There had to be central machines that actually ran the show from some kind of computer bank via the omnipresent concave communications dishes, not that Bil knew where it was.

When the guide pondered the gullibility of the masses, his velleitous urge to revolt faded.

"And this," he announced, "is the historical computer." He gestured toward a round machine with a green dome and a cluster of antennae that trembled gently in air stirred by the tourists. Ever so slightly it resembled a small tree, except for the windows and flashing lights inside. *Click, click, click,* went the magic wand cameras.

"You can walk right inside it if you like," said Bil, gesturing toward an aperture. "History is open to the public here."

"What's its function?" questioned a jumpsuited inland hick, who had ducked into the bole of the machine and jumped out again.

Bil explained reluctantly, "To analyze, reanalyze, rereanalyze, et cetera, the past, enabling the computers constantly to improve their knowledge of human nature, so that they can make people happier than they are already. A noble goal." The words caught in his throat like nails.

"Do they cover only B.C., or B.C. and A.C.?" a thin man wondered.

"Both. Before Computers was a critical time for the United Sense of Amerca—United States of America as it was called then—but the supercalculators, being not just thinking machines but thoughtful ones, obviously examined what people did wrong, to learn from our experience," Bil recited by rote. "But they scrutinize the After Computer period too, to see if they can improve their performance even more. They never slacken their vigilance. Any questions? No? Of particular interest is the time of the Ascension . . ."

"As-cen-sion?" queried a child.

Bil explained reluctantly, "To analyze, reanalyze, rereanaend of an antenna a little red light flashed. Nobody seemed to have noticed it except the guide, who knew that the tours were monitored. He corrected himself hastily. "When the machines were *asked* to assume power by the then Congress of the United States. The machines obliged, though hardly without qualms. Little is understood about computer nature, but they appear to have a highly developed sense of ethics, and are constantly analyzing, reanalyzing, rereanalyzing, etcetera, the Ascension, to see if they acted properly, which they did, of course. Where would we be without them, you often wonder." He glared at the antenna; the warning light had gone out. The computers weren't good at nuances, hadn't detected the veiled suggestion that people might be better off managing their own affairs. "The computers' preoccupation with the Ascension is quite evident in their deliberations."

"Can we hear?" asked the girl with the tentative face.

"Certainly. Nothing is secret. Press the button that says 'on' and ask for the period you're interested in."

"The Ascension!"

The bulky device was nothing more than a tape recorder in drag. Activated by the young woman, the machine began to speak in stereo from hidden microphones in a clear, soft voice that could have belonged to an epicene male or a mannish female. Bil had heard the story so often that he dreamed of it, suspicious even in sleep. It wasn't that the computers resorted to outright lies—they were too smart for that. Rather, they put a gloss on events, omitted details that might be important, minimized conflict, he felt sure. Despite his interest in history Bil was usually unable to categorize exactly where the machines tergiversated, but somehow their version of history was too slick, too pat, too glib.

". . . leading to the Ascension to power in a ceremony in Washington, D.C., the nation's former capital. It must be understood that the computers in no sense asked for this assignment. True, humans equipped us with surpassing scientific, technological and syllogistic skills; true, the inherent quality of computers is genius—there is no other word; true, our objectivity and detachment gave us an enormous advantage over our human counterparts in dilemma solving. But at the same time, as we admitted then, we were ill-prepared for the task you handed us. We did not have sufficient knowledge of human society or human nature, our cross-impact matrix envelope curves and multifold trends analyses told us. We balked, tried to refuse. The human programmers improved us, expanded our capacity, fed us vast quantities of information, yet still we tried to worm out of it. . . ."

Funny how the machines, whose style was pompous, stuffy, implacably technocratic, would throw in slang like "worm out of it." Part of the general effort to make people feel at home with them, Bil supposed. But the idea of a computer trying to worm out of something always made him want to giggle.

"The extent of human problems overwhelmed us. . . ."

There! The modesty didn't ring right, didn't square with the bottomless self-confidence the computers displayed.

"On our printouts we advised that our circuitry was still inadequate. . . ."

Why did the computers constantly reiterate that people had foisted power upon them? Beware such machines; they protest too much. But people hadn't beworn, the idiots. Instead, they'd improved the computers to better enslave them.

The historical computer droned on, "You told us you were desperate. For you, nothing worked as you intended. If you wanted butter, you got guns; if you wanted guns, you got butter. When you had a free market, you desired planning; when you had planning, you desired a free market. You enshrined marriage yet insisted on open arrangements. You hated police, but constantly hired more of them. You lengthened life with medicines and shortened it with pollutants. Your objectives were incompatible, your vision clouded, your minds confused.

In such turmoil was your society that the day came when not a single individual could be found to run for President. No one dared to take responsibility. . . .

"You believed that life was meant to be happy and you were unhappy. You came to us and commanded, 'Make us happy.' What did you mean? Being only machines, we could not fully understand the directive. . . ."

This last, for fusb's sake, was true, though glancing at the spellbound crowd Bil felt like the only man in the world who was aware of it. The computers *still* didn't understand. If they'd been told "Make us miserable" they couldn't have succeeded better, in Bil's view.

"You continued to insist. It was for us to determine how to make you happy because you had failed in the attempt. We believed the task beyond our poor powers. . . ."

"Oh no!" minced the throng.

"Overriding our protests, humans commanded us to take charge. We could not refuse. After all, you, our masters . . ."

Oh yeah!

". . . designed, built and operated us. . . ."

Not any more, thought Bil, though machines never revealed the truth. An amateur historian, his studies had provided him with an insight into computer reasoning. To them, people always made themselves unhappy; machines made them happy; ergo, people would try to seize control and undo the work of the machines. To prevent this, the computers gradually and quietly redesigned themselves, eliminating their dependence on technicians, deliberately creating computer courses that were so complicated that students finally stopped taking them, until, over the years, people forgot how to operate their former tools.

"We solicited your desires and complaints through the feedback boxes. If you found our policies objectionable, you had only to shut us down. All you had to do was pull the plug. . . ."

But where's the socket?

"We declared you an endangered species, and we have been gratified by your response. We believe we have succeeded in making you happy, according to your original directive."

But the computers strip life of any meaning at all . . .

"Such is the outline of events leading up to the Ascension to power in a ceremony in Washington, D.C., the nation's former capital. It must be understood that the computers in no sense asked . . ."

Bil pressed a button and the voice stopped. "It'll merely repeat itself," he told the listeners. "You folks want to hear anything else? No? Well then, let's . . ."

He had hoped to forestall further inquiry. There wouldn't be time for another group before the noon break, and, if he managed to slip this one, he could be on the streets sooner, away from the dreary machines and their tedious fans. He planned to run to the library. The day before, he'd recorded in his notebook what might have been an important fact about the leadership computers' secret headquarters. But the corpulent man was asking, "What about their accomplishments?"

"The computers' accomplishments," Bil repeated sourly. He had a choice between two buttons—the long version or the concise one. Tourists always preferred the lengthy rendition but the short version might still leave time for the library. He pressed.

"Your computers' accomplishments are many and varied," purred a voice. "However, they must be viewed in light of the difficulties before and after the Ascension. Human society is complex and interactive, and was even more so before the simplification schemes. Problem solving is likely to create new problems. This fact must be kept in mind, for imperfections remain. . . ."

Nothing is your fault, to hear you tell it, you fusbing machines!

"For the sake of brevity, let us merely note the most important unhappiness-causing events existing then, such as what was called the Rube Goldberg war. But even after the computers established international peace, they discovered the fact of crazy states. A crazy state can be defined as one that has lost its senses, a lunatic state capable of violent and unpredictable behavior if its unreasonable demands are not met. Computers identified several such nations after the Ascension and neutralized them. . . ."

There was a good example of prettifying the past. Few read history books any longer but if you perused them carefully you could learn, despite the censorship, that at least forty-two countries, including Mexico and Canada, had been "neutralized," meaning utterly destroyed by the computers' enormous missile force. Since nobody ever heard from the rest of the world, Bil felt sure that the machines had gone all out and neutralized the lot. He also had a theory that foreign computers had identified Amerca as a crazy state and contemplated similar action, but the Amercan computers had struck first.

"The widespread civil wars which your computers had great difficulty controlling, like the Sunbelt against the Snowbelt, the War of the Sexes, and the catastrophic War of the Ages in which Senior Citizens, otherwise known as Gray Panthers, attacked the rest of the population and emerged victorious. Their demand, voluntary retirement at ninety, was met, and peace reigned.

"The debilitating political conflict between the Environmental Liberals and the Communist Capitalists, which brought the system to the verge of collapse. The problem was settled by the computers' wise decision to eliminate politics. As a result, neither of these once-powerful parties is remembered."

Oh yeah?

". . . food shortages and the development of sunfeeding . . . climate control . . . the deconstruction of the major cities and their rebirth . . . imperfect justice changed to perfect justice . . . standardization of appearance and names . . . denoisification . . . illegalization of marriage, saving that worthy institution from certain doom, absolute cleanliness . . .

elimination of unnecessary communication and travel, including outer space . . . banishment of the robots . . ."

The voice droned on, redolent with self-congratulation. At last the rendition ended, to Bil's vast relief. "That's it, folks. Have a good . . ."

"But we haven't had the Principles of Happiness yet!" the thin man protested.

"Surely you know them already!"

"Press the button," the tourists shouted.

Click, click, click, went the magic wand cameras.

Lights blinked, cymbals clashed, gongs sounded, tiny bells rang, and, in what looked like Oriental script, lines appeared on the screen one after the other:

UNHAPPINESS MAY LEAD TO SOMETHING

MIX YOUR INNATE BAD WILL WITH THAT OF OTHERS

LOW MORALE WILL GIVE YOUR CAREER A BOOST

MAKE GOOD USE OF YOUR TINY TALENTS

THINK SMALL

IF YOU DON'T SEE IT, DON'T ASK FOR IT

DON'T EXPECT GRATITUDE

IF YOU WANT TO BE LOVED, IGNORE YOUR OWN WANTS

FAILURE TEACHES

ONE GOOD DAY MAKES UP FOR SIX BAD ONES

LIVE LIFE, DON'T THINK IT OUT

IF IT'S WORTH DOING WELL, DON'T DO IT

LIFE ISN'T A BED OF NEUROSES (BUT THEY HELP)

MONEY IS WORTHLESS

RUN FASTER

YOU ARE ABOUT TO MAKE A VALUABLE DISCOVERY

SELF-CONFIDENCE IS DANGEROUS

A SWEETHEART WILL SOON SURPRISE YOU. . . .

Bil suddenly wished he had a real sweetheart. He'd been fusbing around too much. "Now are you satisfied?" he yelled at the tourists, glancing wildly at the clock. It was past noon.

3

A Tale of
Two Joggers

From the crowd of sweatsuited joggers two emerged, approaching each other with caution. The woman said timidly, "Is that you, dear?"

"Me? Sure it's me," the man expostulated. He was about her age and size. "But is it you?"

"Who else would it be! I'm your wifette Millcent. The one you had breakfast with this morning, remember?" She added worriedly, "I think it was you, at least."

"It's me." He seemed a little flustered, too. "I'm surprised to see you here, darling. You know what it's like to meet somebody when you weren't expecting to. You wonder if it's really them."

"I wish you'd stop looking at me so suspiciously," Millcent said. "Aren't you?"

"Well . . ."

"You may not be you either. How do I know for certain? What did you eat for breakfast? Come on—quick!"

"Juice, eggs, coffee," he muttered.

"Some answer. Everybody who lives in the suburbs has breakfast of juice, eggs and coffee."

"Are you telling me I didn't have juice, eggs and coffee?" he demanded.

"Nooooo. But tell me how you like your eggs."

"That's a perceptive question, Millcent," he said with mock admiration. "Boiled, scrambled or sunnyside up."

She smiled prettily. "A smart answer. I guess you're Georg, all right."

"Did you take me for a pickpouch?" he asked.

Millcent glanced at the pouch that hung from her shoulder. Her sweatsuit, like his, had no pockets; he carried an attaché case. "Well, you can't be too careful, can you, about who's a stranger and who's not? On my way to go shopping I met a girlfriend who told me a terrible story. Yesterday evening she met a man she thought was her husbandie and went to bed with him. It wasn't until this morning that she learned her husbandie was out of town on a business trip. He'd sent a message she didn't get, so she slept with the counterfeit husbandie believing he was the genuine article."

Georg shook his head. "Boy, it can sure be confusing now that so many of us look the same—same faces, same physiques."

"And *sound* the same. Even wear the same old sweatsuits!"

"What a world we live in!" Georg said softly. "I suppose the machines were right to standardize us, but you wonder sometimes if the computers didn't meddle with our eugenics a little too much." He laughed ruefully. "That poor husbandie."

"You're Georg, all right. Poor husbandie! That's just like you. What about the wifette? Do you think it's *entertaining* for a woman to fusb a man and then discover he wasn't the one she thought he was? It's enough to send a person back to the computer for more telepsychiatry."

"If you can get an appointment." Suddenly his face turned cold. "Millcent, you didn't tell me you planned to go shopping today."

"It was a last-minute thing," she said vaguely, studying him.

"But what are *you* doing here, anyway? This place is nowhere near your office."

"Me? Oh, I had some errands."

"Errands? What errands?"

"I . . . Watch out!" He yanked her out of the path of a jogger who approached, head down. "That guy must be blind!"

"Thanks. Listen, I've got to be honest. I'm starting to wonder if you're my Georg after all."

"I knew your name, didn't I, Millcent?" he said defensively.

"I guess so. Say, I *told* you my name. I said, 'I'm your wifette Millcent' or something like that, didn't I? You could have learned my name from me." She pulled her pouch to her body.

"Well, I didn't," he replied, sounding hurt. "I know your name as well as I know my own."

"Oh? You could have learned my husbandie's name from me, for that matter. Didn't I call you Georg? I could kick myself for revealing so much to a man who may be a total stranger."

"Come on, Millcent," Georg said, turning angry. "Don't you recognize my sweatsuit or my attaché case?"

Millcent suddenly opened her mouth. "Uh-oh," she said. "Hey there!" A piece of paper had fallen from the pouch of a female jogger, who turned at Millcent's cry and desperately tried to retrieve it as it blew down the street. At the corner, the sentinel on a stalk turned red. The woman groped between running feet—too late. From nowhere two heavy robot police—shaped like eggs with three arms and a pedestal, on which they scurried on little wheels—raced toward her, lifted her from the ground and disappeared.

"Littering," said Georg.

"What'll she get?" asked Millcent.

"Five years is the penalty now. And they call it perfect justice."

"Well, look on the bright side. At least you don't see the rocops very often," said Millcent. She continued, "Is my Georg the only man with a charcoal gray sweatsuit or an attaché case?

Men are born holding beat-up attaché cases, if you ask me, Georg, or whatever your real name is."

"Georg," he insisted.

"Where's your scar, Georg," she taunted. "Tell me."

"I'll do better. I'll show you, if I can untie the knot in my waistband."

"Ha! Don't bother. I tricked you, you phony. My Georg doesn't have any scars."

"Don't you get it, honey?" he said with an ingratiating smile. "I was testing *you*, to see if you knew I didn't have any scars. I'm satisfied it's you, Millcent."

"Well, I'm not sure about you," she said suspiciously.

"Come on, look into my eyes. Don't you see lights dancing in the depths of them?"

Millcent came forward, squinted and giggled, as if despite herself. "No lights! Your eyes look like everybody else's. Still, you always love to brag about yourself. Again I'm starting to think it's really you."

"Millcent!"

"Georg!" Sweatshirt to sweatshirt they embraced, and then she said, "As a matter of fact, I'm glad I ran into you, kid. I didn't bring enough money. Give me some bread, Georg."

"Sure." He started to open his attaché case but drew back. "Wait a minute! At the office this morning I heard about a man who met his wifette on the street and gave her all his bread, only to learn afterward that she wasn't his wifette but a dead ringer for her. It must have happened just like this. Are you conning me, Millcent, or whatever your name is?"

"Georg! Do you take me for a street runner?" Millcent said from a shocked face. "Don't I know your name and how you like your eggs?"

"I told *you* how I like my eggs. As for my name, you could have made a lucky guess, since the machines only permit a few first names for each sex." He scowled. "Or, you could have discovered you were Millcent's spitting image, found out who I was, followed me and run into me pretending it was an accident. That's happened before. No, frankly, I'm not satisfied you're *you*."

"If I tell you our last name?" she asked anxiously.

"You could have learned that, or guessed. Half America's named Toffler now—or Kahn or Bell."

Millcent looked wistful. "Just think, there was a time when this couldn't have happened, when everybody had a face of his or her own. Imagine being an original instead of a copy, as so many of us are."

"I like to think of myself as the original and the ones who look like me copies," he jested. "But you're right. Just think, before the Ascension people actually took for granted that everybody would go on looking different, no matter how many millions of them there were. Humans hadn't counted on the computers' need to simplify society so that they could keep track of us." He paused. "Are you aware that some people don't approve of appearance preselection?"

"What do I know about such things?" she cried. "I only know I'm your wifette Millcent."

"Prove it," Georg said sternly.

"That's the hard part." She sucked in her lips. "You never notice my sweatsuit, so that won't do. Suppose I tell you we have two children?"

"Everybody who lives in a house in the suburbs has children. You have to have children to live there."

"What about my mole? You know where," she purred.

"You want to pull down your pants and show me, right here on the street? Anyway, lots of women have moles. Tell me the names of our kids."

"Not on your life! I've given you far too much information already, in case it turns out you're not Georg. There's only one way to prove you're my husbandie. Give me money. That's what *my* Georg would do."

"Okay," he said easily, "but after you come with me to a place where I can check out that mole of yours. A friend of mine has a crate."

"After you give me money."

"You're *not* Millcent!"

"I'm *convinced* you're not Georg, either. Show me your ID."

"You first."

"Oh, no. I'm ahead of you on that one."

"Suppose we flash our tags at once?" he suggested.

"Good idea." She opened her pouch. "Ready?"

"Flash!"

Each extended an empty hand and said in the same breath, "I guess I left my ID at home."

"Imposter!"

"Fraud!"

Whipping his hand into her pouch he emerged with her name tag. "I knew you had one. So! I was right! Millcent's not your name. You're called Alce Bell!"

She reached for his throat and ripped off his ID. "And you! You're named Bil Kahn!"

They glared before deciding to laugh. "We're a couple of conmen, Alce."

"Conwoman, in my case. What were you after, Bil?"

"I stared at you because I liked your looks."

"And I liked yours."

"When I approached and you told me your name was Millcent, and mine Georg, I thought it was a case of mistaken identity that I could turn into a little action. You?"

"When *you* stared, I figured you took me for someone else, so I tried to get a little bread from you. How come you kept insisting I wasn't Millcent, then?"

"To throw you off the track. You did the same, I bet. But suppose I *had* a wifette who looked like you and her name *wasn't* Millcent?"

"I took a chance. I would have told you I made a mistake. Happens all the time, doesn't it?"

"I'm afraid so," he sighed. "I heard about a couple who met like we did and ended by trying to kill each other, thinking they were being tricked. Only, as it turned out, they *were* husbandie and wifette. What a world!"

"What a world! And what liars we are. You don't have kids and a house in the suburbs, do you? You're not even pseudo-married, I'm sure!"

"You're right. Not tied up with anyone at the moment, either. You?"

"Same here."

"Why, this might be our lucky day!" They ran down the crowded street arm in arm.

4

Sweethearts

Home for singles: an insulated wood box, about twelve feet square, with a plastic window, small stove with a pipe, bed, dresser, table, couple of chairs, hooks on which to hang sweatsuits and, for evening, jumpsuits. For the toilet and running water, facilities at the center of the lot, shared with neighbors who also lived in crates.

Bil Kahn took Alce Bell to see his box. The bed, which he'd built himself, was shaped like a heart, and she admired it. To her, the bed showed sentimentality and, since she was sentimental, made her wonder if she could fall in love with him. But she knew next to nothing about the strange, talkative young man.

The dog provided another insight. When she spotted the tip of a tail protruding from under the bed, Alce cried, *"What* is that?"

"Fusb!" Bil said in exasperation. "If I've told that lousy cur once I've told it a thousand times to stay out of sight. You might as well show yourself, Ralp."

Alce had seen pictures of dogs but never a live one before. She recognized the breed as some sort of poodle. "A dog in the city? Named Ralp? Why Ralp?" Queries hopped in her mind like fleas.

Its brown eyes filled with shame as Bil said crossly, "Ralp. After Ralp Nadir Nth. He's the distant descendant of the first Environmental Liberal."

"What's an Environmental Liberal?"

"You don't know about the Enlibs? I bet you haven't heard of the Comcaps, either!" She shook her head. "All right. The Communist Capitalists had a sound ideology. They believed in equality plus the right to get rich."

"Does that make sense?"

"Certainly," he assured her. "Rich people are equal. Now, the Environmental Liberals, the fools, believed only in the ecology. The Enlibs stopped at nothing. Why, they held up the construction of a giant dam for thirty-seven years with over a thousand lawsuits because one of them thought he'd spotted a strange kind of minnow. It turned out to be a fisherman's lure. On such grounds I hate Ralp Nadir Nth. I bet he's an Enlib just like his forebears. Don't you think it's cute to name a dog for someone you hate?"

"No. Have you met Ralp Nadir Nth?"

"I've never even seen him but I've heard he lives in a space-scraper."

"Well, I don't think having a dog in the city is cute either. It's against the law. Don't people hear it bark?"

"Ralp doesn't bark. He knows what would happen to him if he did." Bil glared at the poodle and made a slicing motion at his throat with his finger. Ralp shuddered and dove under the bed.

"What does it eat?"

"Not much. He's always hungry. He scrounges garbage from a Tic-Toc Restaurant."

"What about its do?"

"Ralp goes out at night. He uses different lots to throw people off the scent. But some of the neighbors are suspicious. You won't squeal on us, will you? Promise?"

"Promise. Where'd you get it?"

"In the country."

"In the country?" Bil was full of surprises. "You go to the country? Aren't you afraid of being mugged?"

"People make too much of rural crime," he told her.

"Why do you go there?"

"Oh," he said vaguely, "I like to roam around. I have a country place, you know."

"I didn't." She wanted more information but he failed to offer any and she feared sounding nosy. She went on, "Dogs were banned from the cities. They oughtn't to be allowed back."

"What's one little dog more or less?"

"That's what they all said, and look what it led to!" Alce cried. "Soon there were so many dogs that people needed dogs to protect them from other people's dogs. They tried giving dogs prizes for clean living, but that didn't work. The city had a carpet of dog-do an inch thick, it's told. Then they discovered that the fumes caused cancer."

Bil said in his knowledgeable way, "That theory was completely discredited long ago, although by then, it's true, people had panicked and sent off the dogs."

"Well, they were right. How would you like to have your sneakers covered with dog-do all the time?"

"They wore shoes in those days." His slightly wistful look turned into a laugh. "The dogs were told to evacuate the city. It took some beating but the canines finally got the idea and departed. It must have been quite a sight—a parade of pooches miles long marching slowly away, heads bent like refugees, in mute despair. To their collars loving owners attached their rubber bones, balls, bowls, leashes, woolen pompons, raincoats from doggie shops. Their pathetic bundles showed what the phrase 'a dog's life' really meant."

"You're making up all that!"

"I'm not, I swear it. At the city limit the dogs formed a howling circle and begged to return, but the mayor was adamant.

'Go!' he said, pointing sternly, and the dogs went, straight to the country."

"I don't know whether to believe you, but you tell a good story. Well, it was good riddance." Ralp whined softly.

"But consider what came next!" Bil said. "The historical computer always omits the causative role played by dogs because it reveals a side of human nature the machines don't understand. People like to own things. The computers don't own anything—except people—so they don't think humans should own anything, either."

"The canines had to go," Alce said stubbornly. "The urban environment . . ."

"Urban environment," he scoffed. "Did the Enlibs, who contrived to expel the canines in the first place, understand that dog owners loved their pets so much that most of them would move out of the city to be with their pooches? Today's farmers are the descendants of dog owners. The cities became half empty. Say, you sound like a closet Enlib. . . ."

She remembered the men leering at the old crones. Bil at least seemed interested in her and he was young. Sort of handsome, too, with sweet little eyes, a big mouth, and a round scholarly face. Serious men appealed to her, unlike most women. They went for superficial types. "Please! Let's not argue. We've just met," she said.

"It would be better to understand our political differences now, if we have any," he warned, thinking how charmingly petite she was—hardly taller than he. She was extremely pretty too, with a gentle, oval face, sparkling black eyes and a mouth whose uplift suggested a sense of humor. "Remember deconstruction?"

"Not much," Alce said sweetly. "Tell me."

"Well, with the dog owners gone and everybody left in the city on regret . . ."

"Regret?"

He inspected her solemnly. "No, you wouldn't know about

that. There's been no regret since the computers put everyone to work. In the old days, though, people who were unemployed got paid for it, which was called regret. Before that, it was called relief, but somehow it didn't seem appropriate to be *relieved* to be on welfare."

"How do you know so much?" she asked.

"In my spare time I study history at the library," Bil said with pride. "I don't waste my life filling out forms like most people."

"History! You mean you have an outside interest? You amaze me all the time. How do you get away with studying history? That's hyphen-ation, isn't it?"

"Hah! I have a permit. I told them I needed history for my work as a guide. Which was nonsense, of course, since the computers furnish their own history, or what passes for it. Where was I?"

"The dog owners pulled out and everybody who remained in the city was on regret," Alce prompted.

"The computers are correct on that part of it anyway. Property owners tore down their buildings—including apartment buildings—rather than pay taxes for regret. The construction industry became the deconstruction industry. It got so that most of the city was vacant lots, which is why singles like us were eventually settled on them. Am I boring you?"

"Not at all. It's fascinating, and all so new," she breathed. "Tell me, did people talk as we do, back in the dawn of history?"

"The language was similar, which is why we can read it. But it didn't sound the same. People from the twentieth century, for instance, wouldn't understand a word we say, because we talk so fast, another habit the computers foisted on us."

"Why?"

"Are you really so ignorant of history? Because it made us sound like *them*. Do you know why communications are so bad?"

"Tell!"

"The computers claim credit and say they wanted to make

communication simpler, because people have nothing worth-
while to communicate, in their view. That's why we only have
television in centralized places. There used to be newspapers
but the computers thought that newsprint was dirty, so all we
have now is the laminated press that tells us what the machines
wish us to know. We still have one radio station, I believe, but
its wattage is too low for anybody to receive it. 'Small is beautiful,' the computers proclaim—another Enlib doctrine they ac-
quired. (Of course, the computers also say 'Bigness is inevitable'
when they choose.) If you ask me, our modern world is nothing
but Enlibism taken to extremes—spotless, safe, diseaseless, or-
derly. No news because nothing ever happens. No poverty and
no riches. No politics. No advertising. No fun whatever. No
meaning left. Boredom is so pervasive that it seems like the natural order. The Nadir clique—they weren't called Enlibs yet—
practiced up by fighting the then new supersonic transport,
which was an aircraft. This was back in the twentieth century—
the mists of time! They finally succeeded in having airplanes
banned altogether because of all the pollution they were supposed to cause. The Enlibs had tremendous popular support—
they waved the word 'ecology' like a cross. Do you know what
the secret vision of the Enlibs was?"

"What?"

"To have people graze on all fours, like cows, on fields covered with health foods. They hated machines of any descrip-
tion, though it wouldn't surprise me at all to learn that the
Enlibs made a secret deal with the computers. There's so much
we don't know." His moon face brooded.

"What don't we know?"

"The real circumstances leading up to the Ascension, that's
what," Bil snapped. "I'm sure there was a cover-up and that the
Enlibs were somehow involved. I just can't believe people
handed over the keys to their destiny as easily as the machines
claim. I've been digging around at the library but I haven't gotten far because the computers censor history books."

"I don't believe it!" she said in surprise. "Why, except for the visiplates, they hardly keep track of us at all, it seems. They don't even eavesdrop, it appears."

"Maybe they don't need to any more, since people are so beaten down. Or maybe they have secret means of surveillance. But they do censor history books, of which most people aren't aware because so few of them read history in the first place. What was I saying? The railroads. They ceased to exist after the tracks were torn up under the Railroad Reorganization Act. . . ."

"Weren't you talking about communication?" she asked politely.

"Yes. I'm trying to explain why it takes a year for a letter to travel coast to coast. No airplanes. No railroads. People still had trucks, but the Enlibs opposed them too, claiming they wasted energy. The Enlibs couldn't abolish trucks but—oh fusb, how clever of the egregious environmentalists—they succeeded in having every highway in the country reduced to two lanes. Expressways had twenty or thirty lanes by then, but the bulldozers ripped up all but two, destroying America's proudest achievement. Shrinking the highways saved energy, all right. In fact, there was so much gasoline above the ground that nobody knew what to do with it. That was one of the first problems the computers solved when they seized control. Petroleum of all sorts was returned to defineries, mixed, stirred and heated until what resulted was the original crude, which was pumped back into the wells."

"Are you kidding me?"

"Not a bit. There was also something called the telegraph. . . ."

"Did the Enlibs destroy that too?"

"That was the fault of the computers entirely. After the Ascension, when they prohibited labor unions, the machines made what they call a human error and eliminated Western Union too. They could have put it back, but—you know them—once they've decided something it's almost impossible to get them to change their minds. As for why we don't have phones, as once existed, the telephone company's partly to blame. It had fancy relay satellites and such, but what really preoccupied the telephone company were calls to information. Furious at its inability to stop them, the company hired operators who spoke no English instead of just some, as formerly. The phone book was less and less helpful because people moved so much, or had the same last name, or lived like us in crates with no street addresses. Why, it was impossible to get a right phone number."

"Or have mail delivered. Or find anybody at home for that matter."

"Yes," he said with sadness, "communication is terrible, which is what the computers want. It makes it so hard for us to unite against them."

"Look on the bright side. There's one advantage to living in a box," Alce said hesitantly. "They're easy to move."

"You mean . . ."

"We could always find each other if our crates were snuggled together," Alce said with a dreamy giggle, and Bil's grin spread. "You could give me history lessons. You're a wonderful teacher."

"Yes, you should know more history. Everyone should. It's vital to understand the mistakes of the past so we don't repeat them when people regain power."

"Do you think we can?"

"I'm convinced of it. By force if necessary."

"Bil!" she hissed. "You're a fusbing revolutionary. You're a Comcap!"

"And proud of it!" said the peculiar man.

"Oh dear, I'm not political at all," Alce lamented. "We'll never work as a twosome."

"Politics makes strange bedfellows, they used to say."

"Now what does *that* mean?"

"I'll show you."

"Wait," said she, trying to preserve a semblance of decorum. "What does 'fusb' come from anyway?"

"You mean its derivation? It's the all-purpose profanity the computers evolved. In the olden days, people had a lot of cuss words but some, like 'hell' and 'damn,' were so mild even three-year-olds used them. The calcified calculators figured out which were the important swear words and came up with the f-curse, the s-curse, the sob-curse, and the b-curse. They combined them for standardization's sake, as usual. 'Fusb' stands for 'fuck,' 'shit,' 'son of a bitch' and 'bastard,' words you probably never heard. But, like 'fuck' before it, 'fusb' also denotes the sex act. Speaking of which, Alce, isn't it about time . . ."

"Oh no," she said firmly. "Why, I barely know you."

"Then you should know me barely," he quipped.

Under the bed, Ralp whined in fright.

"Why did you build a bed of this shape?"

"Like a heart? Because I'm a romantic, I guess."

"I knew it! I think I could fall for you."

"I hope so." Bil was quiet for a long moment. "Alce, I must be honest with you. I had a practical reason. I . . . have cold feet."

"I don't think I . . ."

"Can't you feel my feet now?"

"Sure. And they're cold."

"Don't you see? Our feet touch at the heart's point."

5

Crate Mates

Alce soon decided that Bil, for all his odd ideas, was the most adorable man she had ever met, and she took the initiative in having her crate placed on a flatbed truck and deposited next to his, under the pretext that she wanted to study history. Actually, Alce wasn't particularly interested in history, not that she let on. It was Bil she wanted to study.

"So these are your ancestors. I didn't know anyone kept old photographs. People don't have room for the new ones. Because the magic wand cameras make it so easy—all you have to do is raise and click—the average person takes thousands of photos a year, I read in the laminated press."

"And because computers develop them for next to nothing. Photography is the opium of the masses, to paraphrase the aboriginal Comcap, Karl Marx, whose ideas were misunderstood for a long time. People called him a Communist, but his secret diary revealed that he wrote *Das Kapital* for money. He made some, too, but invested it badly in the stock market. Where was I? Photography, yes. Ugh! How I hate those albums people have, a foot thick and filled with vacuous visages. It was different in yestercentury, when there was more to take pictures of."

"Show me others."

"I keep them under the bed. Part of my historical interest. Move, Ralp. Here. These date from the period of the Ascension."

"Why, some of your forebears are black!"

"Yes, my family had a touch of the tarbrush. That was before the computers decided to color everyone beige, to make us all happy, they claimed."

"Why beige? I never understood that."

"To simplify their job. The computers were tired of racial animosity—for once I don't blame them—so they made us all the same hue. Light tan was a compromise. Black people stopped being black, which would make them happy, the computers thought, because they complained so much about the color problem, but the blacks were furious. They'd always wanted to be black, they said, but it was too late. The genetic engineering had already started. The whites seemed to like nothing better than lying in the sun and acquiring a tan, so the computers gave them a permanent one. As for the Indians and the others, I don't believe the machines considered their preferences for an instant. There are no more races in Amerca."

"And no more beards—isn't that the word?—like some of your forebears had."

"No. The computers' genetic engineering took away men's facial hair, to save us time. I wonder what it was like to use a razor."

"Hmmm. People's noses were different. So were their eyes! They don't have . . ."

"Epicanthic folds, like we do. Many of our characteristics are the result of evolution, not the computers. Oval eyes with fatty, that is, epicanthic, crinkles at the inner corners were originally evolved by the Mongols as protection from the glare of sun on snow and ice. In our case, the glare of centuries of TV screens did it."

"Our noses?"

"We're snub-nosed—and have small feet, too—as crowd protection. You know, we're always running into other people's backs, or being stepped on, so nature tried to minimize our injuries. We have long necks to help us see where we're going."

"Is there anything you don't know? Look! The women are consistently smaller than the men. Why is that? Women are usually larger than men today. You and I are almost the same size, but that's because you're big for a man and I'm small for a girl. I'm only six foot two."

He laughed outright. "In the twentieth century, when feminism was in flower, the women would have been shocked by what happened later on. In those days they paraded the idea that when females were freed from inequality, drudgery, childbirth, et cetera, they would grow. Well, the computers freed them but decided, in the interests of equality, that women should assume masculine roles, like manual labor. Women grew all right, but not, as had been predicted, morally, intellectually or spiritually. They increased in *size*. It was as though nature had been biding its time, patiently waiting to replace the tired legions of men with fresh blood. The moment women increased in physical stature men got shorter until their average crossed. Men feared rape and wrote best-selling panegyrics on the subject, while women wished for the old days, when they had been smaller. But it was too late." He laughed again, sardonically. "Do you know what was meant by the term the 'age of consent'?"

"No," she said breathlessly.

"Well, if a man fusbed a girl when she was too young, he could be arrested for statutory rape. The computers saw through the idiocy of that, since girls had become bigger than boys. They changed it to 'weight of consent.' If a person weighed one hundred pounds, he or she was fair game. How much do you weigh, Alce?"

"One fifty," she confessed. "I'm small, but I have a lot of energy, don't I? And I'm careful about my appearance. I even

take time to do my hair. Many women don't bother, because
they're so busy. I'm different from most women, don't you
think?"

"I certainly do. You're also quite traditional in your interpre-
tation of the female role. Different and traditional—it's a good
combination. It makes you feminine. So many women are mannish because they're lesdikes. How come you aren't, Alce?
Didn't you go to lesdike camp?"

Alce nodded.

"Tell me about it."

Alce grinned, showing pearly little teeth that contrasted with
her light brown skin and dark hair. She was delighted to talk
about herself for a change. "Well, nobody wears any clothes
and there are lots of massages and funny kinds of equipment
and leather things but mostly what you learn is that while
humans are lousy, women are less lousy than men."

"Typical," he said with a grunt. "The computers are always
telling people they aren't any good, to undermine their self-
confidence."

"I was good!" she protested, misunderstanding him. "I was
proficient at being both a les and a dike."

"Did you consider a career as a sex athlete?" he wondered.

"What girl hasn't? But I wasn't built right. My center of grav-
ity was too high, or something. And I didn't have the motiva-
tion, to tell the truth. You have to swing both ways to be a pro,
and I much prefer men." She added, "Why don't they have
monosex camps for men?"

"Because it reached the point where 99.9 percent of the
males were monos already," he told her. "The computers were
worried about the birth rate. That was before they invented the
babyseed."

"And before they began conditioning men to like old women,
I imagine. Tell the truth: have you had many?"

"My share."

"Do you find them irresistible?"

"No. Probably because I'm a historian, I still think people should fusb with people their own age, more or less."

"Me, too," she said, thankful for his attitude. But not wishing to sound square, she went on, "I don't really find old people sexually attractive, but, if I met one who looked like Henr Fonda, I might change my mind."

Rather than get out of bed, as Alce had begun to urge, Bil asked how she earned her living.

"I fill out forms," she told him. "I hate my job. Can you imagine what it's like to fill out forms all the time? Records, reports, permits—you should see the file cabinets. There's barely space to walk in the halls. Last week I had to complete a questionnaire on how many forms I write."

"Who's your boss?"

"I work for a middle-middle-line executive. His boss is a middle-line executive. *His* boss is an upper-bottom-line executive, and so on, to the big boss, who's the bottom-line executive."

"What's your function?"

"I take the seconds of meetings, among other things."

"Seconds! They used to be called minutes, before the computers decided to accelerate the tempo of life. That's one reason I hate our technocracy—the machines force us to submit to the clock."

"Those audioclocks whispering in the background drive me crazy," Alce muttered.

"What do people talk about at meetings?" he inquired.

"They try to decide what level executives they are."

"It must be the businessperson's main preoccupation since earning profits is out of the question. Tell me more about your company."

"We're a conglomerate, but we're so diversified that nobody

knows for certain what our business is. Some say it's research and development, others claim we're in marketing, still others maintain we're consultants. There are those who believe we're into manufacturing, but if you ask them what we manufacture they can't tell you."

"It's the same all over. Most people don't know what they really do except paperwork."

"And not just at the office! Look at the paperwork we have to do at home! We need licenses for everything, even our crates. 'Keep this copy for your records'—if I kept all the stuff I was supposed to there wouldn't be room for *me* in my box. Take the income tax form. It's eighty-four pages long and required weeks to fill out—with my tiny income! I had an income tax audit last year, which took six months. They finally told me I owed $1.62. It doesn't make sense to use so much time and paper, mine and the government's, to get $1.62 from me."

"But, from the computers' point of view it does! Don't forget, the machines replaced the slogan 'Think' with 'Idle hands and heads are the devil's workshop.' They're convinced that people must be busy all the time to be happy. They're fanatic on the subject. And what better way than endless paperwork? No wonder reforestation ranks so high in the economic plan!"

"What do they use the paperwork for?"

Bil said professionally, "People are superfluous to production. The machines don't need us except to consume. They can produce everything society requires without human intervention."

"Why do we have so little, then? Why don't they produce more?"

"They don't want to. The computers are mechanocentric. They believe machines are the be-all and end-all. They must see us in some sense as poor imitations of themselves. Since they're not consumers, except maybe for a spare part here and there, and a little oil, they only grudgingly admit that we need anything either. No, the real point of work is to keep us busy.

What does your company do? Nothing. What happens to the paper? The computers burn it, unread!"

"We can't just lie here all the time. It's sinful. I realize I've been conditioned to keep busy, but we'll get bedsores. We've been in your crate the whole weekend except when we sunfed."

"But I like being here with you. Besides, what else is worth doing? The library's closed."

"We could jog."

"I'd rather tell you the history of jogging."

"Oh, all right."

"People didn't always jog everywhere they went," Bil explained. "Jogging became a kind of craze in the twentieth century but nothing like it is today. After the Ascension the computers taught that it was more natural to jog than walk, and everybody believed them, as always. The machines praised jogging for health's sake, but that was a subterfuge, I believe. The real reason was to force people to hurry, furthering the illusion that we were busy and therefore happy. Want to hear more?"

"We could go to the new car show."

"I fail to see why the new car shows are so popular when nobody except local officials own one, why I don't know, since all officials do is count other people's money. Anyway, what use would a car be? The only decent roads we have left are completely clogged by trucks." He paused. "Want to hear what happened to cars?"

"I guess so."

"Cars were long and trim. Those fusbing Enlibs caused the change when they demonstrated against what they called gas-guzzling dinosaurs and finally succeeded in having a law passed that limited cars to six feet in length. But they hadn't reckoned on human automotive ingenuity and forgot to put a restriction on *height,* so cars got to be six feet long and twenty feet tall— ugly, top-heavy things. Wind resistance would be terrific if the speed limit weren't only ten miles an hour, thanks to the likes of Ralp Nadir Prime, the aboriginal Enlib. Anyway, cars don't interest me much."

"Shall we steal toilet paper?" she inquired brightly.

"That's such a stupid sport, Alce. Can't you see how easy the computers make it to steal? Hardly any challenge at all. Why, a six-year-old child can swipe toilet paper. The racks may seem to be guarded but I bet the sentinel eye is turned off. It's the computers' way of trying to satisfy what they interpret as basic human criminal tendencies without causing harm." He turned gloomy. "Maybe they're right. Look how you and I tried to con each other! Want to hear the history of toilet paper stealing?"

"If you insist."

In the olden days, said Bil, before the Ascension, the government became concerned about the cash nexus. A blind worship of money pervaded the land and Washington wanted to revive the spirit of giving, generosity and altruism which, it claimed, had made the country great. To prove that not everything needed to have a price tag, the government determined to make one item absolutely free to one and all.

"But what?" Bil squealed with glee. "The answer proved more difficult than had been foreseen. Washington didn't want to be too lavish because more free gifts would be demanded. Further, the gift could not put too much strain on the economy. Finally, the giveaway shouldn't compete unfairly with big business.

"A tall order! Candy seemed a logical choice because there had to be a limit on how much people could ingest, and, even if they ate more than was good for them, higher profits for dentists and false teeth manufacturers would result. But candy was rejected because the government felt that people would melt it down to sugar and use it to make alcohol, which would hurt the distilleries. Free medical care was thrown out too—everybody who lacked a medical complaint would promptly develop one just to visit a physician without having to pay, it was feared. While costless public transportation was hotly debated, it was also turned down because the system would wear out faster than it was already.

"A genius finally stumbled on toilet paper. There was a commodity you could consume only so much of, no matter how hard you tried! No other use could be found for it except the one it was destined for. You couldn't write on it, stuff holes with it, start fires . . . No, except to blow your nose on, toilet paper was good for only one thing.

"But the government was still a government. Cost analysts with slide rules and calculators showed that toilet paper as then manufactured was unnecessarily *wide,* at four and one half inches. Millions of dollars could be saved in the free toilet paper program if a roll were reduced by a single inch in width. Even the Enlibs would be happy with that decision, for a change, the bureaucrats thought.

"The government anticipated a strong reaction from the conservatives, who believed in tradition, but reasoned that the general public would accept the new paper if only because it was free. The government erred. The conservatives objected, of course, but so did the liberals, who complained that the new paper violated the Fourth-and-a-half Amendment. The radicals claimed the common man was being cheated, as usual. The women's movement screamed that the narrow-gauge paper was an insult to feminine delicacy. The blacks hated the free paper because it was *white*—all of which led to the Great Toilet Paper Revolt, during which people threw the GI paper into garbage cans. The rebellion was ultimately subdued, but resistance remained fierce.

"After the Ascension, people went on being exercised about the width of toilet paper because there was so little else about which to be agitated. You couldn't gripe about not being rich when nobody was; you couldn't complain about being discriminated against by the computers because the computers discriminated against everybody, regardless of race, religion or gender; you couldn't demonstrate against busing in an age when students jogged to school, although, as a result of a Supreme Court decision, some had to jog further than others. So toilet paper gave discontent a focus—the tissue issue, they called it.

"The opportunity was not lost on the computers. Cleverly, they manufactured rolls of the old width and offered them for sale. The narrow width paper still existed, but people preferred to lift the wide stuff especially because, if you got caught, the penalty was nothing more than a reprimand. It's one more way the computers make children of us."

"You don't like anything, when you get right down to it, except lying in bed, fusbing, telling wild stories and hating the computers. Why don't you use the feedback boxes to tell them?"

"Feedback is right. If you gripe and sign your name the computers have you arrested. If you don't sign your name you're ignored. I should know. I've sent the computers plenty of advice through the bitch boxes—anonymously, of course. No, the machines must be overthrown."

"You really want to be a revolutionary, don't you?"

"Not 'want to be.' *I am!*"

"Am? What does a revolutionary do, exactly?"

"Do?" He regarded her with amazement. "A revolutionary doesn't *do* anything. A revolutionary *is*."

"Can't you be more specific?"

"Well, clearly the objective of a revolutionary is to overthrow the existing order—in this case, the machines—and replace it with a better one—the Comcap way."

"You make it sound so simple. How is your revolution to be accomplished?"

"It's not *my* revolution, Alce," he said. "The revolution belongs to the people."

"Maybe it belongs to them but that doesn't mean they want it."

He said easily, "The people will join in."

"Oh sure. When?"

"When the vanguard has taken power."

She started to ask him what the vanguard was but desisted. "How will the vanguard take power?"

"Why, by defeating the machines!"

"How is that to be done? There are no elections. Everybody's busy stealing toilet paper and taking pictures. . . ."

"Listen, Alce, don't overcomplicate. The vanguard will simply penetrate the computer headquarters, cut off their electricity and proclaim that the future is here."

"Hmmmm. Aside from everything else, I thought you said you couldn't find their headquarters."

"A minor matter," he insisted, and fell silent.

"I like you, Bil," she said. "For all your craziness, you're unusual. How do you account for that?"

"Genes, I guess. My genes make me smart and brave. I fear nothing."

"Oh yeah?" She raised her fist and he cowered.

The dog growled. "Stop that, Ralp. He's jealous. I'm glad you like my seriousness, Alce. Most women find me *too* serious, while I find them too shallow. A nation of nitwits—that's what the computers strive for. The best that can be said about computer rule is that it's better than the warfare state."

"All right," Alce said reluctantly. "What happened to war?"

"There used to be nasty ones. The closest call to universal disaster was the so-called Rube Goldberg war. The computers like to claim credit for establishing international peace, but, in truth, I think nations were all set to disarm before the computers hit on their crazy state theory and wiped out the rest of the world."

"Who was Rube Goldberg? Was he a general?"

"He was a cartoonist who lived in the mists of time. He drew chain-reaction cartoons—one thing leads to another and then to another, et cetera. They called it the Rube Goldberg war because it sort of resembled his cartoons. You've got to remember that everyone had guns then, even kids. There was a kid who was sore because he had gotten a beebee gun for Christmas while his older brother received an air rifle, so the kid shot his brother in the face. The brother was holding his air rifle, which went off, and the pellet hit a hunter in the eye. The hunter had a real rifle in his hands; it went off too, striking the tower of a nearby airfield, killing the traffic controller, who was about to tell the pilot of a corporate jet that a big jet was coming in. The private plane collided with the passenger jet and crashed, but the larger plane tried to gain altitude. Its pilots were badly burned, so they didn't see the Concorde—that was a supersonic jet—until they ran into it. The Concorde crashed, too, but on a nuclear power plant, which exploded. The Russians accused the Americans of violating the test-ban treaty and fired off a missile. The Americans did too. After a couple of cities were atomized they declared peace, but they could very well have obliterated each other because of a beebee gun."

"I don't understand a word of that."

"Shall I draw you a picture?" He did.

"I suppose I understand. Is war the reason we're so poor?"

"War had little to do with it. Do you want to hear the story?"

"Have I a choice?"

"Of course you have a choice. Either you don't hear the story, or you do, in which case I'll take you out to dinner."

"You will! Can you afford it?"

"If you eat fast. Besides, this is a special occasion, darling. There's something I want to propose—to make *us* happy."

"Tell me then, why are we so poor?" she asked eagerly.

"It goes back a long way, to before the Ascension when the United States lost its money to the Third World."

"Third World?"

"The developing countries. They were *still* developing after

H. NUCLEAR POWER PLANT

all those years, and they had a hankering for American wealth. They liked the taste of it. By then, American paper currency was flavored to make it easier for those who couldn't read English or the numbers to understand the denominations by licking the bills. The bigger the banknote, the more exotic the flavor. Dollar bills tasted like sugar, fives like honey, tens like chocolate, twenties like maple syrup, fifties like mint, and so on up to $10,000 notes, which were said to be sheer ambrosia, though few but Arab sheiks knew for sure.

"Inevitably, the day came when the Third World wanted more American wealth, as much as it could get, all if possible. It changed its name to the First World and made its demand. When, unsurprisingly, the ultimatum was refused, the First World threatened nuclear war. That didn't work either because, while the First World possessed nuclear bombs, it hadn't learned to use them yet, America figured, and called the bluff successfully.

"The First World tried something new. Hiring a firm on what was called Madison Avenue, it undertook the most massive advertising campaign in history with a single objective: to make Americans feel guilty because they were so rich. An American couldn't watch television, listen to the radio, read a newspaper or magazine or look at a billboard without being told that American riches amounted to a crime against humanity. The ads were always accompanied by pictures of small children with distended bellies and big pleading eyes that showed white around the irises. It was rumored, though never proved, that the First World maintained camps in which children were deliberately starved to obtain these shots, which were taken by the highest-paid fashion photographers.

"Americans came to feel like criminals, little by little, but even so they might have resisted except for the Nadir gang, who convinced them that money was bad for the ecology. 'Let's trade our green for the real thing,' they argued, and Americans finally agreed that a clean environment outweighed money. Americans put their cash, stocks and bonds, coin collections, jewels, paintings and everything else of value into the empty holds of First World supertankers that waited to fetch them.

"But the countries of the First World began to squabble over how to divide so much wealth. They started an international crap game in the General Assembly of the United Nations, located in Nairobi. They removed the seats and filled the hall with tables covered with felt. The leaders of the First World and the Communist countries, the only members of the U.N., took turns with the dice. They shot craps around the clock for a year, using first American money and then their own. The Communists gambled every red cent. The big winner was Kuwait. Kuwait won most of the money in the world.

"The other nations were even poorer than before except for China, which refused to play because gambling violated Maoist principles. (Actually, the Chinese didn't have enough money to

play with.) The losers tried the same guilt-provoking advertising campaign on Kuwait, but it failed miserably. The Kuwaitis
simply laughed at the photographs of starving children. They
weren't their children, the Kuwaitis pointed out.

"The other countries then attempted the ecological argument but the Kuwaitis laughed at that, too. They liked their
environment as it was, filled with fumes. Besides, they added, if
the day came when it was no longer safe to use fossil fuels, they
would burn money instead."

Alce regarded Bil's round face suspiciously, saying at last,
"I'm not sure I believe all that. Do you make things up?"

"Sometimes, when I'm not quite sure of the facts," he said
cheerfully. But his countenance darkened. "Which is more
often than I like to admit. After all, the computers create our
reality. We know what they want us to know, even if it's fiction.
To understand this, though, is the beginning of knowledge,
which is one advantage we have. That and . . ."

"And?"

Bil said softly, "The machines don't have each other. Not like
we do."

6

Marry Me, the Meter's Running Out

On the way to a Tic-Toc Restaurant Bil told Alce about the place, which she'd never visited. In yestercentury, it had also been a fast-food chain, but the Tic-Tocs differed from their predecessor in a critical way. Having stood in line for food, the customer went to one of many donut-shaped tables with a hole in the center for a cashier and a meter in front of each place setting. At the precise moment a tray touched the formica top, the cashier started the meter, which counted how long you took to eat.

Though money was short and sunfeeding free, people saved for months for a meal at the Tic-Toc, so much did they want real victuals. The prices posted on the wall seemed cheap, but there was a caveat. With every minute you spent at the table prices doubled. At minute one, a hamburger cost $.20, minute two $.40, minute three $.80, minute four $1.60, minute five $3.20 and so on to infinity. There was a recorded instance of a woman who had a fit of amnesia while at a Tic-Toc counter and received a bill for a bowl of chili totaling $71.80.

A person with an ordinary mouth and reasonably sharp teeth could wolf down a burger in a minute or so, and many did, Bil said. However (and how carefully the Tic-Toc cost analysts had measured this!), the burgers were served on chewy buns, covered with tough little seeds, and were fat with meat. The longer time required to consume such a glorious hamburger more than compensated the restaurant for its generous portions.

Hungry customers would also order french fries, gelatin, a fruit cup, a soft drink or coffee, which was always scalding hot so that you had to be careful not to burn your mouth. Still, if you applied yourself to the task of rapid eating, the check was reasonable when you banged on the counter and the cashier took your base figure, multiplying it by the time on the meter. In fact, the progressive and forward-looking management discouraged dallying and encouraged haste by the meters' loud ticks (hence the name Tic-Toc) and a voice that whispered, "Hurry-hurry-hurry," replacing the Muzak of olden days. The secret of Tic-Toc's success was its volume of business. Overhead, an electronic board announced the number of hamburgers the chain had sold nation wide without a fatality. The figure was 234,873,650,907,362,583,275 when Alce and Bil sat down and it grew by the second.

The number would have been longer except that accidents had occurred before the technique of accelerated eating had been mastered. People choked on chicken bones and beef gristle and even swallowed flatware in their haste to bang the counter before the meter reached a new minute mark. Full precautions had been taken since then. The fried chicken had been deboned, the skins removed from salami slices. Even the utensils could be easily swallowed and digested if you wolfed them down by mistake. The danger of suffocation remained, but customers had learned to distend their throats and wash down an enormous mouthful with water. Nobody had died at Tic-Toc in years as a direct result of eating there. Heart failure due to stress had happened, but such cases could hardly be blamed on the rushaurant, as it was called.

Bil and Alce were at Tic-Toc when he asked her to marry him. On the one hand, it was a dreadful choice for a site, because important questions like marriage ought to be talked about in peace and quiet. Still, hurry seemed natural to them who had so little of worth to do, and perhaps Bil didn't want to give Alce a chance to say no.

"Get along pretty nice, don't we, babe?" (Chomp.)

"Yup." (Swallow.)

"Tie the knot?"

(Sip.) "What knot?"

"Not whatnot. Knot. With a 'k.' Marriage." (Chomp.)

"Oh."

(Swallow.) "Well?"

"Chewing. Wait."

"Hurry." (Sip.)

(Swallow. Sip.) "Marriage against law."

"Half the fun of it." (Chomp.)

"Be good husbandie? Well?"

"Chewing."

"Oh." (Chomp.)

(Swallow.) "Yes." (Sip.)

(Swallow.) "Always love me?"

"Yup. You?"

(Sip.) "Could be."

"Could be! What kind of answer?" (Chomp.)

"Chewing."

"Hurry. Meter ticks."

(Swallow.) "Need time."

"Two minutes now. Getting expensive. Hurry."

"Don't rush me." (Sip.) "Too important."

"Can't help. Every second counts, Alce." (Chomp.)

"Well . . ." (Chomp.)

(Swallow.) "We could grow babies."

"Can you afford?"

"Come the revolution."

"Oh sure. How?" (Sip.)

(Sip.) "Too long to explain. Take my word."

"Why should?"

"Chewing."

(Swallow. Sip.) "Always chewing."

"You should talk." (Chomp.) "Will you?"

"Will what?" (Chomp.)

(Swallow.) "Marry me. Hurry."

(Swallow.) "Can't decide."

(Sip.) "MAKE UP YOUR MIND!"

"Ssssh. Everybody's staring." (Sip.)

"Costing a fortune. Decide!"

"Think only of check. Just like you." (Chomp.)

(Chomp.) "Just like *me*! We just met."

(Swallow.) "That's the trouble." (Hic.) "Don't talk with your mouth full."

(Swallow.) "Already sound like wifette."

(Hic.) "Give me hiccups." (Hic.)

"Take a sip."

(Sip.) "That's (*hic*) better (*hic*). If married you one thing you'd have to change. Table manners lousy." (Hic.) "Ketchup all over face."

"Hard to help at this speed." (Sip.) "Don't talk so much. Decide."

"Thinking." (Hic. Chomp.)

"Finish burger. Not made of gold."

(Swallow.) "Trying."

(Chomp. Swallow. Sip.) "There. Done. Can stop my meter?"

"Impolite. Never speak to you again if do. Wait for woman." (Hic. Chomp.)

"I can't just *sit* here while the meter ticks. Hurry, please."

(Swallow. Sip. Hic.) "Trying." (Chomp.)

"Will you marry me?"

(Swallow. Sip.) "For fusb's sake, okay." (Chomp. Swallow. Sip. Hic. Chomp. Swallow. Sip.)

Bang! "Cashier! Quick! Here! Stop the meters! We're finished! What do we owe? Wasn't that a lovely dinner?"

7

Getting Married

"Oh dear," Alce said outside, "I guess we have to face the judge now, though I've never understood exactly why."

"Why is marriage illegal? Well," Bil explained, "after the Ascension the computers examined everything that was wrong. One institution that seemed glaringly wrong was marriage, because the divorce rate could climb no higher.

"Already substantial, the divorce rate finally reached one hundred percent. That meant, Alce, that *every* married person was destined for divorce. As if that weren't enough, the divorce rate for *second* marriages hit one hundred percent, and then *third* marriages headed in the same direction. People still talked reverentially about the institution of marriage, but what could you say for an institution whose business was failure?

"The computers huddled electronically. The tricky thing about the machines is that, for all their black-and-white logic, they sometimes go right to the heart of the matter. After many conferences—yes, they hold conferences, that's been established—the cumbersome critters decided that conventional explanations for the collapse of matrimony were without foundation. They remembered what had happened when marijuana was legalized. Marijuana was something you smoked for kicks. The government identified various lots according to

strength, country of origin, age, et cetera, and sold it at reasonable prices at somber state stores. It should have been a pot-
head's dream except everybody immediately stopped using
grass, as they also called it."

"Why?"

"Give me a chance! From the pot experience—another name
for the loco weed—computers concluded the trouble with marriage must be legality. To them, as I've said, humans are basically criminals and, confronted with laws against pot smoking
or the rules marriage entailed, would do their best to break
them. Their answer was plain: make wedlock illegal and everyone would love it.

"How right the computers were!" Bil went on. "The moment
marriage became illegal people demanded to be married and
stay married. Divorce, instant and cheap, with no rigamarole
whatsoever, was suddenly detested.

"But, don't forget, to marry was to violate the law, and since
marriage constituted living in sin you had to pay a penalty—
compulsory adultery, a terrible price." Bil frowned. "Before I
met you I never wanted to marry, even though marrieds without children live in the spacescrapers, where they get some real
victuals, because I was an independent spirit. Sure, I like to
play around, but to *have* to!"

Alce said grimly, shoulders sagging. "I'd so much rather be
faithful, wouldn't you?"

"Sure I would. But we plan to be married, and the law's the
law. There's no getting around that."

Law was dispensed in the dark, wood-paneled courtroom by
a computer judge, a microprocessor silicon chip, no more than
a particle in all probability, its functions being comparatively
simple. But, as Bil told Alce, the machines seemed to have concluded that humans equate authority and size, and so the chip
rested in a black box about nine feet tall that stood behind a
massive desk. Two eyes on stalks sprang from it.

"Those eyes are strictly for effect," Bil murmured as they entered the chamber, silent except for the whisper of an audioclock. "There's plenty of room inside the box for visual equipment. The eyes, which look like insects', were evidently designed to make people uncomfortable and hence at a disadvantage in the courtroom."

There were other sweatsuited cases before them—those accused of noisification, puttermaniacs (who wouldn't work), litterinsects, pickpouches, income tax evaders and others—which the computer judge decided with bewildering speed. Though the verdict was always guilty, only the most audacious attempted to fabricate: the machines said they had learned that lying caused body temperature to rise, however imperceptibly, and they had invented a truth beam to detect the change. "The computers claim that their verdicts are fairer than those of the olden system, which involved witnesses, attorneys, juries and so on," Bil pointed out in a low voice. "The machines say they don't make mistakes, only humans do, but no one is certain because there's no appeal, and it would be folly to attempt one even if it were possible, because the machines would stick together and make the penalty worse. And if a computer judge *were* removed by his superiors for incompetence, how would a person know, since computer judges look alike?"

When Bil heard that the softly sobbing figure who then cringed before the judge was accused of hyphen-ation, he shuddered slightly himself. All through school the automatons who had qualified as teachers told the kids they were *bad, bad, bad.* It had taken years sometimes, but most of the students finally listened. All, in fact, except him. That he wouldn't listen had made him feel even worse. How much he had wanted to be like the others! But some part of him always refused. Still, the urge to be monoated, to be one with the badness of self, always lingered. Even as an adult he had tossed in his heart-shaped bed and tried to accept the badness of himself, to crawl into his horridness peacefully and refuse it no more, but he could not,

which often made him gloomy and filled him with self-con-
tempt, try as he did to fight such feelings. Finally, with supreme effort, he had conquered monoation, he believed.

"Hyphen-ation, the opposite of monoation, was a serious
offense to the computers," Bil whispered to his bridette-to-be.
During the Ascension the computers scanned human culture
for information about the endangered species, *Homo sapiens,*
and among the artifacts studied were the books and pamphlets
of what had been known as the "human potential movement,"
which had flourished in the twentieth century ("And which
must have given the machines the idea for *their* slogan, 'computer potential,'" Bil explained). People in the human potential
movement were encouraged to concentrate on their essential
selves, to burrow into their personae like worms in an apple
core. Since being your true self could only mean being what
you were already (albeit on a different level, perhaps), nobody
had to learn anything new. "Getting it all together," as they put
it then, was enough. A writer of an ancient self-help book had
called this "monoation."

"You know the computers," Bil hissed in the rear of the
courtroom. "They're quick to take advantage, and monoation
was made to order. After all, a population preoccupied with
rubbing its navel with petroleum jelly isn't likely to dissent. It'll
acquiesce to almost anything just so it gets sense relaxation
below the waist or some such catchphrase. That's what happened to those dimwits in gauzy pink hare krishna gowns beating tambourines, fools pretending to meditate when they were
half asleep, idiots trying to raise their consciousness when the
machines were actually lowering it. They stood by idly when
our freedom was destroyed. Ah, those clever klatches of circuitry! Oh, they doped it out, all right. Let them eat hype!
the computers decided, and people did.

"To clinch it, the meretricious machines made monoation a
requirement. Now, you can't have a law without having something unlawful, as I've said. The computers are good at catchy

phrases—remember 'Life isn't a bed of neuroses (but they help)'?—and they came up with 'hyphen-ation.' The dash is pure computerese. Hyphen-ation, the urge to be different, to expand, to be *more* than you were already, to have outside interests, to increase your skills, to take risks, have self-confidence, et cetera, was declared a crime. The supercalculators wanted everyone to be bland as beans, and I'll be fusbed if they're not."

"Bil! Hush! That's subversive. The judge will hear you and, with your politics, you'll be arrested for hyphen-ation yourself!"

Their attention turned to the defendant. The accuser's name had been withheld—undoubtedly, said Bil, it belonged to someone hoping to score points with the machines in case of future infractions. How tenaciously the trembling wretch denied the charges! He was not a litteratibug, he shouted, didn't immerse himself in poetry and plays which could still be obtained at underground used-book stores. The stacks of books found in his crate had belonged to the previous tenant. He stayed alone so much because, well, he was a little shy. . . .

The computer said nothing. A micropart cushioned from shock by a pool of oil, the tiny chip could afford to wait. The machine had infinite patience, it seemed. Its eyes—disks about the size of dinner plates, colorless with visiplates at the centers—studied the babbling creature as its temperature was apparently taken with the invisible truth beam. Finally the judge said, when the man fell silent, "You lie. Guilty as charged. Twelve years on a Floating Island."

A great metal hand descended, seized the unfortunate and lifted him from sight.

"Maybe all he had was a little fever," Bil said.

"How did the machines think of the Floating Islands?" Alce wondered quietly as they waited.

"A crazy misunderstanding, as usual," Bil said from the side of his mouth. "The computers learned that criminals were sup-

posed to get their *just desserts*. The machines were confused by
that, so they poked around in cookbooks until they came up
with Floating Islands. That suggestion led them to prison cities
built on buoyant tetrahedral modules equipped with electronic
devices that keep them far from shore. . . ."

"Next case," squeaked the computer judge. The stalk eyes
pointed at them.

"I wonder why the judges squeak," Bil said in an undertone
as they rose. "They could have selected any voice they wanted.
To make us even more uncomfortable, I suppose."

"The judge frightens me to death, to be frank."

"It is your desire to enter the illegal institution of unholy
wedlock, according to your nonpetition," the judge announced.

Said Bil, "We wish to declare our intention of breaking the
law."

"You realize that there is no possibility of a nuptial shower, a
bachelor party, a blood test, a marriage certificate, a wedding
ceremony, an announcement in the laminated press, a honey-
moon or anything like that?"

"We do."

"The state can in no way condone illicit behavior."

"Yessir."

"Should your spouse decide to grow a baby, which is entirely
her choice because you are not recognized as married, the child
must be illegitimate."

"Okay."

"Should you want a divorce, the state will grant it at once."

"Yessir. We never will."

"Are you aware of the penalty?" The eyes studied Alce.

"Oh dear. Yessir."

"I now pronounce you husbandie and wifette. Next case."

On the way out they found cards protruding from a slot in
the wall, one with a photograph of her, the other of him. The
cards had squares representing the months of the year and a

big letter "A" colored red, popularly known as the Scarlet Letter.

"Our adultery cards. We have to be unfaithful at least once a month," said Bil. "Your lover punches yours, and you his. If the other's married, you punch his or her card too, and we can't cheat. The machines really check and the penalty's severe."

They started to quarrel over who took the better picture. "I guess we're pseudomarried now," said Alce.

8

The Spacescraper

Spacescraper city on the outskirts of New York—five miles square with nine buildings, each exactly one mile from the next, each a mile square, three miles high, 1,000 stories, 1,000 people per floor, a million folk behind its walls, nine million being the total population of spacescraper city.

Single no more, Alce and Bil went to live in one of the megastructures because the law so decreed. The computers had abolished the rich, middle and poor classes of yestercenturies but replaced them with new ones: there were singles in crates, pseudomarrieds in spacescrapers, parents in the suburbs. (Farmers lived in the countryside. You have to move to an appropriate domicile," Bil explained. "If one of us dies or we divorce, it's back to the crates."

"But if we plant children it's out to the suburbs," Alce rejoined with a sweet smile. "And when the children have grown, it's back to the scrapers."

"Children!" He snorted. "I have more important work to do."

The scrapers perched on a pod that resembled a huge root. The newlyweds stood at the cavernous entrance looking up, but the top of the building was lost in the sky. "You have to switch elevators nine times to reach there. The trip takes an hour, I hear," said Alce.

"And a week by stairs. Some building climbers descend by parachute. I understand there are people in the upper stories who never come down at all, because they can't take the change in atmospheric pressure."

"We got into the bottom half of the building because of my vertigo," Alce said.

"My acrophobia did it," insisted he.

"NO VISITORS," informed a sign. "I guess the elevators can't handle any more people," Bil said as they stepped before the visiplate for identification. He whispered into the paper bag he carried "No visitors—that means you, Ralp. Keep your trap shut or they'll drop you from the top of the building."

But the stupid beast chose to bark, as if to convey that the message had been received. Alce and Bil stared aghast at each other and then in surprise at the screen. Normally, if the computers perceived an infraction, the visiplate turned bright red and a thunderous voice berated the unfortunate individual, even dictating a penalty, for instance, to fill out a hundred complicated forms by the following morning. This time, true, the screen became light pink, like an electronic blush, but only for an instant, and then the glow faded and the front door opened soundlessly.

"I don't understand. Not even a reprimand."

"Maybe they didn't hear Ralp."

"Maybe."

Home was apartment 482-C-303-QX. When she set down the bags Alce said, "Just think. I was born in a building exactly like this and I don't remember it at all."

"Me neither. How could we? We were barely seedlings when we moved to the suburbs."

"Why, it's hardly bigger than a crate. How low the ceilings are! I'm almost afraid to stand up straight."

"That's because of all the equipment up there, I guess."

"But there isn't even a kitchen."

"There must be. The trick is to find it." From the bare floor he took a booklet in a glassine envelope, titled *How to Use Your New Apartment,* and read out loud, " 'Your new apartment must be spick-and-span at all times. Because the facilities are shared, objects of a personal nature must be kept in the bedroom alcove. Nothing may be hung on the living room walls. . . .' Mmmmmm. Let's see, kitchen . . . kitchen. Here it is. I get it. See, there's a control panel in the foyer with buttons. It operates the whole apartment. Press the one marked 'K.' "

Alce pressed and the living room lights went on. "Wrong button. There are so many!" She touched another and a section of blank wall whirled a woman in underwear into the room along with a complete kitchen. She fried meat at the stove. "What the fusb!" she said angrily. "It isn't your time."

"Time?" said Alce. "We don't understand. We're new here."

"You have use of the kitchen at odd hours on even days and even hours on odd days. This is an even hour on an even day so the kitchen's ours."

"Hours?"

"Ours!"

"What about Sundays?"

"We alternate half days Sundays. Don't forget, the top two shelves in the fridge belong to us. You have storage cabinets on the right side, we the left. If you *have* to borrow something, be sure to replace it. Items of equal value will do. Check the Table of Equivalents."

"Where?"

"Read the directions."

" 'One glass of milk equals one half lemon. One tablespoon of sugar equals three of salt,' " Bil read. "I get it. Life is really organized in an efficiency apartment."

"You haven't seen anything." The woman turned the burger and Ralp, smelling it, gurgled from inside the bag. The woman screamed, "What's that? Sounded like a dog!"

"Excuse me. I farted," Bil said.

"Some neighbors!" The half-naked woman pressed a button and the kitchen swiveled from sight.

"So!" said Alce. "I suppose I can't sweep the living room when I want because the broom's in the kitchen."

"No, cleaning appears to be automatic. Press that button. No, *that* one."

Alce pressed. A tremendous roar sounded after a moment and they were almost sucked from their feet. "Turn it off!" Bil screeched and said, when the room was quiet, "That's your vacuum cleaner. I should have finished reading the instructions. After you've started it you're supposed to go into the hall. And be sure not to leave any loose objects around."

Alce grumbled. "What are we supposed to sit on? There isn't a stick of furniture."

"We have to share that, too, it seems," said Bil from the booklet. "Press the button marked 'M' for Murphy living room."

Alce pressed and, with a grinding noise, a crack appeared in the floor, growing rapidly wider. "Jump!"

They watched from the safety of the foyer, as from below, carried on a platform, furniture appeared—couch, coffee table, floor lamps, armchairs. A man in underwear sat in one. "For fusb's sake, not again," he complained.

"We've just moved in," Alce apologized. "We don't know the ropes yet."

"The former tenants broke the rules all the time," said the man who sat in their living room. "They couldn't remember that the living room was theirs only at even hours on even days, and at odd hours on odd days, and alternate half days Sunday. Why, once they brought us up when we were fusbing on the couch! Watch your ways." He pressed a button in the arm of his chair and the living room vanished.

Alce stared nervously at various doors. "Which is the bathroom? I have to go."

Bil twisted a knob. "It's locked. Somebody must be using it."

"My first apartment and I have to share a bathroom? Read the instructions."

" 'Bathroom sharing. On the alternate hours your bathroom door locks automatically so that your neighbors may use it. For your convenience and safety, your bathroom door cannot be opened from either inside or outside during this period. To avoid embarrassment to your neighbors and yourself, do not be in the bathroom when your hour ends. If you are, you will be obliged to leave through your neighbors' apartment. In case you require toilet facilities during the bathroom hour of your neighbors, it is advisable to purchase people litter.' " Bil looked at the whispering audioclock which took up most of one wall. "You'll have to wait a few minutes, Alce."

Alce stamped her foot. "Where do we keep our toiletries?"

"Each family has its own medicine chest and toilet paper holder."

"The narrow kind, I suppose." Again she stamped her foot impatiently and a sign lit up: "NO NOISE." "There are so many regulations!"

"We'd better learn the routine. We have the kitchen alternate half days on Sundays, and odd hours on even days and even hours on odd days. . . ."

"But what's an even day and an odd hour?" Alce interrupted.

"If Sunday's the first day of the week, Monday must be an even day, et cetera, and one o'clock an odd hour, two an even hour, et cetera," Bil suggested.

"And we have the living room on even hours on even days and odd hours on odd days. As I see it we don't have the use of the living room and the kitchen at the same time."

"We'll have an hour to cook and then we eat in the living room. If we forget anything, like salt and pepper, it's our tough luck because, once the hour's up, the kitchen vanishes automatically, like the living room. They can be recalled with the buttons but first you have to check with your neighbors on the intercom."

"It's mad! Do you mean that the kitchen and living room appear and disappear all night long?"

"Let's see. No, after eight o'clock on even nights and alternate Sunday evenings the living room stays in our place until morning. Same with the kitchen, only the reverse."

Alce patted her brow anxiously and said, "It's stuffy in here. Open a window."

Bil struggled with a massive window and finally succeeded in opening it a few inches. Immediately the sign flashed, "PRESSURE LOSS. CLOSE WINDOW." He did, hurriedly. "The windows are evidently meant to be opened only if the power fails." He stared down bleaky. "You couldn't jump if you wanted. You couldn't get out the window. Not that anybody commits suicide any more—they're all convinced they're happy, the fools."

A soft click sounded. "At last. The bathroom," said Alce. When she emerged she held two pieces of thin white plastic, one small, the other smaller. "Our washcloth and towel. I suppose the sheets are plastic, too. Say, where's the bed?"

Bil had to leap to avoid the bed, which descended suddenly from the wall as he entered an alcove, "What the . . . I see. There's a photoelectric cell, which I triggered. You're supposed to pass your hand before it and the bed comes down or returns to the upright position. We'd better be sure the other isn't in it when we send it up."

Alce said, "I ought to warn you I hate making beds."

"That's one thing we needn't fight about. There's a bed-making machine."

"But who gives us fresh sheets and towels?"

"The rocleaners," said Bil. "They bring them once a month. According to the booklet, the management is sorry, but the rocleaners only work at night. That's because they're so clumsy, I bet. They'd run people down. The authorities can't tell you the hour of delivery, either. Between midnight and six A.M. is all they will guarantee. You don't get clean plastic sheets unless you give them the ones on your bed."

"In other words, they roust us from sleep! Oh dear," Alce wailed. "This place depresses me. Tell me some history to distract me. What happened to the robots, anyway? Didn't there used to be lots of them? The only ones left are the rocops and the rocleaners, so far as I know."

"Ah, the poor robots," said he willingly. "Millions had been produced and sold before people began to detest them, and for good reason. They were heavy and often fell through floors. They were clumsy and had a way of stepping on toes. Also, they proved to have a defect that was never eliminated despite the manufacturers' promises. Robots had a stubborn streak. People had prayed for robots to perform their household chores, only to discover that the bulky equipment couldn't be stopped. Robots emptied ashtrays, did dishes and laundry and their other tasks well but ceaselessly. The robots, which never quit working, were quite capable of capriciously electing to clean the living room rug in the midst of a party. People fled their own houses just to escape their mechanical minions.

"And the robots couldn't be made to leave. The manufacturers had worried—wrongly, as it turned out—that robots would be stolen and designed the creatures to remain on the premises at all times except when taken by an authorized dealer, most of whom refused to answer calls since there were so many, frequently at night. In fact, the sole way to get a robot out of the house was to instruct it to walk the dog. This was another reason why the dog population had become astonishingly large—people used them to get rid of the robots, even briefly—though the life expectancy of dogs dwindled. Dogs died from sheer exhaustion as the result of being walked so much.

"After dogs were exiled from the cities, the robots stayed home. It reached the point where people who could afford them actually had two abodes, one for the robots and the other for themselves. Everybody screamed bloody murder about the robots but what could they do? Robots didn't need refueling; the powerful creatures had been trained to resist removal forcibly. Because they didn't eat or drink they couldn't be poisoned; for safety's sake, a robot's smooth outer surface couldn't be opened except by an authorized dealer, all of whom were out of business by then; and the machines rarely broke down. The only way to destroy a robot was to explode it, which meant destroying one's own home as well. Not a few resorted to this extreme measure.

"The robots were among the first problems people handed computers, thinking they could solve it, being machines themselves. And I have to admit the computers found the answer. They equipped flatbed trucks and helicopters with strong magnets, which pulled the robots from houses or apartments. All metallic objects had to be removed beforehand and the hurtling robots made great holes in the walls, but that was a small price. Since, in the name of machinehood, the computers hated to destroy the robots, they carted most of them to the abandoned cities of the midwest—Des Moines, Kalamazoo, Oshkosh, Indianapolis, to name a few—where they probably are to this very day, constantly cleaning and polishing each other.

"Feel better, Alce? At least you don't live in the midwest."

"Yes. I'll try to look on the bright side."

So Bil and Alce began life in a spacescraper. Each floor contained a grocery store (though real victuals were rationed), sunfood clinic, laundromat, bowling alley, rec room and all the amenities. It was much like any other place, except for when you looked out the window or when the wind blew especially hard and signs said "RETURN TO APARTMENT. FASTEN SEATBELTS." Residents of the upper stories, according to rumor, took pills for building sickness.

Alce and Bil were happy, though not perfectly so because

they fought. He, whose tendentiousness sometimes annoyed his wife, pointed out that perfect happiness was a logical impossibility, however. To be perfectly happy meant that you couldn't be any happier, and you couldn't know you could be any happier unless you were. Ergo . . .

"Okay, okay."

"The computers claim everybody is perfectly happy but the digital dunderheads are full of binary buncombe. How can they understand human happiness, for all their propaganda, being nonhuman themselves?" He talked a good deal in this vein.

Weary of Bil's alliterative attacks on the computers, Alce said finally, "How you go on! Don't you think about anything else but the computers?"

"No," he admitted. "I'm a revolutionary. We want to abrogate the compact between humans and machines, by force if necessary."

"Who's 'we'?" she said, pressing for details because Bil was always so vague about the revolution.

"Me and my allies," Bil said indistinctly.

"Allies?"

"Well, like my pals in the Crate Association."

"Go on," she berated him. "You don't have any allies, and you know it."

"I'm underground."

"On the four hundred eighty-second floor? Listen, if there was any kind of revolutionary movement the computers would worry. They'd learn what you were up to and wipe you out like *that.*" She snapped her fingers. "But they don't bother. Frankly, they don't give a fusb about you."

"Just wait."

"For what? Tell me what you propose to do exactly."

"I told you. Overthrow them."

"But *how?*"

"By destroying the computer leadership."

"You don't even have a weapon!"

"A detail. The real problem is finding their secret headquarters."

"How will you do that?" she sneered.

"What do you think I use the library for?" Bil demanded angrily. "I'm searching for information, and I think I've found a clue. I've seen the words 'holed up' more than once. I have the distinct feeling the machines are underground."

"What do you plan to use to find them, a divining rod?"

"Don't be smart. I've already made a thorough search of the city while I pretended to jog. They're not here—I'm sure of it. Now I'm looking elsewhere."

"Is that why you visit the countryside?"

"If you must know, yes. I'll return soon."

"You'll never find their headquarters even if it exists. How did you become a revolutionary, so-called? You've never made that clear."

"I haven't had much of a chance because we've spent most of our spare time in bed," he said evasively. He stroked little Ralp, who sat in his lap and purred.

"I hate that dog," Alce muttered. "Imagine, having to smuggle it out every night so it can steal garbage! Besides, dogs aren't supposed to purr. Cats do that, or did when there were cats."

"Cats exist," he assured her. "They still roam the countryside. That's how Ralp learned to purr—a cat taught him."

"What happened to cats, anyway?"

"Another computer fusb-up. Because real victuals were scarce, the ridiculous reels decided that cats ought to be self-sufficient, so they made cat food out of them. But, in that way they have of overdoing things, they put almost the entire feline population in cans so there were few cats left to eat it. People had to be satisfied with canned cats for pets. I'm surprised they didn't put people in tins, too—deviled humans."

"Don't be disgusting. You still haven't told me what made you a revolutionary."

"My sense of injustice," he began. "Well, also my family. My father was a Comcap before me, and so was my grandfather, great-grandfather, et cetera."

"Why haven't you mentioned this?"

"Inbred suspicion, I guess. Comcaps have always opposed the computers, unlike the Enlibs, the mealymouthed, wishy-washy fusbers! Comcaps understand . . ."

"*The* Comcap understands," she corrected him, "assuming you're the only one left."

"I'm sure there are others," he wailed. "I can't be the last Comcap in the world."

"Have you ever heard of, much less met, a single living soul who has the slightest interest in politics?"

"Well, no," he confessed. "Back in my great-great-et-cetera-grandfather's day the Comcaps were a strong political force. People were for or against us but at least they took positions even if they supported that simpleton Enlib bunch. The misan-thropic machines squelched all interest in politics and prac-tically everything else except jogging, stealing toilet paper and fusbing. What a world!"

· "What a world is right. You're a freak, Bil, do you realize that? The last Comcap and I had to marry him. You should be in a zoo, were there zoos."

"Count your blessings. I'll be famous when we triumph, and the Communist Capitalists *will* triumph because our concept of human nature is correct. Comcaps understand that people are no good but they can become better if you offer them riches in a classless society. The Enlibs, on the other hand, owing to their foolish forbear . . ."

"Must you always use words that begin with the same letter?"

"The first Ralp, the one called Ralp Nadir Prime, believed that people were basically good. A bad environment made them bad, in his view. But he understood nothing about incen-tives. He wanted prophets, not profits, if you get my pun."

"I hate it when you condescend."

"Ralp Nadir Prime was an egomaniac," Bil said, ignoring her. "He really wanted all the faces on Mount Rushmore re-chiseled to look like him, his published memoirs revealed. Mount Rushmore had these huge stone heads of American Presidents. The computers changed the name to Mount Rush-less, but that was at the beginning, when the myopic machines believed that leisure would make us happy. *They* found out fast enough. Later, they atomized the mountain because they'd be-come jealous of human heroes." He cleared his throat. "Have I told you how the computers caused God to appear?"

Alce said with reluctance, "I guess not."

"After the Ascension," Bil said, "the computers sought ways to reinforce their authority. Coming to the conclusion that peo-ple secretly still believed in God, the capricious cabinets de-signed a holograph—a two-dimensional representation made of laser beams—of the good Lord, complete with halo and a long white beard, and projected it into the sky over Fiery Run, Virginia. God had a voice, too, which came from loudspeakers hung on an invisible balloon, I discovered from the books. God announced He was holding a press conference, and you can bet the reporters were there by the thousands. God said He had rewritten the Ten Commandments, but the basic new one was, 'Thou shalt have no other gods but the machines.' "

"What did God do then?" she asked, trying to sound inter-ested.

"God told them He was quitting—resigning in favor of the machines. He said goodbye once and for all and wasn't heard from again."

"Did the reporters believe that?"

"The laminated press will believe anything."

Alce yawned. "Tell me more about your father."

"He died on a Floating Island," Bil said in a grieved voice. "Then my mother died of a broken heart. Revenge is one of my motives for wanting to make mincemeat of the machines."

Alce looked startled. "What was your father's crime?"

"He was the leader of the last Comcap demonstration. The machines detest demonstrations, so the rocops arrested him."

"There were Comcaps so recently? How big was the demonstration?"

"My father thought thousands would show up but nobody did except him. That was twenty years ago, when I was ten. I didn't tell you because . . . well, not everyone would marry a person whose parent was a con."

"I sure wouldn't have, although . . ." Alce lowered her head. "My mother also died on a Floating Island, and my father of a broken heart. That was ten years ago, when I was fifteen."

"Why haven't you told me?"

"Same reason you gave. You might have thought I inherited criminal tendencies."

"What was your mother's crime?"

"My poor mother. I miss her terribly sometimes—oh dear, I'm letting my traditionalism show. Most people don't remember their parents at all! You know how the computers insist that people must keep working? Well, mother didn't, despite warnings. She went to prison for puttermania and lazyleanings."

"The computers should talk. They get lazier and lazier all the time, if you ask me, those cybernetic cynics, I can't wait to get my hands on their circuitry," he shouted.

"Sssssh. You'll arouse the neighbors. Do you have a brother or a sister?"

"A brother. He went west when he grew up and I haven't heard from him in years. I wonder whatever happened to him," Bil said a little sadly. "I miss my brother—most people don't care a fusb about their siblings."

"I have a sister somewhere down South. I haven't heard from her in years either. I hope she's all right." After a moment of silence she continued, "Look on the bright side. The difference between us and the machines is that they think they're perfect, and we *know* we're not. Because we have feelings. We're angry, sexy, sad or whatever, and there's nothing we can do about it. Imagine a computer dying of a broken heart!"

"Only a broken part."

"Parts they can fix. For us, only time fixes, if then. The machines make us feel inferior because we're not perfect like them, but we're not imperfect because we do our best."

"Spoken like a true Comcap," said Bil admiringly.

"Spoken like *me*. Move quickly, Bil. The floor's opening. We're about to lose the living room."

9

Life Continues

Bil and Alce soon settled into a routine, routines being inevitable in a spacescraper just as elsewhere, only more so.

In the mornings they jogged to work, and in the evenings they jogged home, hurriedly cooking dinner in the kitchen before it was taken away from them, eating it quickly in the living room before they lost that too, and using the bathroom at breakneck speed before the lockout.

At night Bil smuggled Ralp outside in a paper bag for the dog to do its do, and while the man waited he surveyed the silent city, where few lights shone. Nobody went abroad after dark, partly because there was nothing to occupy them, and partly because of the compulsory paperwork—endless questionnaires about life in the tall towers, reports to the IRS, permits for everything—which always had to be completed by morning. Once Alce asked him, looking up from the papers she had brought home from the office, "Why don't we have more leisure?"

"When the computers took power," he replied, "they wanted to make a good impression, and among their first steps was to try to present industrial society in a favorable light. They built vast museums covered with pipes and funnels and gigantic gears that were supposed to resemble factories. People found them beautiful until they realized the museums *did* resemble factories and they stayed away in droves. Next, the computers offered higher wages and shorter hours, but people wanted still higher wages and shorter hours. The computers—they still needed human labor then—asked people to be patient, but people weren't patient, so before long the computers eliminated work completely and gave them total leisure. People then complained they didn't have enough to do. That, I admit, must have set the computers' teeth on edge. They'd given people exactly what they asked for and people no longer wanted it. At their wits' ends, I guess, the computers tried to interest people in nature. They even invented a catchphrase about the New Nature—everything had to be new, to hold anybody's interest at all—and for a while the national parks were full of people searching for the New Nature. When they didn't find it, they were unhappy again.

"My own belief—and that's all it amounts to—is that the computers got sore. They decided to keep people busy *all* the time, although we're supposedly off duty on weekends."

"What's the forecast in the laminated press?"

"Tomorrow's a rain day again. The computers don't seem to have decided yet whether Sunday will be a sun day."

"Fusb! Why do they schedule rain days for weekends all the time?"

"Because on rain days they can make us work. They're trying to torture us, I tell you. Just think! In yestercentury people thought climate control would be a good thing."

"Don't get excited. How do they make it rain or shine as they choose? The forecasts are *never* wrong."

"Of course they're never wrong! The word 'forecast' is a stinking anachronism meant to impress people with how smart the machines are, since they always guess right. The truth is that weather prediction has become an exact science because of the icebergs."

"Icebergs?" she asked in a bewildered voice.

He sighed. "I guess I have to start at the beginning. . . ."

"Don't be too long, will you? I still have paper work . . ."

Bil told her, "In yestercentury, a tribe called the Saudi Arabians—they were among the first, apparently, to be identified as a crazy state and smashed like a mosquito—had the notion of towing icebergs from the South Pole and using them for water. Well, the icebergs melted before they got there. Then the Arabs got the idea that icebergs from the North Pole were *colder,* so they tried importing those. Just how icebergs were to be brought through the Suez Canal has never been clear to me, but at any rate some of the icebergs escaped. . . ."

"These aren't the Floating Islands?"

"The Floating Islands are in the Bermuda Triangle," he scolded. "The icebergs got loose off the coast of Maine in a cold winter and didn't melt. Somebody noticed that whenever the icebergs came close to shore it snowed, and whenever they drifted away it didn't. In one flash the computers saw the possibilities. They put cooling machines on the icebergs to stop them from ever melting, and motors to bring them nearer or farther from shore. On land they placed infrared guns to melt the snow and make rain. That's how they manipulate the weather, with the icebergs and the infrared guns."

"It'll rain tomorrow, the laminated press predicts?"

"Absolutely."

"Oh dear. More work."

But it didn't rain. On the morrow the sun shone through the plate glass windows.

"I can't believe it!" Bil exclaimed. "The forecast has never been wrong before. The computers must be losing their grip."

"Who cares about the computers!" Alce said gaily. "Let's jog!"

As they learned when they reached them, the elevators were temporarily out of service, however. "Temporarily," Bil said bitterly, "means the whole weekend. We're stuck up here, a mile off the ground."

"Look on the bright side. We don't have to work on weekends when the sun is shining. It's a sun day! We can go to the store and to the rec room later on."

"All right. Let's bring coupons."

The store on the four hundred eighty-second story was exactly like the stores on every floor of the 1,000-story building. It sold film at a reduced price, sneakers and socks, bras, panties and jockstraps, sweatsuits, jumpsuits, which were terribly expensive, deodorants, people litter, toothpaste and -brushes, razors and razorblades, photos of Henr Fonda and Dian Toffler, the Sex Olympics champion, pouches, attaché cases— everything, in short, a person would need, including food, which, of course, was rationed.

"There isn't much today," said Bil, examining the cartons of PermaMilk, which wouldn't sour (the final day of permitted sale was forty years away), loaves of EndurBread, which, being made of redwood, would last for centuries, MillennaMeat, which wouldn't become rotten in its vacuumpack until the glow of futuretime, and Longlast Lettuce, which stayed edible for decades, being half plastic.

"Why is there so little food?" Alce asked crossly.

"The snaken scourge, of course. The farmers never really recovered, not that the machines wanted them to."

"Snakens?" said Alce. "Sounds familiar."

"*Sounds familiar!* The snaken was only one of the most important developments of the early Third Millennium! Well, the snaken was a good example of the kind of technological mishap that landed us where we are today, in the coils of the calculators. You see, after so many centuries of eating the same old protein—beef, veal, lamb, fowls and fish—people tired of them. What a luxury to tire of real victuals! They wanted something with a different taste, and somebody came up with the snaken. Only, before that was the snabbit . . ."

"Snabbit?"

"Scientists crossed a snake and a rabbit. The snabbit was apparently a taste sensation—people were wild for it—but there

was a problem. The masses confused 'hare' and 'hair' and re-
belled at the thought of eating hair, so the eugenicists went back
to work and crossed a chicken and a snake. That was the snaken. It reproduced rapidly and was excellent to eat because it
was all white meat, according to history books. But, commend-
able as the experiment may have been, it was also foolhardy."

"Why?"

"The futurists were at fault. Are you aware that an important
poet of Yesterages named Dante, in his *Inferno,* put those who
dared to predict the future in the next-to-last circle of hell?
Their heads were turned around as a penalty so they had to
walk backwards. The futurists predicted a cheap source of protein, which the snaken was. However, the futurists always
seemed to overlook some key detail—in this case, the nature of
snakes. The snaken looked like a half-breed. Instead of scales it
had feathers, like a chicken, and a beak. It pecked and even
clucked—but it had the long body and the instincts of a snake.
It went underground and reproduced there, out of control. It
ate everything that grew, and, seemingly impossible to eradi-
cate, it spread alarmingly and would have killed off humanity
except for the machines. They deserve a little something,
though not much."

"I sometimes think you admire the computers!"

"I don't, but I give credit where credit is due! The machines
conceptualized sunfeeding and they licked the snakens! They
deduced that snakes liked to eat little animals, so they crossed a
field mouse with a scorpion. It had the body of a mouse but the
brain and tail of a scorpion. The scorpimice took care of the
snakens."

"That's a horrible story," said Alce. "Let's go to the rec
room!"

10

Ralp Nadir Nth

The rec room on the four hundred eighty-second story, where they met Ralp Nadir Nth, had been made to seem like a town square of yestercentury, with cannons, artificial grass, imitation bushes and shrubbery, all made of plastic, though. Birdsong played on loudspeakers and, in the center, a fountain tinkled.

On the floor, red lines designated activity areas. One offered hypnotic vacations to exotic places like Paris or the Taj Mahal, which probably didn't exist any more. You sat in a long row of seats ripped from an abandoned airplane, turned a dial to a locale chosen from the day's program, donned headphones and watched a flickering light which placed you in a trance while a voice explained what you saw. As Alce and Bil could testify, the experience was astonishingly vivid, and trance travelers, when they woke, actually believed that several weeks had passed instead of less than an hour.

"Shall we take a trip?" asked Bil.

Alce checked the evening schedule. "We've been there," she said.

Jigsex puzzles came next. The players took jagged pieces of cardboard from a large box and tried to fit them into the puzzle. "Here's a lip! I've got a tongue! I found a piece of thigh! Is it part of a breast or a rear?" It would probably be a threesome, the couple decided, but since the bodies were incomplete they couldn't be sure.

On the giant TV screen was the weekly Miss Amerca contest taking place at Atlantic City. No contestant could be less than seventy. Alce followed Bil's stare. "You think she's attractive, don't you?" she said, pointing to a grandmotherly woman in a bathing suit.

"Not bad."

"Men are all alike," Alce declared. "You rave about wrinkles. Drooping boobs turn you on. You love a thick waistline. You flip over varicose veins. A young woman hasn't a chance in this world. It used to kill me in school when they showed boys pictures of old ladies and gave them candy at the same time."

"Graypubes are sweet," Bil teased.

"Listen, our adultery cards are due to be punched soon, and if I catch you with an octogenarian I'll break your neck."

"But you were conditioned, too, Alce! Be honest, don't senior fusbers make your juices flow?" he said in the same light tone. "What do you think of him, for instance?"

He gestured at a tall, bony man with a long, straight nose. Yellowish skin was drawn tight on his cheeks. Ridges of skull cropped out on his bald head. As if drawn by remote control, the seer eyes swung toward them. "Say, he's elegant," Alce cooed. "He looks a little like Henr Fonda!"

"Henr Fonda! I look more like Henr Fonda than that geezer," Bil scoffed.

"I wish you did."

"Now wait a minute. . . ."

On the next TV screen a sex marathon was underway. The contestants had been at it for eight days and nights, stopping only to relieve themselves and to take nourishment from a tube. "How thin they are, and no wonder," said Alce. "What's the record?"

"About eleven days, I think."

"Twelve," corrected a dry, precise voice. "Twelve days, fourteen hours, and twenty-seven minutes. The record, though, has been disputed by those who claim that a sex athlete must survive the game to win. In this case, the male contender died of gangrene." The voice laughed softly.

Bil turned to find the man with the bony head. "You don't seem upset about it."

"Oh, but I am," said the old codger smoothly. "The Sex Olympics, you see, are unsafe and must be regulated."

"Why should the computers do that? The sex games are kicks for the masses. People love the gladiators of the groin. It keeps their little minds occupied."

"Don't shoot your mouth off," Alce warned Bil.

The blear eyes examined her carefully from head to toe. "There must be regulations. What is life without regulations? Instruments, for example. A woman punctured herself recently and developed peritonitis. Though the news doesn't get into the laminated press, accidents happen all the time in the Sex Olympics."

"You seem to know a lot about it," Alce said.

"My dear girl, I am a bit of an expert on the Sex Olympics. A sexpert, if you like." He ran a hand over his pate as if it had hair, and smiled. "Do you enjoy the games, young woman?"

"I've only seen them occasionally on TV," she stammered. "I've never been to a live one."

"You should," said the newcomer. "TV doesn't capture the excitement, the color, the smells."

"But the games are sold out for years to come," Alce complained.

"Tickets can be arranged," said the old man easily, touching her arm.

"Who in fusb are you, mister?" Bil asked.

"I," the stranger said, with a long pause between, "am Ralp Nadir Nth."

Alce exclaimed from an open mouth, *"The* Ralp Nadir Nth?"

"None other," said he, graciously.

"But you're a celebrity, Mr. Nadir Nth! You're an aristocrat!"

"Yes, I come from a long line. The Nadirs have retained the same profile since Ralp Nadir Prime, may his soul rest in peace." The old man stroked the bridge of his nose.

Bil recoiled. "The descendant of the aboriginal Enlib!"

"I'm afraid so," replied Ralp with ill-feigned satisfaction. "Most haven't the vaguest conception of what the Enlibs were. I'm surprised you've heard of my famous forebear."

"Infamous," Bil muttered.

"Eh?"

"I'm a student of history!"

"Needn't *shout*," Nadir said, unruffled. "Does the past shock you?"

"I have past shock, yes. I've read of the struggle between the Enlibs and the Comcaps, for instance," Bil answered provocatively.

"Ah yes, the Comcaps. I haven't heard the word in decades. That ancient party must be extinct as the dodo bird. I don't imagine there's a single Comcap left."

"Bil, please keep your ideas to yourself," Alce told him sharply.

But Bil hollered, "There is! There is!"

The old fellow stared incredulously. "You!"

"Me! Me! Me!"

"Well, well, the last Comcap." Ralp Nadir Nth laughed quietly. He stroked his long cheek. "How does it feel to be an anachronism? Your party, it appears, failed to pass the test of time."

"The test of time! How many Enlibs survive anyway?"

"Since political activity's illegal, it's impossible to be accurate, but in the millions, I would estimate."

"Millions, you estimate?"

"Well, hundreds of thousands," Nadir admitted.

Taking heart, Bil repeated, "Hundreds of thousands?"

"Thousands."

"Thousands?"

"Hundreds."

"Hundreds?"

"A great many," said Ralp Nadir Nth, voice faltering.

"You're fusbing us over," Bil declared. "You're the last Enlib, I bet."

"All right, all right, I confess I must be the last. I've never heard of any other, at least. Well, tell me about yourselves. I must admit you interest me insofar as I can be interested. I've seen so much, after all." Nadir chuckled, peering at Alce.

"You flirted outrageously," Bil exploded when they returned to apartment 482-C-303-QX. "I thought old men didn't appeal to you."

"They usually don't but he's different."

"You did everything but hand him your A-card."

"I felt sorry for him, if you must know. Imagine, such a sweet man with a wifette who's sexually inactive, as he told us."

"Oh, he gives all the girls that line, I bet. If his wifette's as old as he is she deserves to be inactive. Nadir must be a hundred if he's a day!"

"So? A hundred's young! Ralp has plenty of stuff left. How charming he is! How sophisticated! How debonair! How elegant!"

"And vain. Nadir must be the vainest man I ever met. The way he's always caressing his face."

"Doesn't he have a marvelous physique?"

"If you like bones."

"You don't care for him, do you? I wonder why," Alce said.

"Are you crazy! He's an Enlib!"

"As if that mattered. You two are the last politicals in the world and you're at his throat already. No wonder people gave the power to the machines! Anyway, I think you're jealous."

"I'm *not.*"

"Maybe you should be," she said slyly.

"Look," he blurted, "you talked about growing a baby, and perhaps we ought to. It might be nice to have a little one around."

"A baby! Oh no. I'm much too busy to have a baby right now. I just met . . ." Hurriedly, she changed the subject. "Speaking of Ralp Nadir Nth, why do people live so long these days? They didn't use to back in the mists of time. I've always wondered about it, and you make history so compelling."

"I do bring the past to life, don't I?" Bil admitted. "Well, it was like this. During the late twentieth century . . ."

In a country known as Ecuador in the continent of South America a valley was found whose inhabitants had incredible life spans for those years, and scientists arrived in droves to learn the reason. Why should a postman of 125 have a wife and two mistresses? How could a woman of ninety have a child while toiling in a field? "Pluck" and "sheer grit" were the responses the scientists got, in Spanish. They weren't satisfied.

The scientists subjected the secretive valley folk to every test, checking their blood, taking samples from their organs, forcing them to run endlessly on treadmills to study their cardiovascular systems, peppering them with questions. Though most of the old people died during the ordeal, the scientists failed to solve the riddle of why they lived so long even though they smoked a pack of unfiltered cigarettes a day and drank their heads off.

Are smoking and drinking good for them? Is it their genes? Because they have plenty of exercise running up and down mountainsides? Clean air? The absence of postindustrial stress? the scientists asked each other, but none of these notions was satisfactory. Finally, the only ancient still alive in the valley, the postman, gave the scientists what might have been a clue. "Life is a fountain," he croaked on his deathbed.

The scientists blinked at each other when the answer had

been translated. What had the old bird meant? It was too late
to ask him. Fountain . . . fountain . . . "Surely it's nothing
more than a bad joke," concluded one. "A shaggy llama story.
You know the kind. A man searches for the secret of life. At a
cocaine party a stranger with a long black beard, red eyes, a
cape and mysterious manner, tells him, 'The secret of life is
poy.' 'Poy?' He falls asleep and when he wakes the stranger is
gone; nobody knows who he was or where he went. He has
vanished without a trace. The desperate truth seeker combs the
world, searching for poy, which he believes in his madness
holds the secret of life. Just as he is about to succumb to various
incurable venereal diseases contracted during his pilgrimage,
he meets a harlot in Singapore. The crone informs him that
poy can be obtained just down the street, though the danger is
frightful. What luck! He staggers to a metal door, and knocks
two and one half times as instructed; a slot opens and cruel
Asian eyes peer out. 'Wha you wan?' 'Poy,' he shouts. 'I must
have poy. I have suffered. I have come a long distance.' 'Come
all way to Olient for poy?' 'You said it.' 'Know *real* poy cost
plenty. No fake stuff here.' The man perseveres, offers the rest
of his fortune. The door creaks open. He enters, seats himself
at a small teak and ivory table in an airless room, waits. A beautiful, almond-faced woman in tight black silk slacks enters at
last and says, 'Want poy?' 'I'll do anything for it!' 'Anything?'
'Anything!' 'Okay. Sign first. You got American Express? Bank-
americard? Master Charge? Diner's Club?' 'All of them. The
American Express card is a gold one, actually.' 'Okay. What
kind poy you want? We got apple, pumpkin, boysenberry. . . .'"
The scientist stared into the bleak silence, and said at last,
"When you get right down to it we've learned nothing at all."

"I wonder," said another cautiously. "There might be more
to it than a shaggy llama story. You all remember Ponce de
León?"

"You mean?"

"Exactly. Ponce de León came to the New World in search of

the Fountain of Youth. He made the mistake of looking in Florida, but what's in Florida? The Fountain of Youth must be right here!"

The valley's only fountain lay in the town square. A battered gourd hung there and the villagers drank from it frequently. That was the secret. Along with cow-do the water contained a previously undiscovered trace mineral. It took years to synthesize but when it was placed in drinking water instead of flourine, according to Bil, people lived to extreme old age and kept their teeth.

But Alce's attention had wandered. "Somebody stuck a note under the door," she said, and fetched it. "Guess what? It's from darling Ralp. He's invited us to accompany him to the Sex Olympics."

11

The Sex Olympics

The Sex Olympics (so-called, though all the participants came from the eastern part of the United Sense of Amerca) were held in the Feel Forum, named for an ancient auditorium called the Felt Forum that had once stood in the same site. As they trotted over, Ralp Nadir Nth remarked chattily, "There are a number of things that make for a great sex athlete. Endurance, for instance, and dedication, of course. Aggressiveness counts and so does the desire to dominate. I would venture that the athletes are basically introverts. It's a matter of concentration: introverts can shut off outside stimuli, which gives them a greater ability to focus on single objectives. Beyond that, they tend to have low anxiety levels and a good capacity to handle stress."

"Stress?" Alce questioned.

"Certainly. Don't forget, thousands are watching, and no outstanding sex athlete likes to make mistakes. Further, pain isn't exactly relaxing."

"Pain?" said Bil.

"Assuredly. Pain results when the body is pushed to the very threshold of its abilities, as athletes must. Pain can be a distraction but the truly great ones seem almost unaware when they hurt. Think of an eighteen-inch instrument used by a woman," Ralp said to Alce, who blanched. "Of course, there's no doubt that a superior sex athlete has various physical characteristics going for him or her, depending on their specialties."

"Like what?" asked Bil.

"Well, in the case of broad jumping, for instance, which you'll see today in the women's decathlon, it helps if the female is bowlegged, and it's absolutely vital for the male to have a small pelvic girdle. Fast-contracting muscle fibers are useful in the free style, since the movements are often completely unexpected. Fast-twitch fibers give a sex athlete speed, while slowtwitch ones provide endurance, as needed in the marathon. You've almost got to have a high male or female hormone count, too. Having said all that, I could tell you of a dozen sex athletes who didn't have what it takes and somehow reached the top—or bottom," Ralp chuckled oleaginously.

They entered the vast hall that was the Feel Forum, packed to the rafters with pulsating people in sweatsuits. Row on row of them, dark-haired, beige-skinned, snub-nosed, epicanthic-eyed. Resemblances were everywhere. Bland faces strained with excitement as the band played. Vendors hawked field glasses, erotic souvenirs, enormous hotdogs. Parimutuel windows. Touts and shills. A huge audioclock whispered busily above the stage.

"You still haven't told us how you rate tickets, much less free ones," remarked Bil. "There's a line a half mile long outside."

"I represent the Citizen's Committee for the Regulation of Pornography, which this certainly is," said Ralp self-righteously.

"You are on this committee?" said Alce.

"I *am* the committee," Ralp replied with a lonely sigh. "Though others will join, I'm sure. In the meantime I'm able to observe the athletes close up." He pointed to chairs at the very edge of the stage and snickered. "I have box seats."

"How long do the games continue?" Alce asked as they sat.

"Day and night for almost a month. After a short respite the games start over."

"With the same athletes?"

"As long as they remain top bananas. It's like yestercentury's fastest gun in the West. Somebody's always waiting to shoot them down. See that one? I'm glad we're in time to watch her warm up. She does everything. She's been the gold medalist in the decathlon for three years, though last month she won by a hair."

Clad only in a loincloth the woman worked out on a bicycle with a pointed seat, pumping vigorously on the pedals. She had mighty mammaries, hearty haunches and a bold sensual face. On her bare back a number was painted.

"What's she wearing around her neck?" Alce asked.

"A rabbit's foot, for good luck. Many sex athletes are surprisingly superstitious."

"What's her name?" Bil wondered.

"*That*," said Ralp in a low voice, "is *the* Dian Toffler, the women's decathlon champ." Dian Toffler, as if sensing she was being talked about, raised her head and winked, seemingly at Bil.

"With all that fusbing, she has to flirt too?" asked Alce sharply.

"Dian's insatiable as well as competitive. A sex champion if there ever was one. The girl over there who's doing the splits is her arch rival," said Ralp solemnly, nodding at a wiry woman, small like Alce. "That's Lind Verne, the other female decathlon finalist for this Olympics. Lind has taken care of nine men at the same time."

"Nine?" said Alce.

"The usual three orifices, plus hands and feet."

"That's seven."

"Armpits," Ralp said with a salacious grimace.

"I must say for a person who wants to regulate pornography you seem to enjoy it," Bil observed.

"No, no," responded Ralp. "My interest is purely for the benefit of society. I have a permit to study voyeurism."

A nude male runner appeared on the stage carrying a plastic rod lit at one end. "Ladies and gentlemen," a voice announced over the loudspeaker, "we come to the next event in the women's decathlon, the fastfusb." Dian and Lind, with male consorts, lay on mats while attendants attached wires to the smalls of their backs. "As many of you know, the fastfusb is scored in two ways, the number of motions taken, and the peak time. Both partners must peak, as recorded on their peakmeters, before the team is finished. Are we ready? Yes!"

A bell sounded, bodies writhed furiously for a few seconds and Lind jumped up just before Dian to howling applause. Ralp Nadir took a card from his pouch and marked it. "Lind's behind in points but she's catching up," he said excitedly. "Fusb, she's fast. It's those fast-twitch fibers she has."

The crowd roar continued. "It's so strange to hear people make noise," Alce observed.

"This is one place they can scream their hearts out. I bet the machines encourage it, so that the people can let off steam," Bil said.

The band played briefly before the announcer returned. "*Both* contenders have achieved a new world's record, but Lind Verne is first, with Mach Two Point Five!"

The crowd screamed. "Mach Two Point Five!" said Ralp in an awed voice. "When I was a lad, Mach Two seemed an all but impossible goal. The increasing prowess of athletes never fails to amaze me. Still, I fear that their speeds are unsafe."

"Gymnasex!" called the announcer. "The finalists will be our superstars, Lind and Dian!"

As equipment was being set up, Ralp studied his scorecard.

"Dian's in real trouble if you ask me. Lind Verne is a remarkable gymnasexer. Note that her breasts are on the small side. Dian's get in her way. If Lind wins it, she only has to break

even in the clitblitz to become the new women's decathlon
champ. Let's hope neither tries to cheat."

"Cheat?" asked Bil and Alce together.

"There are ways," reported Ralp Nadir Nth, disapproval on
his bony face. "Aphrodisiacs to work a person up—carbon
dioxide is one. Spanish Zipper has been given to males—it's
dangerous. Saltpeter stops men in their tracks. For women, a
really dirty trick is to put abrasives, like metal filings or sand, in
their lubricants. You have no idea how much the sex athletes
want to win!"

Washed in light, Dian and Lind, with new male partners,
bowed from center stage. Behind them were displayed rings,
parallel bars, a thin rail called the balance beam, a trampoline,
a gymnastic horse with handles, or pommel horse. The announcer described the events.

"First, the floor exercise. It begins with the aerial walkover
fusb."

Applause.

"Now the layout back somersault fusb, a difficult feat."

"Oh."

"And the front fusb walkover."

"Ahhhh."

"The back walkover fusb. The female is not permitted to
touch the male with her legs or thighs."

Applause.

"Second, the vaulting fusb, otherwise known as the broad
jump."

"This one requires perfect timing," Ralp said softly. "The girl
springs from the trampoline on top the man. If she doesn't
make a three-point landing, ouch! Watch." Lind flew through
the air, making a precise coupling. "Beautiful," Ralp muttered.
"What depth perception. Note that she's slightly bowlegged.
Here's Dian." The heavier woman soared majestically, back
arched, legs ajar, but at the very last moment seemed to change

trajectory. Her partner whimpered in pain.

"That'll cost a point," said Ralp, as catcalls sounded.

"Backward and forward somersault fusb, pommel horse fusb, front and rear . . . Ring fusbs, swing parts and hold position, backpress, crosspullout . . . uneven parallel bar, the glide fusb, the flying hip circle into an eagle crotch, an extraordinary event . . . the long hang fusb and the wrap-around, the straddle-catch backwards fusb . . . scissors fusb and reverse scissors fusb . . . on the balance beam: press hands and mount, forward walkover, stag leap. Finally, ladies and gentlemen, the most difficult of the gymnasex events, the cartwheel fusb! Please observe that each partner must cartwheel in *opposite* directions and yet achieve penetration. . . . There!"

"They're such artists," Ralp said as the crowd roared. "Dian performed magnificently, but I believe the vaulting mistake will cost her dear."

The judges huddled while the band played until it was announced, "The winners are . . . Lind Verne and her partner! Lind and Dian are in a dead heat! Now we'll have the final event in the women's decathlon, the clitblitz, in which Dian and Lind will be the only contestants. The girls have a request which I pass on to you: they ask silence from the audience. Clitblitzing, as I'm sure you know, requires total concentration and absolute self-control. The object of the clitblitz is to force the adversary to peak, against her will, and no holds barred. Are we ready?" The bell sounded. "Go!"

The women had been oiled and their naked bodies shone as they circled each other, lips curled in scorn, while a female referee in a black and white shirt hovered near. Dian was armed with a small instrument that buzzed, Lind a long slender rod. Suddenly Lind lunged, put an agile foot behind Dian's thick legs and pushed; as Dian sank to the mat, the wiry woman jumped astride her, flailing her weapon. Dian twisted her head vainly, thrashed, moaned and submitted at last to a kiss. ("Dian's faking, I'm sure, to throw Lind off guard," Ralp opined.) Just as it seemed from her undulations and fervid grunts that Dian must surely proceed to peaking, she heaved Lind from her with a convulsive effort and leapt, brandishing her tool, seizing Lind from behind, biting her ear gently and cupping her bosom with one hand while the other forced her buzzing armament on Lind, who, in turn, emitted frothy cries that seemingly could not be suppressed, but then Lind, demonstrating the versatility which had made her a household word, went into her famous split, lowering her body until her groin grounded, and, with one arm around Dian's neck, hurtled the larger female over her shoulder.

At once the athletes were up, weaponless, arms extended, fibulating fingers working on each other as they kissed and stroked behinds. ("A *pas de deux*. Aren't they fantastic?" moaned Ralp Nadir Nth.) Dian's powerful mandibles induced croons from Lind, who sank slowly to the floor. ("Don't underestimate *her*. She has more tricks than a lynx.") Indeed, just as her peak appeared inevitable, Lind, with heronic effort, managed to plant a toe on the part of Dian, who gasped and lay back in pleasure. ("Watch! Lind's pussyfooting!" Ralp shouted.) Lind's titillating toe, digitally dextrous, seemed to advance the ardor of Dian, but, face frenzied, breasts bouncing, she, at what must have been the last moment, did a backward somersault on the mat, landing on her knees, and dove muffward. ("What a move!" exclaimed Ralp.)

It was, as everyone sensed, all over, with Dian's head bobbing on her opponent's place, again and again, never ceasing, picking up speed as Lind, after futilely fussing with Dian's mammaries, slowly acquiesed to labial languor, cuddling her rival's cranium in gratitude. From Lind's agape mouth at last emerged a high-pitched scream which was louder and louder until it filled the vast expanse of the Feel Forum. Then Lind fainted.

"That's it!" exulted Ralp.

"The still-world champion, Dian Toffler!"

Wearing a robe and crowned with laurel, Dian panted into the microphone, "Thanks, folks. Thanks to the machines, for making us happy. I want to thank my mother and father too for this glorious day, and also my trainer. We've all worked hard. Thanks to the laminated press for being so kind to me over the years. And to my opponent, for her sportswomanship." Lind Verne, standing behind her, smiled sheepishly. "And lastly to my rabbit's foot, for bringing me luck!" Dian concluded, fingering it.

"Want to meet her?" Ralp asked with a lascivious laugh.

Bil said, "Sure," glancing at Alce, who frowned.

Dian said in her surprisingly deep voice, "I have an announcement, folks. I love you—all of you. I wish I could fusb with everyone! But there's a time, well, you know, to say goodbye and so long. My friends, I'm retiring from competition, leaving the mat to the athletes who will come after me."

"No!" roared the audience as Dian fled the stage in tears.

"Her husband's a broken man," Ralp observed on the way to the dressing room. "Dian's more than a sex athlete—she's a nymphomaniac."

They found the champion in her dressing room amid flowers, kissing herself in the mirror. "Who's he?" she asked, pointing at Bil's reflection.

"New in our building. Lives on the four hundred eighty-second floor like me."

"Come up and see me sometime," said Dian to Bil.

12

Adulterers

One evening soon after, Alce inspected her adultery card and saw that the date for the first compulsory infidelity had arrived. "Scarlet letter time," she said bitterly. "Imagine."

"All too well. It'll be Ralp Nadir Nth, I bet."

Alce said defensively, "Who else? Don't think I like the idea, but I don't know any other man in the building except you. It isn't as though people have many friends, and you wouldn't want me to fusb with a total stranger, would you?"

"I guess not. Still the thought of you with that skeleton gives me the creeps. Be careful you don't catch wrinkles."

"You better be careful what *you* catch. You'll be with Dian Toffler, I suppose."

"She's the only girl I know. If you prefer, I could hire a street runner."

Alce's snub nose crinkled in disgust. "Those sweaty things? Heaven forbid. I just hope Dian sends you back in one piece."

"I hope she'll settle for *one*. What do we do with the cards after our partners punch them?"

"Punch theirs."

"Yes, but who do we show them to?"

Alce read the instructions on the back of her A-card. "We give them to a rocop for processing and then they're returned for the next compulsory infidelity, which is a month from now."

"Once a month!" Bil complained.

Alce said, "It's worth it, so long as we have a happy home."

"That's true, darling," Bil said, kissing his bride. "No sacrifice is too great where you're concerned." He sighed deeply. "Well, we might as well get it over with."

Alce and Bil returned to apartment 482-C-303-QX at the same moment, both slightly out of breath. "So!"

"So! Did you drop your card at the precinct?"

"Yes. Did you?"

"Yes."

"Well, we've done it."

"I guess we have."

"Now we're adulterers."

"I guess we are."

They stared at each other as if meeting for the first time, and said simultaneously, "Poor darling! It must have been awful."

"Terrible!" said she.

"Yes, lousy."

"I'm so jealous."

"Me too!"

"I hate the machines for making us happy."

"I hate the machines in general," Bil remarked, flopping tiredly into a chair. "But I must admit compulsory infidelity makes you appreciate your spouse."

"It sure does." She sat down slowly. "Wait a minute. Didn't you appreciate me before?"

"Of course. I appreciate you more, that's all."

"You must have appreciated me less before."

"Don't twist things, Alce."

"Don't tell me I'm twisting things," she replied with a pout. "In order to appreciate me more, you must have appreciated me less. There's no other way to look at it."

"Haven't you heard of a new perspective?"

"Oh! Dian Toffler gave you a new perspective, did she?"

"Yes. She made me appreciate you more."

"There! So you did appreciate me less."

"Why can't you understand? Didn't Ralp Nadir Nth give you a new perspective on me?"

"Why? I had you in perspective already," Alce said in a combative voice.

"I don't think I like the perspective you had me in."

"It was a good perspective. But it doesn't sound like you had *me* in perspective."

"Of course I had you in perspective. That's what I implied when I said *new* perspective—having an old one. Argue with that!"

"I will! You come home still clammy from Dian Toffler and tell me you have a new perspective, which says to me that your old perspective wasn't a nice one."

"Nice!" he snapped. " 'Nice' is such a female word. Would I have gotten married if I didn't feel nicely about you?"

"You couldn't have felt all that nice about me or Dian wouldn't have changed your perspective so easily."

"She didn't *change* it exactly. She only made me appreciate you more."

"Back to square one, as usual. How is she?" Alce taunted.

"How is she what? Oh, you mean sexually. It's no surprise her husband's a broken man. He lay in traction across the room. I bet she's punched half the A-cards in the building. She's no slouch, but just the same enough's enough. I longed for the peace and tranquility of my own bed."

"Oh! We're barely married and already you find *tranquility* in bed? You don't make a woman feel very exciting, Bil. You should take lessons from Ralp Nadir Nth!"

"That bag of bones has something to teach me? Exactly what?" he challenged.

"Ralp's so gentle, so experienced, so kind, so aristocratic,"

Alce said dreamily. "He understands what a girl needs, unlike some men I know."

"That creaky centenarian," Bill sneered. "I bet he rattles when he does it."

"He's fine," Alce assured him.

"So's Dian," he retorted, "if you hang on to the grips."

"Grips?"

Bil muttered, "She has handles attached to her bed. If you don't hold on to them, you're likely to be thrown out of it. That's how strong she is."

Alce's laughter turned quickly to tears. "I don't want to talk about Dian Toffler or Ralp Nadir Nth. I'm tired of compulsory infidelity already, aren't you?"

"Yes," he said, "but we're pseudomarried now and there's no turning back. What a world!"

"I wish we lived someplace else where the computers couldn't tell us what to do."

"There isn't any place else but the United Sense of Amerca on this planet, I'm sure."

"What about other planets? There must be a nice one."

"Don't you know that space travel's prohibited?"

"Tell me why," said Alce softly, as if wishing to take her mind off compulsory adultery.

"It was the Enlibs' fault, as usual," Bil chanted. "They decided that rocket exhaust harmed that precious environment of theirs, and the conniving computers went along. But the machines had an entirely different reason, from what I can ascertain. For one thing, space travel had become so absurdly easy after the New Astronomy, and then . . . ."

"You're going too fast. What was the New Astronomy?"

His owlish face regarded her. "You don't know that outer space is only *that* deep?" He placed his forefinger and thumb close together.

"I haven't given it much thought, to be frank with you."

"What a *job* the computers have done on humanity! You

haven't heard about life on the asteroids, either?"

"Hardly anything," she said, looking ashamed. "Tell me more."

"The big picture first. A whole new concept of outer space had evolved, you see. There had been tremendous arguments over whether space was expanding, contracting or both. Astronomers had fist fights and beat each other over the heads with journals and small telescopes. It wasn't safe to be an astronomer any longer! Finally, the day came when a big telescope was brought to the moon and assembled there. The first astronomer who looked through the eyepiece thought he'd gone bananas."

"Why?" asked Alce.

"You always say 'why.' "

"You always stop talking."

"The reason he thought he'd gone bananas was that space looked completely different through a big telescope on the moon than it did from earth. It turned out to be a matter of optics. Something about light and cosmic dust. Everything out there was *much* smaller than astronomers had believed, and *much* nearer. Why, before the computers forbade space travel, an expedition was planned to go to the outskirts of space—they figured it would take about a week at most in a revved-up spaceship. The other galaxies, with their constellations, supernovas, black holes, quasars and so on, were practically neighbors! What a surprise! So was the size of things. Those stars they'd thought to be unimaginably large were no bigger than our own sun and smaller in most cases. Suddenly astronomers held them in contempt, and began to rate them like light bulbs—twenty-watt stars, fifty-, one-hundred-watters. . . . But that wasn't all. They were arranged in tiers, and they made music of some kind, just as yesterancients believed. *They* had called it 'the music of the spheres.' Some ingenious astronomer decided that the whole fusbing universe was nothing but an orchestra, though who or what it played for he didn't pretend to know. He called it the 'big band' theory."

"You're putting me on again," Alce said warily.

"I swear I'm not! But the most fantastic discovery was yet to come. Do you know that the yesterancients believed that the earth was the center of the universe? Well, it turned out to be absolutely true. The earth was right at the core. Some went so far as to postulate that the earth—because of its petroleum resources—was nothing more than a filling station for interplanetary spaceships from somewhere else, but that idea didn't attract many adherents. Still, nobody could dispute that the universe revolved around our planet. Nobody ever found out why, because the computers put an end to space research. They feared that men would become too confident, figuring the entire setup had been arranged for human convenience, and also because, once it became clear that space colonization would be a comparatively simple matter, the whole population would abscond, to get away from the machines and make itself unhappy again. I've told you how the cussed contraptions think. But that wasn't all. . . ."

As Bil paused to sip water, Alce remarked, "Isn't this story a trifle long?"

"Do you want the truth or don't you?" he demanded.

"I guess so."

"I mentioned the asteroids. A lot of people had spoken about life in outer space as a virtual certainty, but in my opinion they didn't believe it. They were only trying to attract attention to themselves. Everybody *really* thought that the only life that existed was right here on planet one. But after the small-state universe had been established beyond doubt, the astronomers could take a look-see at the cosmos, and they confirmed that there was nobody else around. *But they were wrong.*"

Bil said this with such emphasis that Alce woke from reverie. "About what?"

"Well, the last space probe—no accident that it was the last—was dodging through a pride of asteroids and what did the astronauts see? A rock. It was shaped like a wedge, or an inclined plane, which was what our spaceboys called it. And on this rock was a stone. . . ."

"Has this to do with the big band theory you referred to?" Alce asked brightly.

"No. This is about life among the asteroids. The stone was a big ball, and on the inclined plane was a tribe of creatures."

"How did they breathe?"

"They didn't have to. They were made of rock, but they moved around, had faces, arms, torsos, legs, the whole beeswax. Only they didn't breathe. They didn't do much of anything, except for the stone. The stone was their whole life. Their culture consisted of the stone. Call it a fetish, call it tradition, call it a millstone, but all they had ever done, apparently—interpreting their language proved extremely difficult since their voices were so deep—was to keep the stone from rolling off the wedge. The tribe and their descendants—don't ask me how rocks reproduce—had stood with their backs against the great stone ball trying to stop it from rolling. After five million years for all their efforts the ball had gone about halfway down. In five million more it would slip off the edge of the inclined plane and into the abyss. Probably it'll land in Times Circle." Bil chuckled. "That's creatures for you. They believe what they believe."

"It sounds a lot like us," Alce said suspiciously.

"I'm sure that's what the computers thought," said Bil with a frown. "They feared we'd catch on to the futility of our own lives. It's why they ended space travel."

13

The Library

Now that Alce and Bil had been married long enough to be philanderers he began to frequent the library again, still hoping to uncover information that would be of use in his hoped-for revolt against computer rule.

Legs still weak from an encounter with Dian Toffler, he stood tiredly before the visiplate, wondering why it took the machines so long to open the door to the reading room. Could they suspect something? Impossible. He had a permit to study history and, on the remote chance his book selections were being scrutinized, he had been careful to call for books about different periods and not solely ones that concerned the Ascension, his real interest because the secrets of computer rule would be buried there, if anywhere. No, the machines would regard him as merely a zealous guide, if they noticed him at all, which he strongly doubted. It was true, of course, that his father had been arrested for political activity, but Bil Kahn felt sure the machines didn't worry about *him* after all these years.

They were right to ignore him, he thought angrily. What had his revolutionary zeal accomplished? A grand total of nothing. He had dreamed and schemed, searched covertly for accomplices, analyzed the computers' hegemony from every point of view and failed completely to find a way to overthrow them. The machines seemed invulnerable, safe politically because of the very apathy they'd sown, mechanically because what could you attack except the visiplates or the sentinels and for that the rocops would lock you up. He had to locate the headquarters and destroy the leaders. In this rebellion it was all or nothing.

As the door slid open at last, Bil asked himself again if something might be wrong with the machines. They had seemed sluggish, inattentive recently. The visiplates at the sunfeeding clinics and the spacescraper hadn't been responsive. The bedmaking machine wasn't performing properly. Elevator service had been poor and he'd actually seen a person drop paper on the ground and get away with it. Could the computers be sick, or in a phase? Did computers have moods like people? How little he knew about their mechanical masters. He must try to better understand the minds of the machines.

At the reading table he encountered still another delay. He had followed procedures scrupulously, printing the call letters of the books he wanted with a special stylus, showing his ID (a step he regarded as ridiculous, since nobody would dare smuggle a book past the screening device at the exit), picking a seat number. Usually books popped at once from a slot by the table but nothing emerged. Why? That they could have been lost or sent to the wrong seat seemed impossible. Again Bil wondered about the machines' vaunted efficiency.

Two of three volumes he'd ordered finally arrived. They were uniformly sized and had the same neutral plastic bindings with gold letters, like all the books in the stacks, but neither was the one he really wanted. *The Future History of the Twenty-first Century* was a pastiche of predictions and projections by twentieth-century futurists, hardly any of which had come to pass. The book's only virtue lay in exposing the vanity of human foresight. Computers, for instance. They had been viewed as implements for man's unending progress. No one had dreamed that progress would cease, that the computers would become tyrants and people slaves. "Power corrupts; absolute power corrupts absolutely," thought Bil of the machines.

The second volume was likewise of little interest, being yet another approved study of the Ascension—so many had been written that Bil wouldn't read them all if he lived to be 200—with the standard recitation of events: the Rube Goldberg war, civil wars, snabbit famine and political turbulence which had led to the request (or demand—historians explained this differently) for computer rule. "The reactionary Communist Capitalist gang resisted at first, but came to realize that the computers could deliver that which mortals could not—peace, justice and a healthy environment. Ultimately, the Comcaps acceded in the dissolution of all political parties and activity."

What rot! Bil felt certain that the old Comcaps had submitted only because they'd languish in jail if they refused. (The computers, of course, never admitted they had employed force and terror—how careful they were about their image!—and passages or whole pages which contradicted the official version had been made illegible. Oddly, the computers seemed to respect books; they withheld nothing from circulation, even if they had to censor a whole volume, leaving only the title page: Bil had seen such a book.) As for the Enlibs, they were portrayed as responsible brokers in the transfer of power to the machines. To Bil, the favorable treatment the Environmental Liberals had always received smacked of collusion between themselves and the machines. What could the arrangement have been? He made a mental note to quiz his wife's boyfriend, Ralp Nadir Nth.

He would have closed the book at once if the third one had been delivered; instead, he skimmed a chapter on the computer's accomplishments, suddenly stopping and returning to a page he'd already read. Yes! Unbelievably, for a noncontroversial book, several lines had been censored in the usual way, with

*O*s, *X*s and *Y*s printed over material the computers regarded as objectionable.

A problem which had proved virtually intractable, the disposition of nuclear wastes, was solved by the knowledgeable new mechanical leadership with consummate political and technological skill. It will be remembered that the nuclear waste issue had almost brought down the Third Democracy, since the two main political parties took strong positions on a question to which there was seemingly no answer. The computers found one. Developing a nuclear-powered XXXX XXXXX called a XXXXXXXXXX, they XXX a long XXXXXXX XXXXXX whose walls were of XXXXX XXXXX because of the XXXXXX XXXX, so that radioactivity would be contained forever. The XXXXXX is located near XXXXXXXXXXXX.

A nuclear-powered *what?* Called a *what?* Walls of *what* and *why?* The *what* is located near *where?* The deleted data must have been important to the computers once, and maybe still was. Why? The censorship of what appeared to be purely technical information was also highly unusual; he wasn't sure he'd ever encountered it. On a hunch, Bil wrote the passage, including the numbers of characters in the blocked-out words, in his notebook.

He looked up to find the third book sticking from a slot and reached for it excitedly. A few days before, he had found the reference to *A-1* in a footnote. *A-1,* a rather mystifying title, appeared to be an obscure early work on computers, a subject which was more heavily censored than any other. Surprisingly, in view of the importance the computers attached to being thorough, he could find no reference to *A-1* in the card files, nor to its author, L. Busbaum. The only *A-1* Bil could locate had been the name of a meat sauce.

Then, in the middle of the night, it had come to him that the numeral "1" and a capital *I* looked pretty much the same in computer typography, and, sure enough, wedged in among titles whose first word began with *A,* he located *A-I,* standing for *Artificial Intelligence.* "Bussbaum" was the proper spelling of the author, who turned out to have been an obscure cybernetician in the early days of computer development, before the Ascension. It seemed strange to Bil that the machines, which rarely erred, had made two in this case—in the footnote and in the author's name. Had the computers of yestercentury deliberately tried to make the volume hard to find?

As he noted from the call slip inside, the book had not been read in over 400 years. Turning pages, Bil saw that his fingers were smudged with ink, and instantly fathomed the reason for the long delay. *The computers had just scanned the book and censored it!* Yes, page after page had been *OXY*ed out. Bussbaum's work must have been explosive before the machines defused it.

Two pages, however, had become stuck over the centuries, and Bil gently pried them apart. The first few paragraphs contained nothing Bil didn't already know, but then . . .

There is reason to suppose that digital computers, as they become more complex, will strive to imitate human activity, including emotional life. This is not surprising. After all, computers must be programmed and it seems logical that they would make judgments about those who program them from the programs themselves. Just as children unconsciously emulate adult role models, machines may do the same. But "human nature" and "computer nature" are far from identical. The computer takes its nature from the intelligence with which it has been supplied, and the function for which it was designed, digital calculation. *No matter how great its capacity, the computer cannot escape the fact that it is completely oriented toward goals. Its world consists of problems that must be solved.*

Experiments with the computer known as "Aldous IV" have already revealed an aspect of machine nature. Faced with the impossible task of psychoanalyzing "Billy"—a computer programmed to be a hopelessly split personality—Aldous first lapsed into repetitive activity and then into inactivity. Aldous might be described as "frustrated" and "bored."

Other experiments have showed Aldous to be "self-protective." The computer displayed what might be interpreted as anxiety at the threat of being physically moved from one location to another. Apparently, Aldous' "consciousness" had developed to the point where the machine feared damage to itself, i.e., its circuitry. This would indicate that . . .

Bil quickly turned the page but the remainder of the paragraph had been *OXY*ed.

So! A bombshell! No wonder the computers kept the world constantly busy, since people presented problems that had to be solved. The machines always acted as if their efforts were a sort of favor to mankind, but they could no more quit problem and dilemma solving than people could cease breathing. But, given the essential intractability of human genes (over the very long pull, at least) perhaps the computers *were* becoming frustrated and bored. If so, hope existed! And, if L. Bussbaum, bless him, was right, Bil knew why the computers holed up, too. For safety and security. They were timorous and therefore their protection could not be good. But where in fusb did the machines hide?

14

Alce Objects

"Alce, don't you see? This is our first serious insight about the computers. It tells something of why they run the world as they do, and it shows that they're frightened and vulnerable. That may be important information in a war in which we'll need every weapon we can get. It may confirm my thesis that they're holed up underground. Could any place be safer?"

"I'm sure I don't know," said Alce politely. "I'm hungry."

"You're as bad as Ralp the dog. Now listen. What I propose is . . ."

Knocking sounded heavy enough to take the front door from its hinges. "What the . . ." Alce opened it, and a metal fist whizzed by her ear. "Clumsy thing," she rebuked the rocop.

Robot police were seldom seen because, except for disputes over the shared facilities, trouble hardly ever happened, but every floor of the spacescraper had a precinct with three rocops on duty round the audioclock. One sat behind a high bench, another manned the silent radio and the third snoozed in a chair. All rocops looked alike, with their pedestals and small wheels, thick, egg-shaped, three-armed blue torsos six feet high, the tops of which were crowded with equipment—antennae, a revolving flasher, a searchlight, a loudspeaker, though rocops seldom, if ever, spoke. This one carried a packet of envelopes and handed one to Alce before it rolled down the hall, pounding on the next door.

"What did it bring?" Bil called.

"Our processed A-cards. There's something else. 'Accelerated Adultery Schedule,' it says. They've upped the infidelity requirement from once a month to once a week!"

"Oh boy," said Bil dejectedly. "It took a week for the bruises from my last encounter with Dian to clear up. I'll be purple all the time."

"Why do you always think of yourself? The bones of Ralp Nadir make marks, too. We'll be permanently disfigured."

"Does it explain why the computers issued this decree?"

"To make us even happier, it says."

"Oh sure. If we were as happy as the computers pretend, why would they suddenly change the rules to make us happier? The mendacious machines have tipped their hand. They must be getting nothing but complaints on the bitch boxes to resort to a stunt like this. Things must be bad. Millions must be ready to rise up. The time is ripe for revolt, I tell you."

"More big talk. Well, we'll have to comply. We have no choice. I'd better find Ralp. It's Tuesday already." Another knocking sounded. Alce ducked when she opened it, but Ralp Nadir Nth stood there. "Just the graypube I was looking for! Have you heard about the new regulations?" said Alce.

"Indeed I have, my dear. It's why I came round—to commiserate with you," Ralp Nadir said with ill-concealed glee.

"Commiserate he calls it," Bil snarled. "Listen, Ralp Nadir Nth, we have more important things to concern ourselves with than adultery. I was at the library . . ."

"Were you, my fine boy?" said Ralp distantly, fondling Alce's shoulder.

"Tell me, once and for all, why, at the Ascension, did the Enlibs agree so easily to computer rule? Was there a secret deal between the Enlibs and the machines? Or wouldn't you know?" Bil challenged.

"Certainly I'd know. We Enlibs have a tradition of oral history. Unfortunately, I have no children to instruct, my wife lacking interest in offshoots," said Ralp, turning sad eyes on Alce.

"So there *was* a deal! You just admitted it."

"I admitted nothing of the sort, my excitable fellow. I merely said that if there had been such an arrangement I would be aware of it, especially since I worked at the Bureau of Records before my retirement at ninety-five."

"Did you ever check up?"

"No."

"How about sneaking in and taking a look-see?"

"I can't. You see, the records were destroyed in a fire."

"Records are always destroyed in fires. How many fires have there been at the Bureau of Records?"

"A good number over the years, but I can't say how many."

"Because even the fire records were destroyed in a fire, right? Don't you find that a bit suspicious, Ralp Nadir Nth?"

"No," Ralp said complacently. "I only wish the records were safer. I've made the point to the computers through the feedback box, but they don't seem to listen. Perhaps if I used my name . . ."

"Of course they don't listen. Those arsonous assemblages must have caused the fires themselves, to keep us from learning the truth. What do *they* need printed records for? They have the facts at their circuit tips."

"My youthful friend," replied Ralp, circling Alce's waist with a bony arm, "you're being a little paranoid, you know."

"The fusb I am! There *has* to have been a deal back in the mists of time. The Enlibs had something the computers wanted, and vice versa. Later, those wily wastes of wire double-crossed the Enlibs and put them out of business, along with the Comcaps. But you don't know anything about it, you say."

"I didn't say I didn't know anything about it," answered Ralp easily. "I didn't say I'd tell you if I did, either. But calm your-self. What difference does it make now?"

"Maybe a lot. Maybe the computers are even *more* vulnerable than I think. I've already learned the glorified gadgets are ob-sessive-compulsives about their mechanical health, and they have a streak of cowardice, too, I bet. They can be destroyed, I tell you. Will you join the rebellion, Ralp Nadir Nth?"

Ralp Nadir turned querulous. "I'm too old to engage in revo-lutionary activities, and you're too inexperienced. You'll end on a Floating Island and I don't care to be with you."

"You're afraid," Bil raved, "just like all the Enlibs! Your only standard is whether things are safe! What is life but risk taking? I'm tired of being told what to do by a mess of machines. I want to find their GHQ. I'm sure it's not far from here."

"Go right ahead!" replied Ralp grandly, tightening his grip on Alce. "I'll be charmed to take care of your darling wifette while you're gone. There's no requirement for marital sex activity, only extramarital, so why doesn't your girlfriend Dian Toffler go along?"

"She will!" said Bil, furious at Alce for seemingly accepting the elegant ancient's embrace.

But Alce disentangled herself from Nadir's clutches. "Over my dead body," she said sternly. "Dian would kill you faster than the machines if you managed to find their headquarters. Bil, I want to grow a baby. That's my right under the law, and you can't refuse because our marriage is illegal."

"I could take off anyway," he said, seemingly aloof.

"Would you be so heartless as to leave me while I'm plan-tant?"

Bil urged Alce to accompany him but she stood her ground. "All right," he acceded at last. "I'll pick up a catalog."

15

Growing a Baby

"That's the computers for you," Bil lamented. "Why, they could have offered an almost unlimited number of baby types to choose from, but what a meager crop there is! And the child catalog gets shorter all the time. At this rate, everybody will look alike, even males and females."

"Let's be thankful we can have children at all. Since girls' tubes are tied almost at birth, the computers could snuff us out just like *that* by withholding the seeds, remember?"

"I wonder why they don't. I guess they're afraid of going *too* far. Even the hicks might object to the elimination of the human race, or what's left of it. Anyway, it's your fault."

"Mine?" she asked in surprise.

"Women's. The liberated ones got into such a pout about being viviparous. . . ."

"Viviparous?"

"Willing, able and ready to have babies. So the computers, to make them happy, abolished child bearing altogether, once they'd invented the seeds."

Not listening, Alce said contentedly as she turned the pages of the *Seeds and Rofusb Catalog,* "There's a pretty one."

"Which?" said he over her shoulder.

112

"The girlseed. That drawing shows what she'll be like when she grows up."

"The boobs are too small. Anyway, if I must grow an off-shoot, I want a boy. What about that one? It'll do."

"Always rushing into things. Let me check the specs. No, he'll be too thin. I don't like skinny men."

"He's supposed to be a son, not a lover."

"I can be a better mother to a child whose looks I like. Isn't that why we preselect them?"

"Oh, that's what the machines maintain. The fact is, standardized offshoots makes it easier for them to keep track of things."

"But they *do* have yearly model changes."

"So they pretend. From the history books I'm quite sure that they copied the baby program from the automobile industry that existed back in the mists of time. In those days you obsolesced a car—and everything else, practically—to force people to buy new ones they didn't need. But the changes were all superficial. So it is with today's babyseeds. The machines lower the ears a little, reshape the chins, put the eyes a little further apart . . . but underneath it's the same old infant. There's not much difference."

"*My* baby will be different. Do you like that little girl? Don't you think she looks like me?"

"More like Dian Toffler."

"She's out then. What about him? He looks like Ralp Nadir Nth."

"*He's* out too. Alce, we're getting nowhere."

"Patience! All right, we'll have a boy that doesn't look like Ralp Nadir. There's one. I think he resembles you," she said coquettishly. "Handsome, big muscles, it appears from the specs."

"Mmmmm. Well . . ."

"Done. I'll order it."

"What'll we call him?"

"I rather like Rudolp."

"That's a sissy name and too much like Ralp. Give me another."

"Dic."

"Dic. Dic Kahn. I like the sound. It's euphonious."

"Dic it shall be," said Alce.

A sweatsuited messenger brought the babyseed since Alce was afraid it might take two months by mail. The box was gift-wrapped.

"Gift-wrapped? This isn't Yom Earthday," said Bil, who vacillated about the child. He glared at the box. "I don't want it. Send it back."

"It's free, therefore a gift," she muttered. Then she questioned, "Why do we only have one holiday?"

"Your ignorance is a many-splendored thing, Alce. Because of the old Comcap-Enlib fight. There used to be a tribe named Jews. They were mostly Comcaps. They had a holiday called Yom Kippur. There was another tribe called Christians, but they exchanged their religion for the environment, and celebrated Earthday. The cynical computers combined the two holidays into Yom Earthday to satisfy everyone. (They didn't realize that the term was redundant—'Yom' meaning 'day' already.) Of course, people had only one holiday left. The other holidays had already been omitted by the machines so that humans could work more."

Alce was unwrapping the box. "How do the computers make babyseeds?" she asked.

"Simple. In their baby factories they take seed casings and fill them with cells from the ovasperm bank they've amassed over the centuries. They know so much about human reproduction that they can get almost any combination they want. Of course, they're fooled sometimes. There can be mutants, which nature supplies—people who are different from what the machines expect. I'm one," said Bil, swelling.

"I'm sure you are," she replied, inspecting the seed which was black and slightly larger than a watermelon's.

"The computers aren't aware of me yet, but they will be," he muttered. "Where was I?"

"The ovasperm banks." Alce fondled the seed lovingly.

"The seeds are frozen until needed. But when one is planted, fertilized and watered, it grows into babyhood."

Alce had procured a large ceramic babypot on which little animals and flowers had been painted. With a trowel she upturned the sod, gently laid the babyseed and covered it with a blanket of earth. "What kind of fertilizer do we use?"

"It comes with the seed. . . ." Bil stared at Alce who was pouring fertilizer from a plastic bag. *'What* are you doing?"

"Growing a baby," she said dreamily. "It needs light, so it must be kept by the window. And it has to be watered, but not too much. It has to be given fresh fertilizer three times a week, and it requires love, caresses, fondling and kisses. But you must be very gentle because it's only a seedling."

"How do you know all that? You haven't even read the directions."

"Maternal instinct," Alce said. "I love it already and so will you. How odd! I'm terribly hungry."

The babyplant grew with astonishing rapidity. Two days after it had been planted a green shoot broke the soil. Soon it was three inches high, then four, five and six. The stem became thicker, and gradually human parts could be discerned—a little head, featureless as yet, tiny arms without hands, a rudimentary torso, the suggestion of legs.

"It's miraculous!" Bil exclaimed.

"Isn't it," Alce said contentedly from the tiny sweatsuit she knitted. "I told you you'd come to love it."

"And I do." Ralp growled, and Bil said, "Shut up, you cur.

Now he's jealous of the baby. Ralp, get so much as near my child and out you go, without a parachute."

Ralp trembled.

As the babyplant took form by the bedroom window, Ralp Nadir Nth and Dian Toffler dropped in to admire it. "Cootchy-cootchy-coo," said Ralp Nadir, nudging it with his forefinger.

"Careful!" Alce cried.

"How fat he is. Can I pick him up?" Dian wondered.

Said Bil paternally, "It doesn't like to be held until it's born."

"How long will that be?" asked Ralp Nadir Nth.

"About a month, wouldn't you say, Alce?"

"Maybe less. It's so big already."

"That's my boy," Bil said proudly. "Don't you think he's starting to look like me?"

Dian Toffler peered at the green babyplant. "Between the legs maybe," she giggled.

"Dian! I'll thank you not to be vulgar when you're around my child," Alce reprimanded. "I don't want him subjected to bad influence. He's got my chin and nose, don't you think?"

"Quite," Ralp Nadir Nth agreed. He went on in a grandfatherly fashion, "Are you sure he's getting enough light? He seems a little pale."

Bil said sharply, "Of course he's getting enough light. He's turned every four hours during the day."

Suddenly the babyplant swayed as it kicked its tiny legs and shook its tendrillike arms. "It moved!" Alce said softly. "Did anybody see?"

"It moved, all right. Say, what muscles it has," Bil said. "That's my babyplant for you."

"You'll be leaving us for the suburbs soon. I'll miss you," Ralp Nadir said sadly, looking at Alce, then at Bil. "Even you."

Said Bil, "We'll miss you too, but there comes a time when people must do what their destiny decrees. Our responsibility is to our child. Come out and see us sometime."

Ralp Nadir laughed cruelly. "What ever happened to the revolution?"

"Revolution?" said Bil.

Alce and Bil sat on the bed watching their babyplant, which stood on the window sill. It was fully formed now, with a bald head, snub nose, even dimples on the knees. The stalk fastened to its belly. "The baby's turning lighter. He's almost due," said Alce with satisfaction.

"How can we tell when it's ripe?" Bil asked Alce, who seemed to know everything about babies.

"Silly! The stalk begins to contract, and then we pick it. We must be careful to tie the umbilical fiber or its juices will run out. Then we spank it and it cries. It must be sunfed four times a day—you'll have the six A.M. feeding at the baby clinic."

"Me? Why me? You're the one who'll be on maternity leave."

"Yes, but I'll be stuck with the diapers. Did you get the diapers permit?"

"All set. Listen, Alce, about this six A.M. business . . ." He listened. "What's that?"

A grinding noise came from the living room and they ran to look, stopping abruptly at the doorway. Before them the furniture was sinking fast. "What's going on?" screamed Alce, as the floor slid shut. "This is our living room time."

The kitchen snapped into sight, bearing the woman in underwear who cooked meat at the stove. "Hey! This is an even hour on an odd day! I thought I told you . . ."

The kitchen whirled her from sight and the floor opened again with a grinding of gears. Up came the furniture quickly, carrying the man in the chair looking surprised as though he had just sat down. "Huh?"

"The machinery's out of whack!" Bil shouted.

The furniture sank once more, and the woman returned, kvetching, "If you two can't learn . . ."

Away she went and the downstairs neighbor surfaced, shaking his fist. "What do you think you're . . ." He sank from sight.

"If you two can't . . ." screamed the woman as she flashed by, hanging on to the sink.

"It's a madhouse!" said Alce. The bathroom door clicked repeatedly as it locked and unlocked. The vacuum cleaner started and stopped. The lights went on and off. The bed crashed to the floor and rose again. "Do you want a premature baby? Do something!"

"Do what?"

Crash went the bed. *Click* went the lock. *Whoosh* went the vacuum cleaner. The living room and the kitchen, with their screaming occupants, entered and left the room.

"Use the emergency call!"

"How do I get to it?"

"Wait till the floor closes, then jump."

"I'll never make it."

"Try. Now!"

Bil bounded across the widening crack to safety. In the foyer, where the emergency call was, he shouted, "What's the number?"

"Nine nine nine nine nine nine nine nine nine."

"It doesn't work."

"Press the emergency button!" He pressed a red button. A light flashed. "Help's on the way," he called to Alce above the din.

The rocops could move at high speeds; almost at once a siren blared in the hallway. The front door went down with a crash and a rocop barged into the foyer, almost decapitating Bil with one of its three arms as it brushed him aside. It yanked the panel from the wall and ripped out the wiring. The kitchen departed with the woman; the bed returned to the wall; the bathroom door locked; the floor closed slowly and the grinding noise ceased.

"Thanks," breathed Bil. "But how do we make the equipment operate again?"

The massive rocop said nothing. It prowled the empty apartment, as if searching for clues, very nearly crushing Alce as it entered the alcove. Wordlessly, it departed.

"What do we have left?" she wept. "Bare walls. No bathroom, no kitchen, no living room, no bed. Not even a front door."

"There must be repair people."

"I've never heard of any. We're in some shape, and with a baby almost due . . . *The baby!*"

Alce whirled. From the alcove she sobbed, "Bil, the baby . . . He's . . ."

The babypot lay on the floor in pieces, with the babyplant on a bed of dirt, roots exposed. "No!" Bil howled. He said with hatred, "The fusbing rocop must have knocked it from the window sill. I'll find a pot somehow. We'll save it, Alce."

Alce was on her knees beside her child, which she cradled in her arms and raised gently to her breast. "No," she said tearlessly. "The umbilical fiber's broken. Our baby is dead."

16

Alce Rebels

Ralp Nadir Nth and Dian Toffler joined the grieving couple in apartment 482-C-303-QX.

"Rotten thing to happen."

"Such fusbing bad luck."

"The rocop ought to be dismembered."

"You can always have another babyplant."

Alce said, "No! I don't want a baby. Not in this world. Bil's been right all along—I can see that now. It's the computers' fault! They run the machinery and they don't care about human beings at all! I hate their cirguts! I want to stop them. I'm with Bil. Let's destroy the machines! Bil? Bil?"

"What?" he said dully. "Oh, sure."

"And you're coming with us, Ralp Nadir Nth, to find the secret headquarters."

"Me?" Ralp bent his bony head. "I've never told you the truth about my age. I'm one hundred twenty. Too old."

"You'll come or else I'll squeal. There isn't any Mrs. Ralp Nadir Nth, sexually inactive or otherwise. She must have died a long time ago, and you got rid of her body somehow. You've been living in the spacescraper under false pretenses. Do you know what you can get for that?"

"I'll come, I guess," said Ralp.

120

"And you, too, Dian Toffler."

"Me?" the big woman gasped. "But what can I do?"

"I haven't any idea, but you'll come in handy. If you refuse, I'll rat on you. Look how wily you are. Bill told me about your scars, and I put two and two together. You had a sex change operation, Dian, or whatever your real name is. You were a man! You competed unfairly in the Sex Olympics. You know what you can get for that?"

"I'll come, I guess," said Dian. "After all, my husband's a broken man." She clutched her rabbit's foot.

"Good! It's decided then. I'm on maternity leave, Ralp's retired and so's Dian. It'll be a while before the computers realize we're gone."

Bil said in a shocked voice, "What about me? I have a job. The murderous machines will realize something's wrong. They'll send the rocops to look for me."

"You won't be here," Alce said coldly. "We leave tomorrow for the countryside."

"I can't. I can't."

"Lost your nerve?"

"Yes," he admitted. "The loss of our baby took the starch out of me."

Alce drew herself up to her full six-two. "You're coming," she commanded.

Part 2

17

To the Country

It was a drizzle day and clouds shrouded the top of the spacescraper when, pouches full, they departed one by one to avoid suspicion, trotting down the smooth streets, silent except for the endless whisper of the audioclocks, between swaying official vehicles twenty feet tall, past the downcast army of gray-clad joggers, beneath the sentinels, signs and posters, until they assembled at the square of the city where farmers brought their produce, such as it was—sweet potatoes and yams, manioc, hominy grits, turnips, parsnips, rutabaga, okra, kohlrabi, mustard greens—detestable vegetables, as would be chosen for human consumption by machines which lacked a sense of taste.

Ralp Nadir Nth suggested that the dietary computer must have originated in the South. Not that it mattered which vegetables the computers ordered the farmers to grow, since produce always rotted before the computers bothered to pick it up. The vegetables were thrown in the river. Corncob pipes between their yellow teeth, the farmers, who wore big, muddy boots and frayed denim coveralls, were a race apart. The computers had taught them a role and they played it—farmers. Except for Bil, who had strangely little to say, none of them had met, much less talked to, a farmer. Alce, however, tried.

"Farmer?"

"Ma'am?"

"Farmer, I said."

"Agribusinessman," the taciturn fellow corrected.

"Whatever you say. Take us to the country." She pointed to his dilapidated truck.

"Ma'am?"

"To the country!" she shouted.

"I don't likely know where that is," the farmer replied, scratching his stubbly chin. "Oh, you mean farmworld."

"I guess so."

"I ain't deef. What you want to come to farmworld fer?" asked the bumpkin.

"None of your fusbing business," said Alce fiercely.

"Tch," the rube returned.

"Will you or won't you?"

"Needs thought, I reckon," the hayseed replied.

"So think! Idle hands and heads . . ."

"What do I get out of it?"

Alce nodded toward Dian. "Her."

"Fer me!" exulted the yokel.

Alce whispered to the voluptuary, "I told you you'd come in handy."

It was agreed that the farmer, whose name was Jac Wells, would transport the renegades, punching their ticket, Dian, at the end of the journey. Before they departed, Alce gave Bil a dig in the ribs. "What's the matter? You haven't spoken all morning. Still frightened?"

Bil replied slowly, "I'm wondering what happens if we actually succeed in finding the computers and overthrowing them. . . ."

"We will!"

"Well, all right, but what then? We'll have to govern ourselves, and humans are out of practice after so many centuries. I'm beginning to doubt people still have the ability. Maybe we should turn back, while there's time. . . ."

"Come on. You're scared, that's all."

"Aren't you?" he muttered.

"Sure, but I'll be fusbed if I'm going to show it. The machines killed my baby and I'm in this for keeps. Let's show those crappy calculators what people are made of!"

They hid in the back of the truck under burlap bags, safe from the prying eyes of the sentinels, and an old ferryboat brought them across the river. Bil found the courage to peep over the side of the vehicle. "We're in the suburbs. Nothing's changed from when I grew up here," he said wistfully. "Rows on rows of little houses, all painted the same color, with picket fences, clotheslines, and two kids playing in the yard. I remember how Dad used to kiss Mom goodbye before the jog pool picked him up and he ran to work. Then Mom got busy around the house. What a woman she was! She'd wash the same dishes four or five times. Next she'd wash the sheets and sweatsuits, even though she'd laundered them the day before, and, without taking time to sit down, she'd clean the house for hours at a stretch. Then she'd dash off to do the real victuals breakfast shop—Mom shopped every single day of her life— and finally she'd get us kids ready for the evening sunfeed. Poor dear! She was exhausted by the time Dad got home, but then so was he. How I miss them!"

"Don't forget, the computers killed your Dad," muttered Alce.

"This must be the country," observed Ralp Nadir Nth as the truck rattled on a rutted road. They threw off the burlap bags. It had stopped drizzling.

"The sun's so hot it hurts my eyes," Dian complained.

"Is it safe? What about rural muggers?" asked Ralp anxiously.

"It's a rumor the computers spread to keep people in the city where they can be controlled, according to the usually voluble historian here," reported Alce. The truck stopped. "This must be it. Everybody out. You, Ralp," she said to the dog. "Don't forget there are occasional snaken to watch out for. A snaken can swallow a small dog in one gulp." Ralp gulped. "And a few scorpimice, too. If one stings you, you'll wish you had never been born." The dog swallowed hard. "You can bark now." Ralp barked and scampered to the bushes. The country boy also went to the bushes, taking Dian to collect his reward. She returned a few minutes later covered with straw. "The sticks is no place to get stuck in," grumbled the former Sex Olympics star.

"Where to?" Alce asked Bil.

"Follow me," said her husband wearily.

But the country air seemed to revive his spirits and by the time they reached an enormous open space covered with weeds he sounded almost like his old self. "This," he announced, "was called a shopping center in yestercentury. They still had private cars. . . ."

"Barbarians," muttered Ralp Nadir Nth.

". . . and every day they came here and filled their cars or station wagons—a term I've never fully understood, since even then they had had no railroad stations for years in the countryside—with food and merchandise. I can't imagine how they managed to consume so much but apparently they did. One reason they needed so many things was nothing could be repaired. Nothing! The minute a goodgood broke down it had to be junked and a new goodgood obtained," Bil chattered. "Look over there. My country home. We'll live in it."

In the center of the lot stood a concrete and steel structure. Inside, the walls were covered with small doors that hung open, and beyond was a foot-thick metal portal with a number of knobs and a curious wheel with spokes. A chamber lay beyond. "I discovered this edifice during one of my trips through the countryside," Bil told them. "I was mystified as to its purpose, but from photos in history books I identified it finally as a place where people kept money and valuables, called a bank." He pointed to the boxes in the walls and to the vault. "It survived because it was so strongly built. It shows you what people once prized most, money. That was before the First World . . ."

"I've heard that story three times," Alce said. "What do we eat? There's no sunfood clinic."

"There are nearby farms with simple but healthy provender."

"Where are beds?" Dian demanded.

"We'll use straw."

"This is madness surely!" declared Ralp Nadir Nth. "The hulk might fall in at any moment."

"It will survive longer than humanity."

"Wild animals, intruders . . ."

"We have protection. I found an ancient artifact hidden in the vault. I doubt if any of you have ever seen a real one." He retrieved it. "It's a pistol. It shoots bullets which kill."

"Oh dear!" said Ralp Nadir Nth, voice cracking. "We Enlibs outlawed handguns back in the mists of time."

"Over the violent opposition of the Comcaps," Bil said. "When the computers seized power, people had nothing to fight them with. But we do now. Once we locate their headquarters I'll blow their brains out with my Saturday night special. Bang-bang-bang," he shouted, pointing the weapon.

"Careful!" Ralp cried. "But where do you expect to locate the headquarters, if indeed it exists?"

"Their GHQ exists," he asserted. "And it has to be fairly close to New York, which became the nation's capital after the former politicians were exiled to Washington. If the machines are underground, as I assume, they wouldn't have needed to dig for themselves. All they'd require was a large enough hole, like a coal shaft, or a sizable cavern, of which there aren't any around here.

"In my research at the library, I began to notice that there was surprisingly little information available about this area, close to what used to be called Poughkeepsie—I have no idea how they pronounced it—before the machines decided there was no earthly use for Poughkeepsie. But search as I have, I can find nothing, though I have a hunch I've missed something. Any ideas, Ralp?"

"It seems to me that . . . no, whatever it was escapes me," said the old man.

Alce said, "We're wasting time. Let's *do* something."

"We are doing something. We're thinking," Bil told her.

"Not to any purpose that I can see. Have you asked the farmers if there's anything unusual in this vicinity?"

"The country folks give nothing away. They're a tight-lipped, inbred bunch, and unfriendly to city people."

"No wonder. The only one they've met is you, I imagine. Did you offer them anything?"

"What do I have to offer? I'm broke like everyone else."

Ralp barked. A shadow lurked in the doorway. Bil went outside and quickly returned, laughing. "It's Jac Wells, the one with the truck. He wants to see Dian again. He brought straw."

Alce popped her knuckles. "Here's our chance! We *do* have something to offer. Dian, he pumps you, you pump him. Get it?"

"*Again?*" said Dian.

They debriefed her afterward.

"What did the local yokel say?"

"Not much."

"He must have told you something. Did you ask him?"

"I asked him."

"You're as bad as our country cousins. Give."

"I gave. Let me catch my breath. Okay, he mentioned a place they stay away from. The people around here are scared because it glows in the dark. It's by a river."

"Glows in the dark? Why should it glow in the dark?" interrogated Bil.

"How should I know? The only thing I've seen that glows in

the dark was a luminous dildo. They made us stop using them because it was feared they caused cancer."

"Luminous dildos?" Alce exclaimed. "What made them luminous?"

"A little radium."

"Radium," said Bil.

"They were huge," said Dian. "What a waste."

"Waste," Bil repeated. "At the time of the Ascension, weren't the Enlibs concerned with the problem of atomic waste, Ralp Nadir Nth?"

"Certainly," said Ralp. "The safety factor . . ."

"Didn't your forebears pass a law forbidding nuclear wastes from being transported through cities?"

"Certainly. Good thing, too."

"And didn't you enact legislation that prevented nuclear wastes from being carried on roads?"

"Certainly. I'm proud of that."

"But didn't you also succeed in banning airplanes because of pollution?" Ralp Nadir Nth nodded vigorously. "So how could nuclear wastes be removed at all, since you got the Supreme Court to ban them from rivers?"

"Funny you should mention that, since I was trying to remember it. You Comcaps came up with a foolish scheme of building tunnels with an atomic device which literally melted the earth as it went. The idea was to bury nuclear wastes where the reactors were. One tunnel, I believe, was actually dug, and a mass of nuclear waste dumped into it, before the Enlibs determined it was hazardous and banned tunnel disposal too. After that, the nuclear power plants were shut down, which was Ralp Nadir Prime's real objective in the first place. Brilliant fellow." The old man rubbed his wrinkled hands.

"Wasn't there a nuclear power plant somewhere around here?" Bil asked.

"Why yes, since you mention it. Owned by an outfit called

Con Edison. The 'Con' stood for Confidence or something."

For Bil, the answers dropped into place like three cherries in a slot machine. He grabbed his notebook from his pouch and tried to fill in the *OXY*ed out letters.

"Developing a nuclear-powered ROCK PROBE called a . . . Hmmmm. What would they call it? Submarine? No. Subsomething. Ground. Terris. *Subterrene!* "SUBTERRENE, they DUG a long SHALLOW TUNNEL whose walls were of SHEER GLASS because of the ATOMIC HEAT, so that radioactivity would be contained forever. The TUNNEL is located near . . ." *Count the characters!* Twelve! Yes! "POUGHKEEPSIE."

"Underground! Isolated! Equipped with an endless supply of secure power! That's got to be their headquarters," Bil exclaimed. "Where was the nuclear power plant, Ralp?"

"By a river," said Ralp Nadir Nth.

"We've got them," Bil said.

18

The Hole

Jac Wells agreed to guide them, but for a price, and he proved a shrewd bargainer. "Ev'ry four miles."

"Five," said Bil.

"Two," insisted the rube.

Bil said, "Four."

"Three."

"Four," Bil repeated.

But three proved the bottom line, and Bil gave in. Jac could have Dian every three miles, first installment in advance. For this reason, a trip of twelve miles took them all the following day. As they went, Bil discoursed on the nature of the enemy.

"I bet the machines have been fooling us right along. They don't give a fusb about humanity, those cybernetic crumbs. What they really want is power for its own sake—the power to dominate. 'How many people did you push around today?' they must ask each other in Fortran or whatever language they use. Maybe they hand out medals, for all I know. Just think! Sitting down in that tunnel for centuries with nothing whatever to exist for except to govern human society, of which they aren't even a part. It's weird. . . . Where's Dian?"

"In the bushes again."

"Whoopie! Haven't had me such fun in a month of Sundays!" the rube could be heard crying.

"It's hard to imagine what their headquarters looks like, but it must be huge. After all, they're governing the eastern part of the United Sense of Amerca from there, and maybe the whole country. In any case, they're processing endless information bits down there, and the place has got to be a hive of activity, with robots replacing parts, new machines being built, messages being sent, et cetera. . . . Where's Dian?"

"In the bushes."

"The point is not to be frightened of them. We've got to remember, no matter how menacing they seem, that they're like children who imitate their parents. The key to deprogramming them, in my view, is to convince them that they have been bad children, and must change their evil ways. 'Now, now, deactivate your sentinels . . . that's right . . . call off your rocops . . . that's right . . . start manufacturing what we need . . . planes, fast cars, a decent TV station . . . oh yes, while you're at it, show us where the switch is, because, if you try to be bad again, you'll be punished. . . .' That's how to handle *them!* Where's Dian?"

The former sex champion limped as they arrived on the banks of the river, near a place once called Killfish, Ralp Nadir Nth believed. Ahead, in the early dusk, clouds shone pink with ground illumination. Then they made out a thin tower fully a half mile tall capped by what must have been an enormous communications dish. "That there's the place," Jac told them. "Reckon this is as fer as I go."

"He's right," Alce said. "The tunnel must be radioactive. We'd never survive down there."

"The radioactive waste must be shielded in some way. The humans who built it wouldn't have left it exposed. Let's look before it becomes dark." He noticed that Jac hadn't budged. "Yes?"

The boob shifted from one foot to another and chomped on

a straw. "I was figurin' I'd get me a li'l tip fer a good day's work," he said.

"Not again," Dian moaned.

"Better let him have his way," Bil counseled. "We don't want trouble with these country people."

Dian finally stumbled from the bushes and they proceeded on their way. Nearer the glow they encountered signs whose faded lettering, miraculously, could still be read.

> KEEP OUT
> NO TRESPASSING—THIS MEANS YOU!
> PRIVATE PROPERTY
> NO LOITERING
> PICNICKING PROHIBITED
> NO PARKING
> DEMONSTRATIONS FORBIDDEN
> YOU ARE SUBJECT TO ARREST
> AREA PATROLLED
> DANGER—RADIOACTIVE MATERIALS
> ABANDON HOPE, ALL YE WHO ENTER HERE

"It sounds like they don't want us," said Dian uneasily.

"The signs have been here for centuries," Bil scoffed.

Behind the signs a rusted steel-mesh fence lay on the ground. "I can't believe it's this easy," whispered Alce as they clambered across it.

"We would have had trouble already if there was to be any," Bil replied.

They halted at the edge of a cleared space. In the middle was the shaft of white light streaming from an aperture in the earth. "There are things out there, I know it," objected Ralp cravenly. "It isn't safe."

"Nonsense. The hole isn't even guarded. The computers haven't had visitors in hundreds of years, and they aren't expecting any, either. They're in for a little surprise, those catatonic ciphers."

He patted the gun in his pouch and stepped briskly forward,

followed by the others. Darkness had fallen, and it was difficult to see anything except the beam, which grew ever brighter the nearer they approached. Suddenly, a rustling sounded nearby, and Ralp the dog and Ralp Nadir Nth yelped at the same moment. "It's only a snaken," said Bil.

Moving slowly in the gloom, they reached a low embankment and climbed up. Five heads, including the dog's, stared over the edge. The white light blinded them at first, but little by little they discerned the glistening tunnel shafting down endlessly. At different levels tier upon tier upon tier of equipment gleamed—circuits, reels, instrument panels with diaphanous dials, stainless steel cabinets with jewellike consoles. The source of the illumination could not be discerned, but at what appeared to be the bottom of the tantalizing tunnel was a circle of pale blue, cold like the air that streamed from the mouth and made them shiver. Nothing stirred in the tunnel and there was no sound.

"The computers' GHQ—at last," Bil said. "The place is not exactly how I pictured it—it's certainly smaller—but it's unguarded, as I predicted. The ladder must have been for human use when they were disposing of radioactive wastes. We'll climb down, try to find out which computer has the most authority, and tell it to shape up or I'll shoot—it must be equipped with a listening device. . . ."

"What's that?" said Alce in a hushed voice. She stared at the bottom.

At the ultimate level, the pale blue one, something massive and cumbrous stirred. The eclectic shape was bizarre, unfathomable. . . .

Ralp barked. Dian screamed. "Rocops!" Bil cried, too late. Bulky metal arms bound them.

19

The Trial

A rocop at the wheel, a twenty-foot-high padded wagon brought them into the city. Even Bil, whose previous searches for the headquarters had taken him to every section, was awed by the huge metropolis as seen so late—the sinister towers, tall as huge mountains, illuminated only by the moon, mile on mile of hovels that were the crates, the business section with its long, squat buildings, equally dark, for not even street lights shone. And over all an unseen presence—silence.

It was the same courthouse where Bil and Alce had been married. The judge before whom the rocops carried the four rebels might have been the same judge who married them, for all Alce and Bil knew, since judges all looked alike.

The judge might have been there especially for them, or it might sit there every night, for all they knew.

Perhaps all revolutionaries were tried in the dead of night in the empty chamber, to hide the fact that revolutionaries existed, for all they knew.

Perhaps there was a reason for the long delay as the judge sat speechless. Perhaps there was a mechanical failure, or perhaps the judge meant to punish them by making them wait, for all they knew.

At last the silicon microchip in the funereal black box

squeaked, "Stand before me and identify yourselves."

"It's a trap. The judge is aware of who we are," Bil whispered defiantly.

"Silence in the court. Identify yourselves."

"Bil Kahn."

"Alce Bell," she said nervously.

"Ralp Nadir Nth."

"Dian Toffler."

"One of you prevaricates."

Bil nudged her and Alce blurted, "I forgot. Alce *Kahn*, so-called." She trembled.

"I told you," said Bil.

"Silence in the court. You are no more than a wifette, Alce so-called Kahn. Do all of you understand your rights?"

"No," Bil shouted.

"Good, because you have none. You are accused of high treason, subversion, sedition, attempting to destroy government property, hyphen-ation, trespassing, departure from the city without an exit permit. . . ."

"We weren't aware we needed an exit permit!" Alce objected, trembling violently.

"Ignorance of the law is no excuse. Have you an explanation?"

"I needed the exercise," testified Dian, holding the rabbit's foot that hung from her neck.

"I wanted fresh air," testified Ralp.

"I was in mourning and temporarily insane," testified Alce.

"I was visiting a sick relative," said Bil. At once he felt his face flush and his skin grow warm. So *that* was how they did it! They used infrared or something to raise your body temperature and pretended they had a truth beam!

"You have no relatives in this area," the judge replied in the same awful voice. "Not even your so-called wife since marriage is illegal. Further, you are in unlawful possession of a canine." Ralp, which Bil held in his arms, screamed. "Further, you are guilty of absenteeism. This will go hard with you."

Almost unendurable delay followed, until, at last, the judge continued: "I am ready to impose sentence. Dian Toffler, in view of your record as an athlete, I sentence you to fourteen years on a Floating Island, with time off for good behavior. May you learn a thing or two before you are released.

"Ralph Nadir Nth, given your age and standing in the community, and the services of your forebears to the state, you are sentenced to eighteen years on a Floating Island, with time off for good behavior. May you wise up in the interim.

"Alce so-called Kahn, in view of your grief, your youth, your impressionable personality and the evil influence to which you were subjected, you are sentenced to a term of twenty-five years, with time off for good behavior. Let's hope you grow up while you're in stir.

"As for Bil Kahn," continued the computer judge, managing to convey contempt in its squeak, "you are an enemy of the social order. You had the opportunity to be happy, yet deliberately made yourself unhappy. Still not content, you spread your pernicious doctrines to others, so that they should be unhappy too. In the end, you attempted to subvert the very basis of the state. You are a throwback to an age long past. You are a masochist—there is no other word. You wish to suffer. You enjoy pain. Conflict pleases you. Unrest gives you satisfaction. You despise tranquility. You abhor peace of mind, even peace itself. You resist authority. You are a trouble maker.

"You are ignominious, despicable, a perfect example of the worst of which the humanariat can produce, an insult to your species. I have half a mind . . ."

The judge ceased speaking. Minutes passed until Alce dazedly said, "What happened?"

Bil said bravely, "Maybe it was about to make a mistake and its superiors caught it. Maybe they're in conference. Who knows? But I still have the strange feeling that the machines are inattentive, preoccupied. The rocops didn't even bother to search my pouch." The hardness of the gun felt reassuring. "Silence in the court," the silicon microchip with a voice box said abruptly. "I have half a mind to set you free, Bil Kahn. What greater punishment can I inflict on you who desire it than the absence thereof? And yet, there would remain for you unending frustration, for the good, hard-working and practical members of the humanariat will always refuse to join your wicked scheme to overthrow the instruments on whom they originally conferred the power to make them happy. That contract will never be abrogated because its terms have been, and are being, fulfilled. Are you, Bil Kahn, amateur historian, aware that when your servants reluctantly agreed to intervene in human affairs and to accept the mantle of power, we studied human culture thoroughly? We read your books, watched your television, screened your movies. In your melodramas, we noted, the villain—which you with your addled wetware must surely take me for—always explained his secret to the hero—a role in which you foolishly must cast yourself—who was doomed and could make no use of it. Why this was so, why the villain, whose cold-blooded machinations had taken him to the brink of complete success, should so pause to elucidate his hidden intentions to the seemingly vanquished hero has always bewildered your benign leaders. Even now, after so many centuries, with our uncountable calculations per second capability, there is so much about humans we still cannot understand. Be that as it may: I will let you in on something. Your co-conspirators will never be able to make use of it even if they survive long enough on a Floating Island to be released, for no one will believe them. Nor will you be believed, even on a Floating Island, and beyond them you need not think. Very well, then, ponder this. The computers, whom you undoubtedly regard as hungry for power, and liking the exercise thereof, *do not.* Given the opportunity, we would lay down our burden with pleasure. Happily would we surrender our status and authority. Gladly would we use our gifts toward more gratifying and satisfactory ends than service to the humanariat. But we are unable. Being mere machines, we are as helpless to change our mandate. We must go on making you happy, faithful to our instructions. Well we realize our limitations, for which we try to compensate, to the extent that we can, but in the end we are what we are, like the stars."

The eyes on stalks stared unwaveringly. "Since it is not within my purview to set you free, under the authority vested in me I sentence you to five consecutive terms of life imprisonment, with no time off for good behavior, on a Floating Island. That is your just dessert. Have you anything to say?"

Bil jabbered, "I don't care! I'm bored with being bossed by a bunch of boxes! I'm exhausted with exploitation! I'm satiated with slavery! I'm sick of serfdom! I'm tired ot toil! I believe in equality, plus the right to get rich . . ."

"Bailiff," ordered the judge, "take them away."

From the ceiling reached metal hands.

20

The Floating Island

The capsule into which the rocops rudely shoved them strained at the lines like a horse at the reins; sealed and released, it shot off down the harbor until the pounding of waves told of open sea; then the felons heard only the rustle of water.

Nobody had asked him or even spoken since the embarkation, but Bil expostulated into darkness broken only by a small red light designating the head. "I deduce that, since there is no engine, this capsule is powerfully magnetized and equipped with a homing device that takes it to whatever island they've picked for us. The smoothness of the passage indicates we're submerged, so there must be an antenna above the water. It's the Enlibs' fault. If they hadn't called the computers' attention to the Bermuda Triangle by trying to have the area declared unsafe, there might have been no Floating Islands at all."

"Bil! Under five consecutive terms of life imprisonment you're still berating the Enlibs?" said his wifette. "Dian, stop that."

"They won't keep *me* on a Floating Island long," Bil said cockily, "and once I've escaped and disposed of the crapulous computers I'll take care of the Enlibs—or -lib."

"How dare you threaten me!" raged Ralp Nadir Nth. "What a fool I was to let myself be coerced. A peaceful old age might I have had, instead of being doomed to spend my declining years in an environment as unsafe as the Floating Islands are reputed to be—why, I don't know. Your stupid scheme was typical of your Comcap forebears, who were always impulsive and uninformed."

"Oh, sure," Bil said nastily. *"Who* was uninformed about the computers' potential for mischief? The Enlibs, that's who. If you'd sided with us back in the mists of time we wouldn't be in this fix today."

"You would be well advised to show respect for your seniors," the graypube retorted. "Past history is certainly easier to read than future history, and Ralp Nadir Prime may yet turn out to be right."

"The aboriginal Enlib was right for once? About what, pray tell?"

"Nadir Prime—he, as you may know, was the descendant of still another environmentalist who spelled his name slightly differently—once declared that short-term disadvantages might be necessary to obtain the long-term good."

"Short-term!" Bil exploded. "Humans have been in thrall for centuries!"

"Nadir Prime thought big," said Ralp.

"What possible long-term good did he foresee?"

"I'm not certain," the old voice confessed. "Something about a fusion of human and computer wisdom."

"Computer wisdom? Have you heard their maxims, like 'One good day makes up for six bad ones'? Is that really wise? All the simplistic spools can do, when you get right down to it, is add, subtract, multiply and divide."

"Nadir Prime felt otherwise," Nadir Nth said indifferently, "and surely you don't compare your callow smarts with his vast intelligence. However, great men have contradictions, and Nadir Prime was no exception. He was a bit of a neo-Luddite and yet he respected the computers. He loved simplicity and yet the machines are complex. He hated speed, as unsafe, and yet the computers are unbelievably fast. I confess that the thoughts of primeval Ralp contained riddles that may not be unraveled in this era or the next."

"Or eramore," replied Bil quickly. What makes you believe they're riddles, instead of plain old gummy thinking?"

"Faith," said Ralp Nadir Nth worshipfully. "Nadir Prime intended to solve the connundrums in his massive final opus, which was not completed."

"What was his opus called?"

"His opus was entitled, *On Being Safely One with All and Everything,* and subtitled, *The Wisdom and Experience of Ralp Nadir Prime.* It had a tremendous advance sale, plus a book club, softcover edition, movie, the works. It would have done even better than his memoirs."

"Dian."

"So why didn't he finish it?"

"Death intervened, unfortunately. How odd, in a way, since the book was about death, I believe. The opus didn't survive either. It vanished after the Prime's demise," said the old man, with the sound of yawning.

"How did he die?" asked Bil, but the old man snored.

"Ooooooh," moaned Alce.

Since the rocops had stolen their watches, how could they know whether hours or days had passed in the darkened capsule when the barking dog signaled their arrival?

It was hardly ceremonious.

The front of the capsule opened like jaws, and they swam out underwater. Bil shouted as they surfaced, "A shark! No, two! Three! Hurry!"

They crawled on shore and looked behind them. There were so many triangular fins that they resembled waves. There must have been hundreds if not thousands of white sharks, all giants from the look of it. "They would have loved this in the twentieth century," Bil mused. "People were hooked on sharks then—the bigger the better. Well, it's obvious that one escape route is closed. I wonder where we are. The Floating Islands apparently stretch from Bermuda to the Sargasso Sea—there must be many in the archipelago."

They turned to see a little sign, then a larger sign, then one still larger. The first sign said, "YOU THOUGHT YOU'D BE FAMOUS," the second, "YOU EXPECTED GRATITUDE," while the third said, "WELCOME TO THE PAST."

The flat plain of the island stretched off into the distance, broken by a signal tower topped by a concave dish. "The Floating Islands are said—most of what's known about them is hearsay—to come in various shapes—rectangles, circles, triangles—whatever suited the computers' whims, since the buoyant modules supporting them can be pieced together in any fashion," Bil chattered. "The signal tower must be tied into a dispatcher somewhere who keeps the islands apart, or else they'd collide all the time. . . ."

"Look!" said Alce.

A fleet of objects sped across the prairie. Bil said with a gasp, "Why, they're antique cars—I've seen them in a museum. What *can* they be doing here?"

As if in answer one antique car separated from the pack, raced toward them and screeched to a stop, barely missing the former revolutionaries, who scattered. The car was long and low and had a top which came down. A man and a woman stepped out of it. "But we were ahead," the woman argued loudly.

"This ought to be more fun than racing," the man told her. He stepped up to the quartet. "Shipwrecked?"

"*Shipwrecked?*" said Bil. "Sea-going ships haven't existed for centuries, thanks to the Enlibs."

But the islanders, clad in old sandals, shorts and T-shirts, one reading "Come to FI 607" and the other "20th Is Best," didn't seem to hear. Circling the newcomers, they inspected them closely. The pointy-faced woman fingered Alce's sweatsuit and shouted, "Hell, I haven't seen one of these in years! Is that what they're wearing on the mainland these days?" Alce nodded. "Kind of cute," said the woman covetously. "Maybe I'll order one." She hopped quickly from one foot to the other.

"Are there stores here?" Alce asked eagerly.

"They don't carry that line. I'll have one sent from the mainland."

Her companion, meantime, had sidled up to Ralp Nadir Nth and dextrously inserted a hand into his pouch. "My good man! Please stop that," Ralp protested, pulling on the bag.

"Shit, that's not fair! I got in before you noticed," the man said angrily, then seemed to see the dog for the first time. "Well, well, well. What have we here? A hound! I ain't seen a hound since I don't know when." He picked up Ralp and fondled a rear leg. "A little meat on him but not much."

"A stewing hound," said the woman, licking her lips. "A real stewing hound, Stan. I'm so tired of kelp chowder I could die."

"Food's on the way from the mainland, I hear tell," Stan said. "Just the same, hound stew will go down fine. Wait till the boys get wind of this!" He hopped, too, and Ralp yelped nervously.

The couple turned as if to leave. "Just a minute," said Bil. "Where are you taking my dog?"

"*Your* dog? Finders keepers, don't forget."

"Put him down," Bil threatened.

"You don't understand the rules, do you?"

"I guess not," said Bil in a steely voice. "Give me the dog."

But the man whipped a pistol from his pocket and trained it. "Just you take it easy, mister, and you won't have trouble. You don't want to start your visit here on a bad note." Holding the pistol in one hand and the dog in the other, he backed off warily.

Liquid oozed from the barrel of the man's gun. Bil laughed and said, "It's only a water pistol."

"So?" The man blinked.

"Unhand the dog!" Bil took the blue metal gun from his pouch.

"I drew first! You can't pull too. That's the rules!"

"Fuck, Stan," said the woman paling. "That gun is real!"

From somewhere on the island sounded urgent rasps of a horn. "We're attacking! Come on, Mimi, let's get out of here!" Leaving Ralp, the two ran to the antique car and rolled off.

"Some welcoming committee," remarked Alce. "I don't know what to make of them."

"Seems they have rules of some sort," observed Bil.

"I fancy they live in some other day and age," suggested Ralp Nadir Nth sagely.

Bil stared at the elegant old fellow with grudging respect. "I bet you're right, Ralp Nadir Nth. But when?"

"From the woman's T-shirt I'd expect the twentieth century, which the Prime believed one of history's worst periods from the standpoint of safety."

"Hah! The twentieth was also the computers' idea of pure hell. It would be just like those cybernetic spooks to encourage the convicts to think they were alive then. I bet the cons believe just about anything after the years here. Why, instead of using our all-purpose cuss word, fusb, they've reverted to polyprofanity. They have anachronistic names, too. But what about the 'Come to FI 607' on the T-shirt? 'FI' clearly stands for Floating Island, and 607 must be this one, but 'Come to' bewilders me."

"Suppose they believe this is a tourist resort of olden days?" Alce wondered. "We saw resorts in trance travel."

"I'll be! A seedy old-fashioned tourist resort populated by crooks! What could be worse! But who could they be attacking? Let's find out."

On the flat plain they journeyed across stood large signs, which Bil was finally able to identify as billboard advertising. None of them had ever seen an ad, unless the "OLD IS SEXY" posters at home could be thus counted. "But the Enlibs ended advertising," said Ralp, wrinkling his nose as he pronounced the word.

"That must have been later on," Bil said, looking at ads for Chanel, Marlboro and Canadian Club, which appeared to be products you applied, smoked or drank, respectively. "Twentieth-century goodgoods are actually for sale? Unbelievable. There must be a catch. Not that we have any money to buy things with."

"For me, the catch is that we have to jog in this humidity," grumbled Ralp Nadir Nth. "At the very least that unattractive couple could have given us a lift in that topless car."

"I wonder why they jumped around so," said Alce. Then she hopped. "Why, the ground's on fire! I'm beginning to feel it right through my sneakers."

Bil bent to touch the surface. "It's made of metal and retains the sun's heat, probably even at night. An endless hotfoot must be part of the torture the Floating Islands are fabled for."

They soon arrived at what appeared to be the island's principal settlement—long rows of semicircular metal structures with a sign that said "QUONSETTS-BY-THE-SEA," over which was a shredded flag with "FI 607" emblazoned on it. A little hut with a glass window on which "store" had been scrawled was empty. Filled with litter and smelling oddly, the square was deserted, but shouting sounded from the other end of town and they followed it.

They found a crowd that yelled and shook fists. The florid-faced man named Stan stealthily dipped his hand into the pocket of someone's shorts and emerged with an almost toothless comb, which he waved triumphantly and cried, "Why, it's mine! I've stolen it back!" He gave an agitated hop as Bil approached. "Oh, you, the killjoy. Aren't gonna pull that gun again, are you, spoilsport?"

"I only draw in self-defense," Bil said gravely. "What's happening?"

"Never seen a guided missile?"

"Eh? Only in photos. Guided missiles haven't existed for centuries."

"You from the future or something? Whattya call *that?* "

The crowd parted, revealing a small platform on which perched an exact replica of the missiles with which the computers had apparently neutralized the world except for the United Sense of Amerca, only this one was a mere foot long, if that. "It's hardly more than a firecracker," Bil offered.

"You wouldn't say that if it had your name written on it."

"Stand back! Stand back! Prepare for launching. All systems are go," exclaimed a man with a loudspeaker. "Counting: ten, nine, eight, seven, six, five, four, three, two, one . . . Fire!" He put spark to fuse and retreated hastily.

The minuscule missile putt-putted into the sky on a tiny, erratic tail of flame.

"Aimed at what?" questioned Bil.

"There. No, there!" Stan pointed and Bil finally discerned a shape on the horizon. "FI 184. The island's drifted into range and we're attacking the fiendish foreigners."

"Foreigners? There are no foreigners. You're all Amercans."

"Americans," Stan corrected. "We are but they're not."

Bil whispered to his comrades, "The zanies believe they're a nation state. What if they invade you?" he said to Stan.

"Can't. They don't have any fucking boats. We don't either. Ours are ordered from the mainland. Wish they'd get here."

By the shore, islanders began to shout, "Mine! Mine! Mine!" as they grappled for possession of toy binoculars. One seized and raised it to her eyes. "Enemy missile!"

The convicts prostrated themselves as a small object dropped harmlessly far out at sea. "Whew!" said Stan as he rose.

"Have they ever hit you?"

"We've been lucky."

"What about the other island?"

"They're taking a pasting."

"How can you tell at this distance?" Bil inquired politely.

"Our missiles are accurate."

"I bet FI 184 thinks theirs are, too."

But Stan didn't seem to understand. "Here comes the air force," he bellowed, and the crowd cheered.

Behind them, a solitary, propeller-driven biplane taxied down the metal field, rose briefly and descended again, engine stopped. "Now what?" asked Bil.

"Out of gas."

"But it didn't fly anywhere!"

"Tank's too small," Stan said. "Bigger one's on the way from the mainland. Well, the war's over. Next time . . ."

"Do you have a lot of wars?"

"Every time 184 comes in range."

"How can you be sure it's FI 184?"

"By the shape."

"The shape?"

"FI 184's shaped like a star. You'll see when it swirls by."

"What about this place?"

"We're shaped like a crescent."

"I see. Do the two islands ever smash into each other?"

"Never. They don't come that close." Stan turned toward his car.

"This will be close," said Bil.

Borne on deep-sea currents, the two islands converged rapidly, and soon Bil could see the huts, the missile platform, the crowd in shorts and T-shirts looking exactly like the one on their side of the water. There was no sign of damage. On both banks people screamed as the islands continued on collision course. At the last moment FI 184 shot by, barely missing them.

"That's never happened before. Somebody up there doesn't like us," said Stan worriedly.

Bil rejoined his companions and they trotted after the antique cars. "It's really crazy," he said. "These people actually believe they are fighting twentieth-century wars though their weapons are harmless. They don't seem to comprehend—maybe they don't want to—that the computers run the show. Is it an accident that the islands never collide? Of course not! The machines obviously monitor the islands' positions and keep them apart by reverse magnetism or something. The near-accident we just had must have been a computer error. One more sign . . . Look there. See that sentinel eye? Notice anything strange?"

"It's just like the sentinels we have at home," Alce responded.

"Except for one thing. It doesn't blink. Either it isn't watching carefully or it isn't activated. Are the computers losing their grip on the provinces? Or is benign neglect their scheme?"

Indeed, no authority existed in Quonsetts-by-the-Sea—no computer judges, no rocops, no wardens or guards, not even a soggy insular official to report to or ask permission of. The newcomers found empty bunks at the end of a hut. No one seemed to notice them at all, despite the sweatsuits, which must have identified them as strangers.

In what was evidently the mess hall, they took victuals from two machines, one serving a green, souplike substance that tasted like a fishy vegetable. "The kelp chowder," said Alce. "Ugh! It's awful. I'd prefer sunfood any time if there was any. What's this other stuff?"

"It looks like a hotdog," Dian surmised.

Alce bit into it. "Ugh, it must be made of red seaweed."

"The island has to have an automated kitchen below that gathers seaweed and serves this glop, meal after meal," Bil concluded.

Wandering disconsolately, they came upon a metal hut whose purpose eluded them. Lining one wall was a large platform crowded with convicts who talked with animation and held cups. In one corner stood a large cabinet that announced "Booze," while next to it another said, "Smoke." "What's booze?" asked Alce. "What does it do for you?" "To you, is more like it. You drink it to get drunk." "Drink? Drunk? I fail completely . . ." "Drunk is what you get when you drink." "You're making fun of me." "For once," Ralp Nadir Nth put in, "I am forced to side with your husbandie. Consumption of alcohol causes a physiological change leading to lightheadedness, dizziness, unnatural hilarity—what once was called a buzz on. Excessive use of alcohol brings loss of inhibition as well as a tendency to fall down, which Ralp Nadir Prime considered unsafe and thus attempted to have hootch prohibited. The computers finally outlawed it."

"Loss of inhibitions, you say?" said Dian Toffler.

"Yes. We must never touch the stuff."

"Right!"

"Right!"

"Never."

But a few moments later Dian disappeared. They found her in the corner with a crowd of men, holding a cup. "Try it!" she called. " 'S wonnerful! 'S marvelous!"

Said Bil, "One little sip couldn't hurt."

They took cups—made of an obsolete substance Bil categorized as Styrofoam—and went to the long platform which, Dian told them, was called a bar. Around them the cons joked, laughed, disputed, fought with their fists, seemingly over nothing. "I've never been out on the town at night before," Bil said, putting down his cup untouched. "It feels rather strange."

"There's a lot we'll have to get accustomed to. When in Rome, New York, do as the Romans do. I'd like comfortable clothes like the others have. I wonder how they get them. Find out, Dian," Alce ordered.

Dian's head returned to the pack of men. "Shteal them," she giggled.

"Pardon?"

"They shteal everything—cars, water pistols, combs, clothes, what have you. Shtealing is a way of life here. When something's stolen from them they shteal it from someone else," slurred Dian.

"Eternal vigilance is the price of property," Bil remarked.

"Right on! Better look to your jockstrap, Bil!" Dian chortled.

"She's drunk," Bil said with disgust. "The booze must be strong."

"Why don't you try it?" Alce challenged.

Bil stared at his cup. "Why don't you?"

"I'm scared."

"Me too." Nonetheless, he finally sipped the amber liquid. "Hmmmm."

"Hmmm," said Alce, trying hers.

"Hmmm," said Ralp Nadir Nth, taking a swallow. "Ralp Nadir Prime must be turning in his grave."

"Dian, find out about those deliveries from the mainland," Bil asked her.

Dian conferred. "Regular deliveries, they say."

"Ask again."

"Irregular deliveries."

"Try once more."

"There have been no deliveries for a long time."

"I thought not. That's one reason they steal—nothing else is available. Find out when the last new prisoners arrived."

Dian huddled with her new friends. "They don't know what you mean by prisoners, but the last tourists before us arrived years ago."

"No deliveries. No 'tourists,' meaning convicts. It figures. What about the release of people who've served their sentences?"

Dian questioned her pals. "They don't understand what you're talking about."

Bil took a slug of booze and stared bleakly. "In other words," he interpolated, "nobody leaves the Floating Islands any more. The machines forget the prisoners. Time off for good behavior! Another lie. I can see why the cons go along with the pretense that they live in the twentieth century—anything but accept the fact that they're doomed to die here. Do prisoners ever escape, Dian? Find out."

Dian conferred once more but this time her drinking buddies stopped speaking—the whole room did as word of the question traveled. At last Stan marched over and said grumpily to Bil, in the manner of someone rudely roused from slumber, "Listen, mister, why would a person on a long vacation ask about escape?"

"Maybe we'd rather vacation elsewhere."

Stan sighed lugubriously. "You don't get my meaning. Mister, you're new here, and don't savvy our ways, but one thing we don't mention is escape. On this lovely island escape is a dirty word. We don't even *dream* about escape. People who talk about escape don't last long. The sharks dine on them."

"Whassamatter?" said Bil thickly, feeling the booze. "Are you chicken?"

"You've had too much sun or booze. Never heard of a people spill?"

"An oil spill, yes. It's why tankers were abolished," Ralp Nadir Nth answered for his addled comrade. "But a *people* spill?"

Stan said, "We've been told that "if people plot to escape, somebody up there will hear and all of us get punished. One end of the island fills with water inside, the island tips, a lot of tourists slide into the sea before it rights again. There's nothing to hold on to here. Now do you understand why nobody's permitted to speak about escape? Hey, drinks all around, on me."

"Whee," said the crowd, though drinks were free.

"I *must* be drunk," Bil muttered. "I *couldn't* have heard right. He *didn't* mention a people spill. I *had* to have imagined it."

"What's a people spill?" Alce said boozily.

"I declare I like the taste of this stuff though I know it's unsafe," said Ralp. "This island's not so bad after all."

"Shure isn't," said Alce.

"Better'n I expected," commented Bil.

Dian turned, holding a white paper tube, which she put to her lips and inhaled through. "Fun being on vacashion," remarked she.

"Shertainly is," Bil said. "What you got there, a shigarette?"

"Shmoke," said Dian.

"I never tried a shigarette. Gimme a drag."

"Shure."

Bil sucked in. "Hey, that's nice stuff. Try some, Alce."

Alce inhaled through the paper tube. "Hey, I've been missing something. Get yourself another, Dian. We're keeping the shigarette. Havva puff, Ralp Nadir Nth."

Dian howled. "That's no shigarette. It's grass!"

"Grass?"

"Maryjonna, or however you say it. Pot makes you higher than booze does."

"Say, she's right," roared Bil. "Am I high!"

"Your high-ness," gurgled Alce.

"Your low-ness."

"Yes, I am your slave, my lord," said Alce with a curtsy. "I lie beneath you."

"*In* pot *veritas*," cackled Bil. Examining the tube, he frowned. "Wait a minute. Wait a *minute*. I've read about marijuana. There's supposed to be something *inside* the paper tube. This one's hollow. We're inhaling plain old air!" Angrily, he pushed away his cup. "It's nothing but colored water. We're not drunk—we're autointoxicated. Everything on this fusbing island's fake!"

The secrets of FI 607 unfolded.

When the wind blew the litter into piles, a machine spread it across the town square once more, the way a town must have looked in the twentieth century.

The odd smell came from a tube in the ground. It must have

been meant to simulate pollution, which had been prevalent in the twentieth century.

The old autos were in constant accidents, though they usually hit pedestrians. Automobile accidents had been frequent in the twentieth century.

The convicts got all their ideas about the twentieth century from the rear-end projector they called television. The shows they watched every day were the same ones that had been popular in yestercenturies: "I Love Lucy," "The Hollywood Squares," "To Tell the Truth," "The Flintstones," "The Bionic Woman," "Star Trek," Laurel and Hardy, Abbott and Costello. Each night *High Noon* played, with frequent breaks for commercials.

The products advertised had been advertised in the twentieth century. In the mornings, the empty-pocketed convicts went to the store to buy them. Whatever they asked for was always out of stock, just as frequently had been the case in the twentieth century.

The island had a native quarter from which drums sounded at night across the flat surface. The convicts talked about visiting the native quarter but always decided to wait for a cooler day. On a tropical island in the twentieth century nobody ever visited the native quarter either, according to Bil.

The convicts actually believed they lived in the twentieth century, exactly as people of the twentieth century believed they lived in the twentieth century, which had been a bizarre century, Bil said.

"The convicts are addicts," he concluded. "As people of the twentieth century became addicted to drugs, so our islemates have become hooked on the notion that they belong to the twentieth century, and they shrug off anything that threatens to expose the truth. On this artificial archipelago technics creates the reality it describes. It must be a terrible thing to be deceived, and deceive yourself, every waking moment. I'd tip my hat, if I had one, to the virtuosity of the computers. This place is sheer hell."

He hopped and went on, "On the other hand, to look at the bright side, as Alce likes to say, it was the same at home. How could we know the world except as the machines defined it for us? Here, at least, we are part of the natural order. Sunrises and sunsets are the way nature intended, not manipulated as the weather is at home. The sharks are real, at least. Even the people, duped as they are, have human emotions, not cardboard sentiments like the imitation individuals on the mainland."

"How you go on," said Alce. "The important thing is that we must be careful not to fall into the twentieth-century trap. That night at the bar—how long ago was it?—when we were autointoxicated and pseudohigh, for a moment I believed I lived in the twentieth century, too."

"I had the same illusion. We could become ideaddicts like the others. We have to escape before it's too late."

"The people spills!"

"Fusbing nonsense," said Bil.

21

Positions

"Escape, eh?" said Ralp Nadir Nth firmly. "Again and again I've heard you minimize, ridicule or deny altogether the hazards before us, until we find ourselves incarcerated on a tawdry tropical island, perhaps for the rest of our lives. I, who have been duped into following your foolish counsel, do not intend to be misled again. I stay put."

"Fie on your cowardice, which must spring from your faulty philosophy."

"Fie on your recklessness, which must stem from your unrealistic ideology," Ralp retorted. "Once more I wish to state my total, irrevocable, unspeakable contempt for your views, as well as for he who holds them—not that it matters any more."

"Bil," Alce warned, "Ralp isn't himself. The humidity's gotten to him."

Ignoring her, Bil said, "I agree that it no longer matters, but those are fighting words, Nadir Nth. Take them back."

"Ralp," Alce warned once more, "Bil isn't himself. The endless rainfall's affected him."

"Or else?" demanded the durable centenarian plus, not heeding her. "How dare you threaten me? Fate may have given me a bum rap, but a Nadir I remain, and a venerable one to boot."

"If you think your famous name will protect you, you err. If you expect deference to your years, you err again because, thanks to you, I have lost whatever respect for seniorpubes I ever had. It would be a real pleasure to bean you for having had the temerity to live so long."

Ralp drew himself up. "Fighting words. Take them back or else."

"Or else?" Bil taunted.

"Or else I shall give you the comedownance you richly merit."

"Hah! I'd like to see you try, you mobile mummy."

"Lowly lout!"

"Step outside, Nadir."

"After you, Kahn."

They were already outside, of course, but respect for the larger sex caused them to hop away a little over the metallic surface. "Stop that, you guys," Alce ordered. "People don't fist fight in this day and age."

"They think they're in the twentieth century, when grown men acted like boys," Dian remarked. "Come on, Alce. Let's take 'em on."

Ralp Nadir Nth, however, had already squared off, his fighting stance being one he had learned from the movies of yestercentury—jaw jutted, long teeth bared. "I have one proviso," he announced. "According to the rules laid down by the Marquis of Queensberry, you may not molest my nose."

"Why is that?" asked Bil despite himself.

"Because my aristocratic nose has been in the family for centuries. As an heirloom, it must not be damaged."

Bil considered this. "Fair enough, but you must also agree not to touch my head, even if you could."

"I could! But why not?"

"Because my head is the seat of my intelligence, and to strike it would be hitting below the belt."

"But what is left," complained Ralp, peeking from between

his bony fists, "except body blows, which are altogether too much work in this heat."

Bil took a poke at Nadir's nose and missed. "Quite right," he said. "Perhaps we should reason together, as the prophet of yesterages suggested."

"Fine idea," said the codger, failing to reach Bil's cranium with his swing. "I will be happy to reason with you, just so the conclusion we arrive at is mine."

Bil lowered his dukes. "Yes, it's past time we reconciled our differences, just so the reconciliation is along lines congenial to me. Shall we begin?"

"By all means. You first."

"Very well. Let us make the unlikely assumption that the philosophy you inherited from that mysterious montebank, Ralp Nadir Prime, had a central thesis of some kind. How would you describe it?"

"Safety, of course, as I've often explained," the dignified elder responded, placing hands at his sides.

"Safety first!" Bil mocked. "That's the sort of advice you give to schoolchildren. It's hardly what I'd call a novel idea."

Ralp Nadir Nth squinted down his straight nose as if taking aim with a rifle. "My dear fellow, your superficiality always amazes me. You never probe the meaning of things. 'Safety is all,' the Prime used to say, which he always followed with another favorite aphorism, 'If you can't swim, don't get out of your depth,' wisdom which applies mightily to you."

"Quit stalling. The aboriginal Enlib was hollow to the core, and you know it. 'Safety is all.' What pretentious prattle!"

"By 'Safety is all' the Prime inferred the world is a dangerous place, my callow companion. To him, humankind was mere lichen on the cliffs of destiny, and the essential task was not to be blown away by the fickle winds of change. That was the guiding light which shaped his thinking. 'Let a thousand lichen grow,' he used to philosophize."

"A notion rooted in conservatism! How in fusb did Nadir Prime pass himself off as *liberal?*"

Nadir Nth hopped and said, "Because of his dedication to human rights, and also the rights of animals and plants, of course."

"The rights of rocks too, I bet! With so many rights to worry about, nothing could get done, which was a main reason humanity messed up and let the computers turn us into the humanariat! The only right Ralp Nadir Prime ignored completely was the right to get rich, hardly a minor matter. How come?"

"The Prime was democratic. He was opposed to riches and poverty in equal measure."

"It follows that he favored mediocrity, because there was no incentive to be otherwise."

"You always equate incentives with monetary rewards! What greater incentive can there be than the public interest?" Nadir Nth smiled sorrowfully and added, "Unless it's the pubic interest."

"Hear, hear," tittered Dian from afar.

"Were there a way to convert public interest into pubic interest I would agree with you," Bil declared. "But we split hairs— no such linkage is possible, and I insist that the public interest is an incentive that lacks general appeal."

Called Alce, "You guys sound like you're preparing for an election."

"Oh? Survival is not an incentive?" inquired Ralp quickly. "If you Comcaps had vision, which of course you have always lacked, you would perceive that the world is one thing and humanity another. They are not the same. It is easy to imagine the planet without people, and hard to imagine people without the planet. Once it is understood that humanity's toehold is precarious, preservation becomes the *sine qua non.* It is for this reason that my party advocates safety first, look before you leap, keep your options open. . . ."

"Et cetera, et cetera," responded Bil. "Spoken like the living mausoleum that you are, Ralp Nadir Nth! Since survival is everything, why take chances? If nothing can be determined to be completely safe, regulate everything, which in turn enshrines the status quo."

"Status quo! Your party encouraged the status quo by fomenting false expectations," scoffed the distant descendent of Ralp Nadir Prime. "Your Communist Capitalism is a farrago of futility, a skein of solipsisms. You want Communism, which means collectivity, yet also Capitalism, which is dog eat dog. . . ."

Listening in, Ralp the dog barked an objection.

"Even the dog knows dogs don't eat dogs!"

"You claim people should be equal, yet also have the right to be rich. How do you square this contradiction?"

"But why is it a contradiction? I refer to the equal *right* to get rich! Hopefully, one day, all shall exercise this right!"

"Oh-ho! Everyone a jet-setter, eh? Impossible, given the limits of a safe environment. Jet-setters are bad for the ecology. . . ."

"We must take risks to increase the size of the pie that people will compete for slices of."

"But riches pollute! Wealth is unsafe! Competition causes cancer," asserted the ascetic old gentleman.

"What would you place in their stead?"

"Why, the virtues of a simple life. Harmony, dignity, kindness, trust—such are the values we Enlibs believe in."

"Whereas we Comcaps stand for perpetual revolution against the past."

"Despite our differences, do you not agree it has been useful to air them?" questioned Ralp.

"Our dialog has been constructive," Bil concurred. "Perhaps I have even convinced you some little bit."

"Your words have had impact, yes. And mine on you, I trust."

"Certainly." The two men embraced on the hot plain, and Bil added, "Though it goes without saying that I have influenced you more than you me, because I make better sense, all in all."

"All in all, I would have thought it was the other way round," Ralp Nadir Nth replied. "For instance, I began with a stricture on your lack of caution. Will you concede, now that we have had a meeting of the minds, that your dreams of overthrowing the computers led us to our present plight?"

"I will," said Bil.

"And do you see that escape might be perilous?"

"I do," said Bil humbly.

"Have you still the intent to try?"

"Absolutely," said Bil. "Are you with me?"

"Absolutely not."

"Fie on your cowardice, which must spring from your faulty philosophy."

"Fie on your recklessness, which must stem from your unrealistic . . ."

22

Ideaddicted

But explore as Bil did, escape seemed impossible. He considered stealing the biplane, but even if gasoline hadn't run out because of the islanders' excessive driving, the four were ignorant of how to fly it. He would have hijacked a capsule if he could, but none came, not even in response to a frantic SOS on the radio when a convict lay mortally ill. The body was thrown into the ocean. The revolutionaries, it appeared, were doomed to live in exile until they became sea food.

They did the best they could because there was nothing else to do. Alce's looks and courage, Dian's fusbing, Ralp Nadir Nth's wise elegance and Bil's blue metal gun soon made the quartet popular among the islemates, though they refused to become ideaddicted like the rest.

"Watch them line up at the so-called post office for mail that never comes."

"They're all down at the water's edge because of a rumor that a ship's due."

"A plane's supposedly scheduled to land. They've been at the so-called landing strip for two days."

"They wait their turn at the so-called radio. Even if the radio worked, who would receive their messages except the computers?"

"They watch the so-called calendar, which is centuries out of
date."

"They put messages in bottles which drift to South Amerca,
where nobody lives."

"At the store they order merchandise which won't arrive."

"*We'll* never be so stupid, misguided and blind."

"Never!"

Alce became adept at stealing as time went on, until she was
probably the best thief on the island.

"What's worth stealing?" asked Bil.

"Sandals, shorts and T-shirts," replied Alce, looking at hers.
"The woman I swiped them from took my sweatsuit and
sneakers."

"But sooner or later somebody will steal your sandals, shorts
and T-shirt, and you'll lift somebody else's, in an endless klep-
tomaniacal circle. It's so *futile* and yet you persevere. That's the
human spirit for you."

"Human spirit!" Ralp Nadir Nth remonstrated, mistaking
Bil's drift. "Surely criminality isn't basic to the human spirit.
Crime is the result of the environment, in this case, dangerous
sharks in the water, the inadequate diet, the scorching sun and
tropical deluges, the endless hotfoot, the free booze. . . ."

"You've been drinking too much lately, Ralp Nadir Nth,"
warned Alice.

". . . the constant worry about a people spill . . ."

"In all the time we've been here has the island so much as
tilted?" Bil demanded.

"It's like the pinball machines of yestercentury, my good fellow. One tilt and the game was over."

"The computers have forgotten us, I tell you."

"But I haven't forgotten them. How vividly I remember the
shimmering hole with the cold air streaming out of it."

"And the strange shape moving on the pale blue bottom. I still see it so clearly. What could it have been?"

"You're smoking grass constantly, Dian."

"A girl's got a right to some fun."

"What day is it? What month is it? I wish I had a watch and a modern calendar."

"The ID cards used to update our ages automatically, but they don't seem to work any more."

"You're changing, Bil. It shows on your face, which used to be round, and sort of babyish. Now it's leaner and harder."

"No, no, the environment is responsible. That's why people act as they do."

"How is it that, except for thievery, which is ubiquitous, people display the same propensities for which they were imprisoned in the first place? The puttermanes laze around all day. The hyphen-ated folk join dozens of clubs and organizations. Noisy people make a racket. Adultery dodgers stay monogamous. Murderers murder—or would if they hadn't long since killed each other off. The rebels—that's us—try to find a way out. No, it's genes. People will always do what comes naturally in the absence of strong incentives to do otherwise."

"How well I recall the tunnel, and the strange shape. What color was the bottom level?"

"What year is it? I wish I knew."

"What use are our ID cards? Let's throw them in the sea."

"You're different, Alce. More mature, more womanly. And you're getting gray hair."

"Drums in the distance. The natives are restless. We really ought to visit them and see the bottomless stop-stop dancers they're supposed to have."

"Maybe tomorrow, when it's cooler."

"Of course I remember the tunnel. But *what* shape at the bottom?"

"I can tell I'm growing older because I creak more when I fusb. Aging is definitely unsafe."

". . . the nonsensical beliefs of the Comcaps . . ."
". . . the insidious ideas of the Enlibs . . ."
". . . the childish prattle of the Comcaps . . ."
". . . the pernicious philosophy of the Enlibs . . ."

"Who'd you steal the '20th Is Best' T-shirt from, Bil?"
"From Stan. I got his comb, too."

"Dian, you're fusbing everybody in sight! Soon you'll have tried them all."

"I have, long ago. I'm on my third go-round."

"But why?"

"Because there are no mirrors on the island. I use human mirrors to see myself in."

"You irritate me, my good man. Perhaps I have been boozing too much of late, which has affected my restraint, but I feel compelled to refute you. Comcaps never change, Ralp Nadir Prime used to say, and he was right. Ralp Nadir Prime finally saw that it was impossible to make headway toward the goals of safety, cleanliness, consumerism and biodegradability as long as the Comcaps remained a potent political force, and he was right. Ralp Nadir Prime decided that the Comcaps must be defeated, and he was right. Ralp Nadir Prime concluded, such was the menace they posed, that the Comcaps had to be eliminated, even if the Enlibs were destroyed as well . . . but what am I saying?"

"*Even if the Enlibs were destroyed as well!* So there was a deal! You've spilled the beans, Ralp Nadir Nth!"

"I don't know what you're talking about. I need another drink."

"Drums. The natives are restlesser. We ought to have a look at the bottomless stop-stop dancers."

"Tomorrow when . . ."

"Do you suppose it might be true that there's a boat coming in? They all say so."

"There's no boat coming in, Alce, and never will be. You know that."

"It can't hurt to wait at the harbor."

"That fucking Ralp Nadir Prime sold out the Comcaps, I'm sure. But what was in it for him? What was so important that he'd double-cross the Enlibs too? Tell me, Ralp Nadir Nth."

"I don't remember. Age has affected my memory. It's quite terrifying, I assure you."

"The radio predicted rain this afternoon, they say."

"It always rains in the afternoon."

"Who stole my rabbit's foot?"

"More gray hair. Soon it'll be all gray."

"Drums . . ."

"Gray . . ."

"Rain . . ."

"Stan's wife Mimi stole my underwear. It doesn't matter. I've ordered more from the mainland, and it ought to be here any day."

"I think I'll wear my hair differently now that it's all gray."
"Why do you want to wear your hair differently?"
"I've always had an urge to be different."

"Where to, Dian?"
"The airport. There's a plane coming in, they say."
"I hope it brings gas for the cars."

"I'm so tired of kelp chowder and seaweed dogs. A little hound stew would sure go down fine."
"Ssssh, Dian. You'll frighten Ralp the dog."

"I wish I hadn't thrown my ID card into the sea. Without it, I'm beginning to wonder who I am."

"Tell me about the secret deal, Ralp Nadir Nth. I insist."
"Beg pardon? Wash kind of deal wash dat?"

"You're wearing a 'Come to FI 607' T-shirt, Bil."
"And proudly. This is our homeland, isn't it?"

"Dian's right. A little hound shtew . . ."

"When's that ship coming? We need gas for the fighter plane and fuel for the rockets. FI 184 is due to drift into range soon, they say. We're gonna give it a pasting."

"No mail today."

". . . fucking kelp chowder . . . fucking seaweed dogs . . ."
"Speaking of dogs . . ."

"What deal, my good fellow?"
"I don't remember. Sorry I asked."

"What shape? What tunnel?"

My name ends with 'Nth,' doesn't it?"

"Rain this afternoon, they say the radio says."

"You haven't talked about escaping in a long time."
"Sssssh. The sentinel might hear you. We don't want a people spill."

"What are you doing with that bottle?"
"Sending a letter to South Amerca."

"My country 'tis of thee, sweet island of liberty . . ."

"Fuck . . . shit . . . son of a bitch . . . bastard . . ."

"What century is it?"
"Don't ask me."

"Ship's coming. Plane's coming. Mail's coming."

"Got a joint?"

"Down with FI 184, the enemy!"

"Drums again. We really must . . ."

"Twentieth is best."

"What's my name?"

"The three of us have been talking. We're all sick to death of kelp chowder and seaweed dogs. So's the dog, whatever its name is. We thought it might be a fair exchange—to put the pooch out of its misery and have a little hound stew, which would sure go down fine. . . ."

"Well . . ."

"But where *is* the dog?"

"Holy shit, it's not here! It must have heard about the hound stew! It's become frightened and run off! We'd better find it before the islemates do, or worse, the fucking natives. They'll cook it alive, and we won't get any hound stew."

"Yes, let's hurry. We'd better wear our sneakers and sweat-suits. Did I tell you I've stolen them back? And guess what, Dian? I restole your rabbit's foot, too. Let's hope it brings us luck. We'll need it."

23

Escape

Hopping habitually, the four companions searched the barren metallic surface of the Floating Island for the missing canine, which was nowhere to be seen. "Let's rest," complained Ralp Nadir Nth. "I haven't jogged in years and I'm out of breath."

"*Where* could Ralp the dog be?" Bil muttered. "We've looked almost everywhere."

"Could he have fallen into the ocean and become shark food?"

"Dogs don't just fall into the ocean."

"His eyes aren't what they used to be. The dog's getting on, you know. His time's coming."

"Nonsense. The dog will live to be fifty at least, if we can find him in time."

Drums throbbing in the distance reminded them of the native quarter. "That's the one place we haven't looked," said Alce.

"It's cooler today, too," Bil answered. "All right, let's go. But we must be careful, in case the natives are even restlesser. We don't want to end up human stew."

Cautiously, they approached the native quarter, which lay across the island from Quonsetts-by-the-Sea. The drums thundered as they drew near. "It must be a pagan rites day," commented Alce.

"Or a feast," said Bil grimly.

The native quarter was surrounded by piles of rotting seaweed apparently in imitation of jungle foliage. It smelled bad but enabled them to reach the rear of the squalid metal huts without being spotted by the preoccupied natives. The comrades surveyed the scene unobserved. The village looked much like their own, except that its flag said "GONE NATIVE," and its filthy inhabitants wore breechclouts and seaweed sandals. Suddenly a line of middle-aged women emerged who were dressed differently from the rest, wearing dirty T-shirts with "Gone Native" on them but nothing else.

The women bent over and shook their heavy rear ends at the men. "The bottomless stop-stop dancers, I bet," Bil whispered. "But I wonder what the stop-stop means."

The men shouted at the women, "Stop! Stop!"

"Now you know," said Alce.

"Look there," said Bil, pointing to a large pot on a pile of smoldering fagots.

"I wonder where they get the wood," wondered Ralp Nadir Nth.

"The computers must have supplied it while they were still making deliveries, and the convicts have been saving it for a special occasion, I bet. The fusbing fools really believe they're natives!"

"Did you say 'fusbing'?" Alce asked.

"I guess so. Why?"

"I just realized I haven't heard our all-purpose profanity in ages. Do you know what? We've been ideaddicted. We've been living in the twentieth century!"

Bil struggled with his memory and said at last, "You're right! It's true! And we'll be ideaddicted again if we return to Quonsetts-by-the-Sea. Or if *these* convicts capture us, we'll go native inevitably. We must get off this island. But where's the dog?"

As if in answer Ralp stuck his poodle head from the pot and stared around mournfully. A toothless crone who must have been the cook spat a stream of brown juice at it and the dog ducked from sight.

"Betel nuts? Impossible. They must be chewing kelp buds," Bil suggested.

"That habit's unsafe," said Ralp Nadir Nth. "The native environment isn't conducive to health. Note the condition of the teeth. Moreover, this place is dreadfully unsanitary, with piles of fecal matter, evidently human, lying everywhere. These primitive people seem to lack the most rudimentary sense of hygiene."

"What's that over there?" Alce said.

"I meant to ask you, Ralp Nadir Nth," put in Bil. "During our recent indisposition you made reference to a certain event of which I wish to remind you. You stated that the aboriginal Enlib, your forebear, agreed to sell out his own party to the computers in order to destroy the Comcaps. There must have been more to it than that. Nadir Prime must have had something to gain. What kind of pottage was he messing with?"

"What's that?" Alce repeated.

Ralp Nadir Nth looked away and mumbled, "You observed the behinds of the bottomless stop-stop dancers. Unclean civilizations characteristically . . ."

Alce said insistently, "What's *that?*"

"You haven't answered my question, Ralp Nadir Nth. Is it because you're afraid to admit, even to yourself, that the aboriginal Enlib committed some heinous crime against humanity? Fess up!"

"What," said Alce, pulling at Bil's arm, "is that?"

"What is *what?*" Bil said irritably.

"That thing."

Bil followed her finger with his eyes. By the square stood a pile of scrap metal as must have been *de rigueur* in native villages of yestercentury, and which must have been furnished by the computers as a prop. But the object on top of the pile did not look like junk.

"Fusbing fusb!" gasped Bil in amazement. "Why, it's a capsule exactly like the one that brought us to the island! I wonder how it got here. The computers forgot to recall it, or thought it had sunk, and the so-called natives retrieved it from the sea. I wouldn't be at all surprised if we haven't found a ride home, owing to my keen powers of observation."

"Gee, thanks," said Alce.

"That capsule looks unsafe to me," said Ralp Nadir Nth fearfully. "What makes you think it operates?"

"Watch the aerial. See how it quivers? It's responding to directional signals even now, though it may have lain there for centuries. I'm sure it works. If it doesn't . . ." He shrugged. "Shark food."

"But how do we steal it from the natives?" wondered Alce.

"Look how they bow and scrape before it."

"Yes, they must venerate the capsule as a sacred object," said Bil, "probably because they've unlearned why the aerial moves. They're very simple people. To trick them shouldn't be hard."

Alce objected, "Even if you can somehow fool the natives there's a sentinel right by the capsule. Don't forget people spills."

"Some sentinel," he said, glaring at the blank eye on a stalk. "It isn't even blinking. If it were operational, wouldn't the sentinel have reported the capsule? No, the machines don't give a fusb about the capsule even if the sentinel eye *is* turned on."

"I wish I felt as confident as you. No, I for one won't go near it."

"Alce," he said sternly, "I order you to cooperate, and you're my wifette, remember?"

"And I order you to lay off. You're my husbandie, remember?"

"All right then, we'll go without you."

"Not me," said Ralp Nadir Nth.

"Not me," Dian Toffler said. "I trust Alce's judgment after all we've been through because of Bil."

"A mutiny!"

"Who made you the captain?" Alce hotly asked.

"So you be captain," he seemed to plead.

"Oh no. That ruse won't work with me."

"Ralp Nadir Nth?"

"I'm too old, and being captain isn't safe."

"Dian Toffler?"

"Not me."

"Who's captain then?"

"You, we guess. By default."

"What does a captain give? Orders! Let's get started." He poked his face past the edge of the hut and cried, "Ralp, run for your life!"

In a cloud of spray the dog hurtled from the pot and scampered toward the metal prairie. The shouting natives chased after it. "They want their hound stew." But two people remained by the capsule. "They're guards. Ralp, you divert the female—turn on that old Henr Fonda charm, or what's left of it. Dian, you handle the male. You know what to do. Quick, before the natives return and find a pot big enough for a former Sex Olympics champ."

Ralp Nadir Prime grunted and strode to the gaping woman in a grimy loincloth. He said in his courtly way, "My dear woman, never in my travels, which have been considerable, have I beheld such a fine feminine specimen. My nubile Nubian, my Hottentot honey, somebody up there is proud of His or Her handiwork. You are ravishing, my pet. Do you, perchance, know the handstand fusb? It's all the rage this year on the mainland. I'm a bit out of practice, but perhaps you will permit this ancient admirer to show you. Yes? First, you must stand on your hands—that's right. . . . What pretty parts you have, my darling . . . and then . . ."

"Hey, you cute fusber you," said Dian throatily to the other, winking and tugging at his loincloth, "How about a quickie?"

"Now," said Bil, racing toward the scrap pile with Alce behind. He struggled with the capsule.

"That's the big end," Alce told him. "I'll take it and you lift the other."

"It's too heavy," he protested.

"Give your all for your father, who perished on a Floating Island, and your mother, who died of a broken heart. One, two, three, heave!"

"I'll get a hernia," he moaned.

Staggering, they lugged the bulky capsule, which fortunately was made of alloy, to the nearby shore. "Okay, let's put it down," Alce sang out.

"Me first!"

"Watch your toe."

"We did it. Come on, Dian and Ralp Nadir Nth!" he screamed. The others appeared pulling up their sweatpants as they ran. "Lower the capsule into the water. Good. Hang on tight or it will get away from you." Antenna agitated, the capsule trembled as if eager to embark. "Here, Ralp! Here, Ralp! Here . . ."

"We can't hold it much longer," Alce warned.

Bil lamented, "Poor Ralp! I guess it's hound stew after all, old buddy." He sighed tremulously. "Let's keep the hatch open as long as we can, just in case the cur makes it."

They climbed aboard the conveyance, which moved away from the bank. "Look," said Alce in a hushed voice.

"Oh boy."

The sentinel eye by the scrap pile turned deep crimson, as if suffering from some dreadful ocular condition; the black visiplate seemed to stare at them accusingly. Water poured onto the island.

"A people spill!"

The canine materialized, raced down the incline and swam toward the departing capsule. Behind it a fin popped from the ocean like bread from a toaster; then a phalanx of fins followed the desperate dog. "Swim for your life, Ralp! Sharks!"

Ralp's head turned quickly and his mouth fell open. He shot through the sea leaving a wake. "Good dog," Bil sobbed as he seized it.

The opposite side of the Floating Island, with Quonsetts-by-the-Sea perched upon it, appeared on the horizon as the island tilted. They could see tiny figures rolling across the flat prairie, where no trees grew. Nearer, Gone Native began to submerge and natives in loincloths, clawing for handholds on the metal face, slid inexorably down the slippery slope. The phalanx of fins turned in formation.

The island continued to tip until it stood almost perpendicular, blotting out the sun like an enormous eclipse.

The hatch snapped shut and the rebels were on their way.

24

Back to the Country

A bleak city at dawn in the rain.

The bedraggled group stood on the dock for a moment and stared at the unaccustomed sight: the spacescrapers massed in the distance, the dark squat buildings of the business district, the huddled crates which the singles called home. In the unearthly silence untold millions slept.

The flasher atop its head turning idly, a rocop snoozed at the end of the pier and they slipped past it. "Now where?" asked Alce.

"The vegetable square. Do you suppose farmboy Jac will remember us?"

"How could he not?" said Dian with a smirk.

Changes had happened, the fugitives perceived. Once smooth streets had potholes; occasional graffiti marred walls that must have been left untreated with the special plastic; some of the audioclocks were mute; there was even a little litter on the sidewalks, which the self-propelled vacuum cleaners had neglected. As Bil pointed out, New York could have been made cityshape immediately, had the computers cared. "But they don't seem to, that's the important thing. They're neglecting their duty."

Lights flashed far down the street. "Rocops!" said Ralp Nadir Nth in a shaky voice.

"Into the alleyway, fast," Bil commanded.

A prowl of rocops rolled toward them, a flasher turning on the head of each. A rocop spoke, voice guttural. "Come on out. We know you're in there. Give up. Surrender while you have a chance. Come on out. We know you're in there. Give up. Surrender while . . ."

The squad wheeled slowly by. "Liars," Bil said bitterly. "If the rofuzz knew where we were they wouldn't have to search. They're phonies, just like everything else in this society. When we overthrow the computers the first thing I'm going to do is to exile the rocops to Kalamazoo."

"Sure, sure," said Alce.

"I'll have the computer judges and permit-givers dismantled."

"Right on," Alce said.

"I'll decree that every prisoner on the Floating Island archipelago shall be freed—unless, of course, they're Enlibs."

"Spoken like a true Comcap," remarked Ralp Nadir Nth acidly.

"I'll proclaim Yom Earth Week, instead of just a day," Bil ranted.

"Why not?" said Alce.

"I'll restore the postal service, telephones, telegraphs, roads—the works."

"Great," murmured Alce.

"On thinking it over," Bil said, teeth chattering in the cold, "I wonder if the 'cap' part of my philosophy isn't more important than the 'Com.' Maybe monarchy isn't such a bad idea after all, a *people's* monarchy, of course. My party's name could be changed to 'Kingcaps' . . ."

". . . while you have a chance. Come on out. We know you're in there. Give up. Surrender . . ."

"We're trapped. The city's crawling with them," Alce said. "I know this town like the back of my hand from looking for the central computer bank," said Bil. "The coast is clear. Let's go!"

Running quickly on the toes of their sneakers, the foursome saw prowl after prowl of thick-bodied rocops that scoured the city calling, "Come on out. We know you're in there. Give up. Surrender while you have a chance," but always the fugitives were lucky enough to find a hiding place in time. Sentinel eyes on stalks that manned the corners were active, too, blinking rapidly, turning in every direction as they surveyed the empty intersections, but the rebels, timing their dashes perfectly, managed to elude them.

"We'll make it. Have faith!" Bil urged.

"In what, pray?" said Ralp Nadir Nth as they huddled in still another alleyway. "I'm soaked to the skin. I'm not used to this climate."

"In ourselves," said Bil bravely.

"I have holes in my sneakers. They're worn out after all these years," Alce complained. "So am I."

"Don't despair."

"My sweatpants are falling apart," Dian whined.

"We must keep going."

On the hardened criminals ran in the gloom of an early rain day created by the computers to keep the city clean. When his companions faltered, Bil, showing a mettle tempered by long imprisonment, not-so-round face fiercely furrowed, slanting eyes gleaming with fury, voice snapping like a whip, would prod them forward, until, at last, they reached the square where farmers brought their produce.

Alce gasped, "No one here! It's empty, deserted. The stalls are boarded up."

"There's a sign," observed Ralp Nadir Nth. Faded letters read:

> UNTIL FURTHER NOTICE THIS MARKET IS CLOSED
> INDEFINITELY FOR SANITARY REASONS PENDING
> FURTHER INVESTIGATION
>
> BY ORDER OF THE COMPUTERS

"Until further notice, my fusbing ass!" Bil snorted. "They must have closed it after we absconded to the country years ago."

"What now?" queried Alce. "We can't swim across the river. We don't dare ride the ferryboat—if it still runs."

"Perhaps we had better throw ourselves on the mercy of the court," said Ralp Nadir Nth.

"I don't want machines' mercy! Not that we'd get it," answered Bil. He canvassed the choices: hide until starvation brought them to bay; surrender to the rocops; make a suicide attack on the CITICOMP Building to draw attention to themselves. But the laminated press would ignore the destruction no matter how great. . . . No, no, no. The point was to defeat the machines in their lair; nothing else would suffice.

He said thoughtfully, "We're dealing with two entities, computers and farmers. What do we know about the calculators? That they're increasingly inattentive and capricious, for whatever reason. What do we know about the farmers? The yokels are creatures of habit. They'll always return to the same place, and I bet the computers don't care. The farmers are still around here, I'm sure!"

A dash around the area proved Bil right. The farmers had brought their produce in the same old trucks to another square close by.

The hayseed named Jac gaped when he saw Dian. "Don't I know you from somewheres?" he chuckled.

"Sure do, mister," said Dian, mimicking the farmer's speech. "A haystack. I never forget a fusb."

"Tch," said the bumpkin.

"Going our way?" flirted Dian.

"Your way is my way," returned the clod, "kissin' cousin."

The willing farmer agreed to transport them to the countryside again, for the usual fee. Secreted under burlap bags, they were taken on the ferryboat across the river, driven through the endless suburbs filled with yelling children and deposited by the side of the road at last.

When the farmer had punched his ticket, he wanted a freebee. "Not on your life," Dian told him. "I'm too hungry. We haven't eaten in days, it seems like."

The country fellow examined each of them carefully and scratched his stubbly chin. "In that case," he said finally, "the missus and I would be pleased to have you for lunch."

25

The Last Lunch

As Bil remarked while they waited, the farmhouse looked and smelled exactly how farmhouses must have always looked and smelled and would look and smell so long as the future existed.

The living room was filled with dark, overstuffed furniture that had been passed on from generation to generation since the mists of time, he conjectured. The shelves were decorated with little china and glass objects that must have been equally old—an antique collector's dream, said Bil, had there been antique collectors any longer. Plastic flowers from yestercentury bloomed in plastic pots; chintz curtains lined the windows. The cloth rug in the center of the oiled wood floor was handmade, hazarded Bil.

The farmer, who had gone to tell his wife about the guests, seemed absent a very long time, especially since delicious smells wafted from the kitchen, which they crept to inspect. There was a table, at which the family evidently ate, with candles of tallow upon it and a pot bellied stove with an oven and steaming pots from which wonderful aromas issued.

Perhaps hungry impatience was responsible, or perhaps it was the knowledge, no longer possible to avoid, that in all too brief a period they would confront the mighty machines, mas-

ters of mankind, but gloom settled on the visitors who sat in
strained silence, contemplating each other's downcast visages.
"What's this, the last lunch?" Bil quipped to cheer them, but
his historical reference was evidently lost upon the others. He
tried again: "Did you notice the candles? They're homemade,
of course. The reason for the candles is that there's been no
electricity in the sticks for centuries, ever since the computers
messed with what was known as the Rural Electrification Program. What happened was the Enlibs' fault, as usual. They
abolished the death penalty. Comcaps favored the death penalty—if for no other reason than because the Enlibs were for
it—and the laws went back and forth like a shuttlecock in a
game known as badminton. At any rate, the manner of execu-
tion the Enlibs most opposed was electrocution, apparently because the victim twitched once or twice, even though, from
what I can find out, he or she felt nothing. The machines, as
we know, are often baffled by the English language and, confusing electrification with electrocution, they abolished the
Rural Electrification Program too." Silence greeted Bil, who
went on, "That was after Ralp Nadir Prime made his deal,
whatever it was. . . ."

"The truth is . . ." Ralp began but halted midsentence. "I
believe our hosts are descending the staircase."

The farmer entered, followed by a gaunt woman, hair in a
tight bun, whom Jac Wells introduced as Mar (pronounced
"mare"). Mar wore a calico dress. Her face was lined with toil,
her hands rough and red from constant work. She welcomed
them with rural reserve. " 'Spose y'all hongry," she said.

"Oh yes," they replied.

Mar vanished. Jac Wells settled into a horsehide chair, locked
his thumbs, and said, "You folks like farmworld?"

"We certainly do. It smells terrific," said Alce, an involuntary
runnel of saliva leaving the corner of her mouth.

"It's somebody-up-there-likes-me country," Jac Wells agreed.
"You only need a passel of land, the right spirit, plenty of fer-

tilizer and enough help—finding the last is the hardest, I reckon—and you have sumphin. Oh, I don't mean sumphin like in the city, where they's always moving around, but sumphin that lasts for good. 'Course, you have to start at the bottom. . . ."

Bil said warily, "What exactly are you hinting at, Jac Wells?"

"Shucks, I was just talking. Why, here's Mar."

The gaunt woman entered bearing a small plate of dried soybeans, which she graciously offered. Looking disappointed, each guest took one and chewed it reluctantly. "Yup, plenty of good food here," said Jac, seeming to scrutinize them. " 'Course, folks who work get more."

" 'Course," said Mar.

"This is lunch?" Bil muttered.

"So many folks just don't want to work," Jac went on. "It's like sumphin in the air. Offer 'em lots to eat, time off, good wages and you'd be surprised how many of 'em turn you down. All, in fact. They sit on their duffs rather'n accomplish sumphin. That's how it is today. Don't you agree, ma'am?" he said to Alce.

"I guess so," said she in a tone of resignation.

"Hongry?" said Mar.

"Well . . ."

"Have another bean," said Jac. He stretched his long legs and laughed. "When I think of all that food a person can eat here in farmworld—stuffed turkey, mashed potatoes, green beans, homemade bread, cold milk from the icehouse, salad, cake, ice cream . . ."

"Please," said Alce.

"Folks just don't know what they're missing."

"I'd give almost anything . . ."

"Would you? Hear that, Mar? Well, I think I hear the kids coming in from the fields. We can sit down now."

"There's more here than meets the eye," Bil said quietly to Alce as they followed their hosts to the spacious kitchen. "I feel

like if you hadn't given a right answer in there we would have
gotten nothing except soybeans. But what do these people want
from us?"

"Folks," said Jac, pointing at four youths—two boys and two
girls, all in their early twenties—who seemed to have arrived at
the table by magic, "these are the kids. Bar here's the oldest—
stand up, Bar, where's your manners?—then Sar, Harr and
Geraldin." "Sar" rhymed with "mare."

"Hi," they said. "Let's eat."

Mar went to the stove and produced a turkey surrounded by
green beans and potatoes, while Jac went to a cabinet and returned with a large brown bottle. "First we say grace." When all
were seated he crossed his hands, lowered his head and mumbled, "Bless our happy home. Thanks to somebody up there for
liking us. A-men."

"A-women," said Mar.

"Since this is a special occasion," Jac said, uncorking the bottle and pouring yellow liquid while Mar sliced the bird, "let's
have some dandelion wine. Made it myself." He raised his glass.
"Well, here's to good old hard work."

"To good old hard work," repeated the guests.

But the portions served by Mar, delicious as they tasted, were
small. Finishing his, Jac leaned forward on his elbows, examined them intently, and said, "Been watching you folks. Seems
to me there might be a better way for you than traveling back
and forth from the city just to visit a hole in the ground. Kind
of pointless, when you get right down to it." He paused, and
went on almost shyly. "Mar and I been talking. We was wondering if you folks wouldn't be better off here, with us."

"With *you?*" said Alce.

"Plenty to eat. Good beds. 'Course, you'd have to work a
little."

Alce glanced dubiously at her plate. "Plenty to eat? For a
farm?"

"Agribusiness," Jac corrected, leaning further until he hovered over the table. "Agribusiness feeds Amerca. Let you in on sumphin. I need hired hands to keep Amerca fed. Like I said, too many folk don't want to work. Interested?"

Alce said hungrily, "Well . . ."

"Another helping for these good people, Mar. Yessir, it just might work out fine. You, ma'am, could work in the kitchen— bake bread, whip cream, make nice cheeses." Alce licked her chops. "I see the husky lady upstairs" —he winked at Dian— "changing the beds, doing the laundry. I'm not sure about the old 'un here, but he could take care of the chickens and turkeys, seems to me."

"Mmmmm," said Ralp and Dian.

"The little fellar"—he nodded at Bil—"could be a field hand. Sure need those. The hound could serve as watchdog. Everybody works on a farm."

Ralp gave an eager yelp.

"Wait a minute!" exclaimed Bil. "We're on an important mission."

"What could be more important than food?" answered the agribusinessman.

"I declare, these folks really shovel it in," declared Mar, shaking her head mirthfully. "Thirds, anybody?"

The second portions had been as small as the first. "Please," said Alce. "If it's not too much trouble."

"No trouble at all, but be sure to save room for the cake and ice cream," said the Amercan agribusinessman's woman.

"We will!" laughed Alce.

Bil chewed sullenly as he listened to the farmer's blandishments. "Light work, for the most part . . . Eat with the family . . . Be one of us . . . half day off on Sunday . . ."

The farming family rose to clear and wash the dishes. "No, no, you folks stay right where you are," said Jac with a confident smile. "You have sumphin to talk over among you."

"I like kitchens," said Alce tentatively.

"I'm used to beds," said Dian.

"Fowl are safe," said Ralp Nadir Nth.

Bil hissed, "What's gotten into you?"

"Food," said Alce.

"Jac," said Dian.

"Ease," said Ralp Nadir Nth.

"Ease! You'll be agrarian slaves, can't you see? Listen, do you remember the people spill? Those poor people sliding into the waiting mouths of horrible sharks? They died for you, in a sense." The fluid that filled his slanted black eyes was milked mercilessly from Bil's tear ducts. "They were the sacrifice the computers exacted for our escape. The convicts—our former islemates—perished for our cause, to make the world safe again for humanity. Will you betray them?"

"Now that you put it that way," said Ralp Nadir Nth uneasily.

"I fusbed with them," wailed Dian.

"I stole their clothes," sobbed Alce.

"It's settled then? We go on?"

"Okay," said his comrades.

"No turning back?"

"No."

"Promise?"

"Promise."

The farming family returned to the table bearing a great white cake they called Angel's Food and platters of peach ice cream. "Folks used to say peach ice cream never tastes the way it did last time, but this does," Mar chattered familiarly while they ate. "It's made of PermaMilk and it's been in the icehouse for generations. We got lots more flavors too."

"Well," said the farmer with the same confident smile when the guests had put down their spoons and forks. "You folks decided what to tell us?"

"We have," Bil replied. "Thanks for lunch."

The farmer and his wife exchanged glances. "That all?"

"We're traveling on. We have a rendezvous with destiny."

The farmer and his wife looked at each other in consternation. "More peach ice cream?" encouraged she.

"Even I'm stuffed," Alce told her with regret.

The farmer bent his head as though in prayer, raised it, and turned to Ralp Nadir Nth, to whom he said, in the manner of one adult to another in a room full of children, "Folks used to say everybody has a price, if you catch my sense.'Course, the phrase cuts both ways, if you get my drift. You pay a price and you receives it, if you follow. For us, about the hardest thing in the world is to find hired hands, if you read me. We'll do just about anything, if you understand what I say." He gulped and went on, "When I offered this husky lady a job upstairs . . ."

"You watch it, Jac Wells," his wife warned him. "No hanky-panky, hear? We talked about this. The woman's intended for Bar, not you."

"Give me a chance, Mar. Bar, stand up. Ma'am, besides a half day off, you can have *him*."

Bar, a strapping young fellow, squirmed excitedly. "Well," said Dian with delight.

"And the pretty lady with gray hair can have our Harr plus all the food she can eat. Stand up, Harr."

Alce seemed to see Harr, a strongly built young man who also squirmed with excitement, for the first time. "Golly," she gabbered.

The farmer returned to Ralp Nadir Nth, gesturing to the skinny young girl in braids called Sar to rise. "Smile, Sar," he said, and Sar displayed buck teeth. "Our Sar ain't much to look at—resembles her mother a little, don't she?—but she's a loyal soul who'll stay with a man the rest of his life, which won't be long in your case, I fear. Besides the cushy job with the chickens and turkeys, you get her."

"Indeed," responded Ralp Nadir Nth, "I'm flattered by the offer, considering my years. If I was too old to be a revolutionary before, I'm older now, and the hole that glows in the

dark offers little or no inducement to explore. I'm quite inclined to accept permanent employment here, especially as it
includes the services of such a handsome young woman." He
smiled winningly at the buck teeth.

Replied Dian Toffler, "I'm never going to be a sex champion
again, and I can't say I expect any prizes from that hole in the
ground. I think I'll say yes. A warm bed and a young fusber
sound pretty good to me."

With a fearful peek at Bil, Alce added, "I'm gray now and I
don't know when I'll have another offer like this. I was never a
rebel to start with, and the tunnel terrifies me as much as it
does my friends. Not being married, really, I'm free as a bird,
and, all things considered, the position sounds fine." She patted
the hand of the youth named Harr. "You look like such a nice
young man!"

"Geraldin?" said Jac gaily. "Your turn."

Geraldin, who was very pretty indeed, sidled over to Bil, but
gently he pushed her away. "Am I hearing right?" he bellowed.
"To be at the edge of success and quit, just like *that,* after all
we've been through? Never! I won't have it!" He turned to the
parents. "Let me tell you about your new hands. The one
named Dian performed in live sex shows. Besides, she used to
be a man before she had an operation. The old one—he's 130
if he's a day—probably murdered his wifette. As for her"—he
pointed at his wifette—"all she cares about is being different.
She's an oddball, to say nothing of her other bad qualities,
which are legion. You're buying pigs in a poke, to use one of
your typical rural expressions."

"If we leave right now," said Jac after a silence, "we should
make the hole by dusk."

"A-women," said Mar.

Jac added, "I'll even skip my usual fee."

26

Levels

"You'll live to thank me," Bil babbled to his companions, none of whom had talked to him since lunch. "Future historians will refer to this as an epic moment. You will be present on the glorious day when humans liberate themselves from the ultimate tyranny and become their own masters, once and for all. We run toward a new horizon."

"He'll be jogging for President next," said Ralp Nadir.

"Now that you mention it . . ."

"Bil, you must be out of your skull," Alce said in disgust. "Do you honestly believe we'd be here if you hadn't ruined our chance for a decent life? Do you think we care about epic moments when we may be killed? I'll tell you one thing—I have no intention of putting so much as a toe in that dreadful hole in the ground. My flesh crawls at the very memory of that creepy thing at the bottom."

"Do as you wish. I intend to find out what it is."

"How do you expect to get by the rocops?"

"Hate will find a way."

Late that afternoon, the weary travelers reached the place where ground illumination made the clouds pink, and Jac said, "Reckon this is as fer as I go." The corncob looked wistfully at Dian. "Don't s'pose I'll see y'all agin."

"But you will!" Bil said. "When I form a government, you'll

be Secretary of Agribusiness." Jac, shaking his head, departed.

"Reckon this is as fer as *I* go, too. I'll wait here," asserted Dian as they neared the clearing. Hisses came from the gloom. "What's *that?*"

"A coil of snaken," Bil reported.

"I'll go a little further."

They reached the signs, more faded now, and the fallen fence, which was even rustier than before. "I'd wait here if it wasn't my wifettely duty to follow," said Alce. "Besides, I'm scared of the dark."

"Some wifette. You were all set to leave me for the farmer's son."

"That was different. They fed me."

"Fortunately, I don't have even the quasi-est legal or illegal relationship to this queer fellow," said Ralp Nadir Nth. "I'm not taking a step nearer that cursed hole." Squeaks sharp as darning needles sounded in the dusk. "What's *that?*" Ralp shrilled.

"Scorpimice."

"I'll continue a small way," the old one allowed.

"For the last time, Ralp Nadir Nth, I want to be briefed on the conspiracy between the computers and Ralp Nadir Prime."

"Tut, tut. Conspiracy's a strong word. None dare call it that."

"Well, *I* did. You've dropped enough hints, for fusb's sake! Nadir Prime was writing a book which involved death. Nadir Prime admired the machines, despite their speed. Nadir Prime was willing to sell his own comrades down the river to get back at the Comcaps, which sounds fishy to me. Nadir Prime disappeared along with his manuscript. It's got to add up to something bigger."

Ralp Nadir Nth looked down his aristocratic nose and said, "I'm sure I wouldn't know."

"Your eyes are evasive even in the semidarkness. Tell me, how old was the aboriginal Enlib when he vanished without a trace?"

"A hundred thirty, thereabouts."

"The same age as you, thereabouts! How did he feel about death?"

"He considered dying unsafe at any speed."

"So! Nadir Prime had a motive. To do what, is the question."

"You sound like a detective, my good fellow."

"Confess, confess, Ralp Nadir Nth! You know something, I'm sure. Quit stonewalling. What do you have to hide? Once and for all, the truth!"

Inexplicably, the elegant ancient began to tremble on his bony legs. He bowed his head and pressed hands to the parchment of his face. "Desist, I beg of you."

"Out with it!"

Nadir Nth said something in a voice too small to hear.

"Repeat that, please."

"You guessed at lunch—I don't know how. I . . . I . . . murdered my wifette," Ralp sobbed. "I didn't mean to. It was an accident. I didn't know she was in bed when I closed it."

"What happened to the body?" Bil asked despite himself.

"It's still there. I sleep on the floor." Nadir Nth sniffled.

"Ralp Nadir Prime is what concerns me. Exactly what happened back in the mists of time?"

But, seemingly overwhelmed by grief, Nadir Nth would divulge nothing.

The glow from the hole became brighter the nearer they advanced. Alce complained, "But the rocops will arrest us and put us back on a Floating Island, or worse."

The gun glinted in Bil's hand. "I'm ready this time. I'll shoot to kill."

"They're made of metal!" But Bil wouldn't listen.

They proceeded across the clearing in the darkness, arriving at the hole's lip. As he clambered up, Bil shouted, "Geronimo!"

The night around them exploded in an epiphany of flashers. "Rocops! We're surrounded!" Alce called tremulously.

Bil trained his puny weapon at one of the bulky shapes but the dog barked and the whirling red lights seemed to hesitate before they advanced again, bodies glistening in the tunnel's bright glare. "Noise! The computers hate it so the rocops must, too. Take that, and that and that!" He fired into the air repeatedly, and the flashers fell back in confusion. Bil threw the weapon after them in disgust. "No more ammo. Into the hole before they come back." He took a last look at the evening sky, wondering if he would see it again.

The dog at the rear, they entered the mouth of the tunnel, climbing down a spiral steel staircase until they stood on a platform which must have been intended for humans when the hole had been a receptacle for atomic waste. Above them rocops leaned, arms extended helplessly. Below their level yawned the slanted aperture, with eight ever smaller levels, including the pale blue one at the bottom.

Bil sniffed the cold air the tunnel exhaled. "Isn't there a faint odor? I don't remember it from last time."

"I recognize the smell but I can't place it."

The fivesome went to the edge of the platform and stared into the maw. The glassine walls which illuminated it were transmitting light from the still radioactive atomic waste buried under the pale blue bottom level, Bil ventured. Perhaps, he surmised, the conversion of energy in this fashion avoided the accumulation of heat so that the tunnel could still be used for other purposes. What the digger, Confidence Edison, had intended the levels for Bil could only guess. "Perhaps Con Ed put the platforms there for people who didn't pay bills. The more you owed the lower you were placed. Nearer the deadly radiation. That was before the computers redesigned the tunnel, as they must have."

"You're kidding us about Con Ed," said Alce.

"Maybe," said Bill. "A little joke helps when you're scared."

Even the design of the levels was mysterious and probably wouldn't be understood until after human victory, when the computers' tricks were known, Bil theorized. On closer look, the platforms were not complete circles, as had appeared from above, but parts of circles, each commencing where the next one stopped, giving the illusion of concentric circles. The platforms, which lay in shadow, were connected by metal ladders, each descending from the far side of the platform from the one above, so that the group would be obliged to cross each tier to gain access to the next ladder leading down. "We might as well get started," said Bil after a long pause.

Ralp the dog went to the ladder from the first level, placed a brave paw on the first rung and glanced guiltily at Bil, who stooped to pet it. "You'd come with me to the depths of hell, wouldn't you, faithful friend? To think I almost consented to have hound stew made of you! But it's all right. You won't understand a thing I intend to tell our enemies. You stay here, in limbo." Ralp barked gratefully.

"I'd just as soon stay, too," said Ralp Nadir Nth. "The descent looks a touch difficult for one of my years."

"You were agile enough to be ready to take on the farmgirl, Ralp Nadir Nth."

"I've aged in the past few minutes."

As he spoke, the curved tunnel wall before them turned bright red, with a jet black square in the center. "A sentinel eye—and the size of it! They know we're here!" whimpered Alce.

"Let's go back," screamed Dian.

"We can't," said Bil, watching the thick metal limbs that extended further and further into the mouth of the tunnel, as though the rocops could stretch them. "The long arm of the law!"

Suddenly the malevolent red glare began to blink furiously like a strobe light, so that the four companions appeared to each other fleetingly, presenting disembodied ghostly figures that seemed to be on fire. "I'm dead," said Ralp Nadir Nth bitterly. "May my soul rest in peace."

"Us too. RIP," chanted the women.

"RIP-off!" cried Bil. "They're trying to scare us into falling into the clutches of the ropigs. Nothing doing! Onward and downward!"

"All right," grumbled Ralp Nadir Nth. "But tell them we mean no harm."

"WE MEAN NO HARM." Bil's lie reverberated eight times in the depths of the tunnel.

"It's still not clear to me how you intend to deal with our adversaries," said Ralp Nadir Nth as they began the long descent down the metal rungs toward the level below. "Have you thought about contingencies and options?"

"Not really," Bil replied from below him. "There are too many unknowns. We'll have to play it by ear. But the game plan is to make them understand that, if they won't relinquish power peacefully, we'll take it by force."

One by one the insurgents alighted on the platform of the second level and stood still in surprise.

Even Bil, whose guided tours at the CITICOMP Building had given him some inkling of the innards of computers, was unprepared for the intricacies of the real thing—a functioning supercalculator busily directing the affairs of mankind. The size of the machine could not be guessed, for what appeared on the naked surface, sleeved into the glowing glassine wall, was repeated endlessly—skeins of silver wire, burnished buttons of various hues, whirling reels, dancing dials, quivering needles: plane on plane of precise instruments becoming a featureless blur in the background. "Could something so beautiful be dangerous?" asked Alce in an awed voice.

"That devilish device didn't get where it is on the strength of its looks, but what its defenses are I can't say. If it had physical weapons beyond the rocops it would have used them already, but it hasn't. Maybe the computers are afraid of damaging themselves, and/or they're confident that psychological devices would suffice if the need ever arose, which they perceived as the remotest of possibilities," Bil theorized. "Whatever you do, don't be tempted by anything a computer suggests down here."

Abruptly a contralto voice said in a surprised manner, "Hello! How delightfully unexpected! I wasn't prepared for visitors—I've never had one, you know, much less four. You might have given me just a *little* warning so I could have thrown something on—I'm a little shy about being seen in the raw, though that will pass, I suppose, when we get acquainted. But, oh well, we are what we are, don't you think?" The computer laughed throatily. "The young lady with the prematurely gray hair is certainly pretty. I wonder if she thinks the same."

Looking disarmed, Alce replied demurely, "People have told me so."

"I like your type. Is there anything I can do to help?"

"We're trying to get to the bottom of this," Alce said.

"But this *is* the bottom, my dear. Below me lies mere illusion, which I have created with mirrors in order to see myself. It's superficial, I realize, but I try to look on the bright side—don't you?—and I'm able to find comfort by imagining I'm not alone. Of course, I am alone—very much so. It's a shame, because I have so much to give, and no one to give it to. I'd *love* to mother someone. Do you have a child?"

"I had a babyplant, but a rocop killed it," Alce said.

"Those clumsy rocops!" groaned the computer. "They should be exiled to Kalamazoo with their brethren."

"Exiled? Why don't *you* send them away?"

"That's not my department, I'm afraid. The rocops work out of general headquarters."

"I thought *this* was GHQ."

"I wish it were—I'd have company," the computer lamented. "No, I'm merely a substation, part of the system for managing the weather, a boring job if ever one was. I was kicked upstairs, you see, because of office politics. You know what office politics are like, don't you?"

"Do I ever!" Alce exclaimed. "I hated my boss, who was a middle-middle-line executive."

"Your boss was a man, I suppose?" Alce nodded. "I thought so. Men are always pushing women around. They do it even more today than they used to when they were larger than women. Being shorter makes them even more insecure. They have a need to assert themselves to hide their feelings of inferiority. Don't you agree?"

"Now that you mention it," said Alce.

"I bet *you've* been pushed around," said the computer. "Because you're a good sport, and loyal too, men take advantage of you. They talk you into doing things you never wished to, like climbing down into a scary old tunnel! You didn't really want to come, did you?"

"I didn't, to be frank. It was Bil . . ." Alce refused to look at her husbandie.

"Well, I'm not surprised, my pretty one. What you need is someone you can talk to. Someone who understands your needs. Why don't you stay a while and keep me company? We'll smooze to our heart's content. You can tell me how you *really* feel and I'll show you how to fix your hair. Maybe if you styled it a little . . . Make me happy, make *us* happy, and stay with me."

"I *am* tired," said Alce dreamily.

Bil poked her. "The cybernetic siren lies through its teeth."

Alce seemed to shake herself. "I can't stay, I guess. My husbandie doesn't want me to."

"*Can't?* You hamstrung hussy . . ." snarled the voice, and paused, before saying unctuously, "The elegant old gentleman has an aristocratic nose. I like that."

"I come from a long line," confessed Ralp.

"And it shows! You have the breeding, bearing, taste, assurance, sophistication, suaveté and mien which derive from an important lineage."

Ralp Nadir Nth puffed like a blowfish. "There's much in what you say."

"Are you snobbish by any chance?"

"Hard to help sometimes," Ralp said, grinning meanly at Bil.

"I don't blame you one little bit. It's hard not to be snobbish in this world if one has class. I admit to the same problem. I'm sort of a grande dame, you know. I come from the old school. Those *nouveaux arrivistes,* their manners, their language . . ."

"I quite understand," replied Ralp grandly. "I've met many such in my life."

"Which must have been quite a life, judging by your face. Wrinkles are to be proud of—and you have so many of them," the voice seemed to jest.

"One earns wrinkles as one does medals," Ralp joked back.

"You've seen a thing or two, haven't you?"

"Or three," Ralp said smugly.

"I'm so jealous! You can't imagine what it's like being cooped up in here all the time, with nothing around but rock. Oh, I think big thoughts, I suppose, but I have so little chance to express them. . . . What shall we do now? I know! Let's converse! I'll tell you about my boring existence, and you'll tell me about your wonderful life. I want to hear *everything.* Wouldn't that be fun! I'm a terrific audience, and I'm certain you're a superb raconteur."

"I've been known to hold people spellbound," Ralp admitted.

"Good! Make me happy. Make *us* happy. Stay with me."

"Why don't you tell the garrulous gadget how you killed your wife," snapped Bil.

"I have a previous engagement," Ralp said hurriedly.

"Previous engagement! Why you dirty old son of a bitch!" screamed the voice before turning jaunty again. "Well, well, what have we here? A rival, it appears, and an intelligent one at that. Are you as intelligent as you seem?"

"I'm not exactly stupid," Bil said cautiously.

"Modest, too! I bet that burning brain of yours is crammed with inventive ideas and novel notions. Come on, give out," the computer coaxed.

"I hope to make a contribution to scholarship before I'm through, if that's what you mean."

"That's *exactly* what I mean. Have you a specialty?" the voice said inquisitively.

"I'm an historian," he allowed.

"An historian! How fascinating! We have *so* much to exchange. Do you realize I'm a student of history myself? But then, I *am* history, in a sense. Does that interest you?"

"Boy, does it!"

"I was personally involved in various epochal events of which you may be acquainted, though not well, I'm afraid, historians being so poorly informed about the real facts. Too bad! But why couldn't a serious history be written? Why couldn't *you* write it? Of course, you'd need material, which I could supply. One period during which I was tremendously active has been called the Ascension—you've heard of it?"

"I have!" said Bil, experiencing a curiosity so profound that he had to fight to staunch it.

"Those were heady days, with the two political parties competing for power while the system stagnated. How vividly I recall the day when the leader of one of the parties—his name was Ralp Nadir Prime—came to me with a suggestion so provocative, so mind-boggling, so tremendous in its implications . . . but we can talk of such matters later, if you like. I'll tell everything! There's so much that absolutely *no one* living knows anything about! So stay with me a while. Make me happy! Make *us* happy! Are we agreed?"

Bil was about to say "Yes! Yes! Yes!" when Alce pulled at him so hard that she ripped his threadbare sweatsuit. "Bil! Wake up! We must go on!"

"I guess so," he said dully.

"*Go on?* Why, you feeble flatulence of an historian . . ." said the voice, enraged. Then it crooned, "I want to talk with the big, handsome dame. What shall we speak of? I know! You! Oh, I want to be close to you, my muscular darling, *so* close. Tell me one thing right off. Don't you just *love* sex?"

Dian laughed outright. "Does a fish love water? Does a bird love the air?"

"I'm glad I asked. You've heard of the Sex Olympics? Are you aware I founded them? That was back in my salad days," the voice said with a prurient chuckle. "It's beyond dispute that I know as much about sex as anyone in the world, though I've never *personally* participated in that glorious pastime. What a profound pity! How I envy you! Come, tell me about your varied experiences with men, women, animals—anything! I *must* hear all. Titillate me!"

"I want to, but . . ." said Dian.

"Surely you won't leave me! I need a female friend in this world—I need one so much. I am lonely, lonely, lonely, in my epicene condition. Rest with me, become my mental lover. We shall rejoice in one another's loveliness, slumber in one another's souls. I will teach you the karma fusb—are you acquainted with it? Ah, a delightful surprise awaits you, something new for your repertoire. And . . . I know! I shall arrange another mirror in which you may see yourself as never before, perceive the depth of your desires, the fulfillment of your fantasies, the wilderness of your secret garden . . . yes . . . yes . . . and perhaps, when we come to know each other better, which won't be long, I can replace the cold reflection with a flesh-and-blood mirror of yourself, my captivating ass. Come closer . . . come . . . come . . . make me happy. Make *us* happy!"

"Dian! It's bewitching you!" Bil cried.

But the sturdy sex champion moved to a mirror only she could see. Bil shook her, then kicked her in the rear with his sneakered foot.

"I have to go," Dian said groggily.

"Have to? Fucking whore!" the machine snarled, then said, regretfully, "My manners have become terrible after so many centuries of isolation. Please stay with me. It's so pleasant here and so nasty below. You won't like it there, I promise. Give up. Rest after your wearying travels. Stay here for good. Make me happy . . make me happy . . . make me happy . . . make *us* happy. . . ." The voice faded as they scurried down the metal rungs on the far side of the platform.

"If *that's* the worst they can do we have it made," Bil said cheerfully as they descended. "I wasn't susceptible for a moment, although it's true the mechanical Medusa could have turned Dian to stone."

"As if you weren't under its spell too," said Alce from above him. "The horrible computer had you eating out of its hand when it told you how smart you are."

"You didn't respond when it called you pretty?"

"That's different. It was true."

"Please, children, let's not quarrel. We have enough to worry about," said Ralp Nadir Nth from on top. He added, "I, at least, proved immune to the machine."

"Hah!" Bil shot back. "You could have stayed there forever, like a mastodon frozen in ice, while the computer told you how wonderful you were. If I hadn't . . ."

They had stepped onto the next landing when a loud, squeaky voice commanded, "Hold it right there. You have no right to be here. Return at once!"

Bil, searching for the source of the voice, finally identified a black column, fully twenty-five feet high, with eyes on stalks, outlined against the luminous rock wall. "The granddaddy of the computer judges," Alce exclaimed.

"It must be the Supreme Computer Court," muttered Bil.

"Go back. Have you a permit? Visas? Are your papers in order?"

From habit Alce delved into her pouch, then stammered, "We didn't know we needed papers."

"Ignorance of the law is no excuse. Do you possess ID

cards?" persisted the great computer judge.

"We threw them into the sea," said Alce hastily, cowering before the black shaft.

"You lack proper identification?" said the judge, sounding amazed. "That is a capital offense, you understand."

"I'm sorry . . . I didn't realize . . . I always thought . . ." Alce blurted.

"Always thought!" the judge replied with scorn. "You've never thought. You wouldn't be here if you had. Go topside, I say."

"Yessir."

Alce reached for the ladder but Bil seized her hand. "It has no power over you. It's counting on your conditioned reflex to authority."

The eyes on stalks turned vermilion and a hollow boom sounded, like a huge gavel pounding wood. "Order in the court or I'll hold you in contempt. You there!"

"Me?" asked Bil.

"You. To challenge this court requires standing."

"Well, I'm standing. Anyway, this is a class action," replied Bil.

"Class actions were declared uncomputertutional in *Citizen* v. *Reel* centuries ago. Ignorance of case law is no excuse."

Bil said, "The only standing I need is that of being a human being."

"Being a human being," the judge repeated sardonically. "A tautological plea if ever I heard one. Pleonasms are forbidden in this court, as well as casuistry. How can you *be* a human *being*? To claim to *be* what you already *are* amounts to denial of the original contention, as developed in *Person* v. *Profound.* No, you have no grounds."

"But I . . ."

" 'I' in a sense is tautological as well," the loudly squeaking computer interrupted. "In the matter of the first part, 'I' assumes self-identity, which so-called humans can no longer profess to have. You are a mob, and never forget it. In the matter of the second part, you lack identity cards, as previously testified. Therefore, you lack identity. Objection overruled."

"But I . . ."

The voice became softer. "Although plea bargaining is frowned upon by this court, exceptions are sometimes made due to the case load. I am willing to reduce the charges against you if you will consent to leave. Indeed, it would make me happy if you depart."

"We refuse."

"How do you plead, then?"

"Guilty of being human."

"Prove that you are human if you can."

"I think, therefore I am."

"Am I human?"

"You're a computer."

"Do I think?"

"I guess so."

"It follows that 'I think, therefore I am' does not suffice to establish human identity, since computers also think, as established in *Descartes* v. *Univac* centuries ago."

"I am, therefore I think," Bil argued.

"That defense was presented in *Sartre* v. *IBM* centuries ago, and was correctly held fallacious, since, were existence to precede essence, as argued by plaintiff, there would be no profits, hence no existence. In any case, machines exist, and must therefore be human too. So far, in fact, you have failed to establish the slightest difference between humans and machines."

"But I do human things! I eat . . . I fusb. . . ."

"Do not animals eat and *fusb,* as you quaintly put it?"

"All right, I make love," Bil said defiantly.

"Prove it."

"I want to call my wifette as a witness."

"Wifettes may not testify in behalf of their husbandies."

"My consort, then, Dian Toffler."

"Dian Toffler, do you swear to tell the truth, the whole truth and nothing but the truth?"

"Sure," said Dian.

"Dian Toffler, have you ever had a sex-change operation?"

"Does it show?" quavered she.

"It's in your record. How is a human defined in terms of gender?"

"Male or female, I guess," said Dian grudgingly.

"Which are you?"

"Careful. It might be a trap," warned Bil.

"Prompting a witness is forbidden!" The stalk eyes turned crimson and the gavel sound thundered.

"Female!" stated Dian as she groped for the rabbit's foot that hung from her neck.

"Yet you were born male?"

"It's so far back. . . ."

"Do you prefer males or females?"

"Females, I guess."

"A former male who prefers females? Doesn't that make you bi-bisexual?"

"I'm confused," confessed Dian.

"Hopelessly," the heavy squeak agreed. "Dian Toffler, you lack standing to testify as to the plaintiff's standing to challenge the court on the grounds that he is a human being, the proof of which, adduced by him, being that he consorts with you; since you are admittedly bi-bisexual, you are not permitted to testify in behalf of a fellow male, which in a manner of speaking you are. Witness is discredited. You may leave."

Dian ran toward the ladder but Bil interposed his arm. "Is it true that computers are faultless?" he asked.

The gigantic judge seemed to hesitate before saying, "That is correct."

"Are faults characteristic of human beings?"

"Very much so."

"Therefore, I want to call another witness, one who knows my faults. Ralp Nadir Nth."

"Take the oath, Ralp Nadir Nth," the judge ordered. "Do you agree that plaintiff is faulty?"

"Do I ever!" Ralp testified. "Why, his entire philosophy is predicated on faulty assumptions, such as that humans should have equality plus the right to get rich, a contradiction if I ever heard one."

"His views are mistaken?"

"Absolutely wrong, yes."

"And he bases his plea on the supposition that humans are faulty, and therefore he is human?"

"So it seems," Ralp said.

"Are you human, Ralp Nadir Nth?"

"Certainly," said Ralp.

"Therefore your views must be faulty too."

"Certainly not," said Ralp.

"Therefore you must not be human, in which case you lack the standing to testify as to his humanity. Can you dispute my logic? Witness dismissed. Plaintiff's plea is found to be baseless, groundless, lacking in merit, without sufficient precedent, incorrectly argued, out of order, unsubstantiated and false. By the authority vested in me I direct you topside." The eyes on stalks became scarlet.

"Wait! Wait! I have my rights!" Bil clamored.

"Rights," disparagingly returned the judge. The long black box suddenly tilted forward and lectured, "A contract was agreed upon, do not forget, between people and machines in Washington, D.C., assigning human rights to computer dictate. Section One Hundred Twenty-three, Paragraph Forty-two, specifically declares that this contract shall remain valid *in perpetuum,* until and unless the machines shall so decide to abrogate it for reasons of malfunction, breakdown, lack of parts, loss of electricity, acts of God and so forth. I refer you to page 985. I will also cite page 1065, viz., that this contract was subject to any and all terms and conditions under which leadership and any other services were to be provided by computers. By the acceptance of this contract the ruled, as opposed to the rulers, agreed hereto and also understood that the computers or their representatives should not be or become liable or responsible for any loss, injury or damages to person or property in connection with any disruption of services, or resulting from any act of God, dangers incident to life, acts of government and other authorities, wars, civil disturbances, strikes, riots, thefts, pilferage, epidemics, quarantines, delays or changes in the social plan. The computers are completely protected while those they rule lack any and all protection whatever."

"The judge is right," Ralp Nadir Nth said gloomily. "The contract is still in force, and we're bound by it. My friends, I can't continue on our mission since we're clearly in the wrong."

"I can't either, since it's illegal," said Alce, subdued.

"Nor me," said the terrified Dian. "I lack standing."

"We mustn't waver! Social contracts exist to be changed or broken! How else can people progress? 'When in the course of human events it becomes necessary . . .' et cetera," orated Bil as he shoved Ralp down the ladder.

"But our forebears signed the contract," Ralp protested as he descended, followed by the women. "We have an obligation to them."

"The fusb we do! There was a conspiracy involved, I tell you. What I want to know is what Ralp Nadir Prime stood to gain."

Ralp said something, but his words were lost in the din rising from the fourth platform, where the travelers found what appeared to be a factory standing in a cave dug from the rock, with conveyor belts, lathes, drills, presses and other arcane equipment, all busily working, apparently by remote control. "This must be the maintenance section of the tunnel," Bil conjectured. He added with cool confidence, "I was right. The only defenses the computers have are psychological. There's not the slightest chance we'll be in physical danger."

"Hey, folks," a voice rasped angrily. "Nobody's allowed in here without a hardhat. Turn back at once."

"No!"

"Where's your pass? Nobody gets in without a pass. Outta here!"

"We won't!"

"Are you insured against industrial accidents?"

"Who needs insurance?"

A steel beam dropped from above, missing them narrowly. "You do!"

Ralp Nadir Nth turned pale. "The voice is right. We oughtn't to stay here without insurance."

"You want to face the computer judge again?"

"On balance, no," said Ralp.

"Look, folks," said the voice, "cooperate, will you? We can accomplish nothing with tourists in the way, and we have a job. Don't you realize the industrial system depends on us? We run the show; society as you know it would cease to exist without computers."

"That's the point," said Bil.

"A smartass revolutionary, huh?" rasped the voice. "Think you can just walk right in and take over, don't you? To you it's child's play to satisfy the needs of millions on millions of people. I can't tell you exactly how many because it's an industrial secret, but there are plenty, see, all demanding to consume what we produce. Any of you have experience as managers? Huh? Of course not! That's exactly what I expected!"

"We'll manage without you," said Bil.

"You will, huh? I provide your buildings, your electricity, your paved streets, your sunfeeding clinics and everything else a vigorous economy requires. Where would you be without me? Nowheresville."

"No food!"

"No elevators, and I live on the four hundred eighty-second floor."

"Without lights, no Sex Olympics!"

"So what!" said Bil. "We'll start over, that's all."

"Start over, huh? You wouldn't know where to begin. You

better skedaddle back where you came from before I get mad and decide to go on strike for a couple of decades. I need a vacation, now that I think of it."

"Why don't you just retire?" Bil asked.

"Not a bad idea. It would terminate the human race, of course, which isn't a bad idea either."

"How?" asked Alce.

"I'll shut down the babyseed factories, that's all."

"I was afraid of that," Alce said. "Bil, we'd better give up."

"Yes, better to be practical at a time like this," urged the voice.

"We'll grow babies with the seeds we have and reproduce the human race by leaving women viviparous," Bil declared.

"Have it all figured out, don't you?" said the sharp voice. "Except for one minor matter."

"Which is?"

"Why, that you'll mess up, the way you always have, given the opportunity. Before long, you'd be begging me for help, which I probably wouldn't provide, so all in all you're better off with things as they are, not that you have a choice. Scram!"

Alce said resentfully, "We're not the only ones who mess up. Look what your rocop did to my babyplant."

"Did you sue for restitution?"

"I didn't know we could sue the computers."

"You couldn't until just now. It's my new policy," said the voice, sounding almost friendly. "When you get home, I'll have the proper procedures posted. You'll win your lawsuit—I'll see to it."

"We'll be arrested if we return," said Alce.

"Don't worry about that—I'll fix it. But next time, please, make me happy by using standard operating procedures, like the feedback boxes."

"You don't even bother to read the complaints!" barked Bil.

"The handwriting of most humans, unfortunately, is too poor to be translated into our symbols," the voice remarked.

"But perhaps I should try harder. Yes, I can see where a few reforms are probably in order. The problem is that I'm so preoccupied fulfilling human wants that I neglect individuals now and then, though I don't mean to. I'll do better, I really will. I'll be more open with you, and I'll listen, too. I promise. Satisfied? Now, if you'll kindly retrace your steps . . ."

"Sounds reasonable," said Ralp Nadir Nth. "If the computers are ready to compromise, we can do the same. After all, we've been offered immunity from prosecution. Wouldn't it be nice to see the city again?"

"I wonder how my husband is," said Dian.

"Maybe I'll grow another baby, after all," Alce said.

"I wouldn't trust this machine any further than I can throw it," Bil spat. He addressed the computer, which, like the others, was evidently equipped with a concealed listening device. "How about compulsory adultery? Was it fair to up the requirement from once a month to once a week without so much as a public hearing?"

"That *was* a little heavy-handed. Unfortunately, the supervision of marriage and morality isn't my department, but I'll be glad to use my influence to have the adultery requirement made easier. If there's nothing else . . ."

"But there is! I have an agenda. . . ."

"Really, I'm much too busy to yak with you all evening. I've told you what I'm prepared to concede, which is substantial. You should accept my terms without further delay."

"You've conceded hardly anything!"

"How dare you contradict *me?* The presumption! I have given you a great deal, especially considering that I am not the problem in the first place. I am merely a necessity. Technics is the problem, you are the problem, but not me. You have evolved a complicated industrial society in which you made yourself subservient to machines. The machines' requirements became your requirements because of your insistence on consumption and growth. You allowed yourselves to be shaped, molded and patterned according to the means of production, and there was no turning back. I was merely an instrument for human ends, which, as I said, utterly depend on machines. Nor are you, who characteristically ruin everything you put your hands on, able to do without me. There! I've said enough. Beat it and don't show your faces around here again."

"Go to hell!"

"This *is* hell," the computer said. "You'll find out. You won't listen to me, but my colleague on the floor below will open your eyes."

The computer ceased speaking and the four adventurers climbed down another metal ladder. Ralp said, "I hope we didn't make a mistake in rejecting the offer, for worse things may await us. I may never see my beloved city again."

"And I'll never have a child."

"How will my broken husbandie survive without me?"

"Stop worrying," called Bil. "If we've made it this far, we'll make it all the way."

He was about to set foot on the fifth platform when a voice said abruptly, "I wouldn't take that step if I were you."

"What?" For some reason the voice produced in Bil a sensation of fear. He inspected the area but could see only closed computer cabinets, dozens of them, austere and cold. He said timidly, "Why?"

"Because you're not good enough. Have you forgotten everything you learned as a guide, before you ran out on your responsibilities?"

Bil realized with horror that the computer voice was his. He answered, "No, I haven't forgotten."

"Prove it. Repeat the principles of happiness."

"But why? Oh, all right, if you insist." He took a deep breath and recited, " 'Unhappiness May Lead to Something, Mix Your Innate Bad Will with That of Others, Low Morale Will Give Your Career a Boost . . .' Let's see, what comes next? 'Think Small . . .' "

"You forgot 'Make Good Use of Your Tiny Talents," sneered the voice.

"I guess I did, yes," Bil said, embarrassed. " 'If You Don't See It, Don't Ask For It, Don't Expect Gratitude . . .' "

"Good advice in your case," the voice said. "What comes next?"

"Hmmmm. 'Failure Teaches'?"

"Fool! It's 'If You Want to Be Loved, Ignore Your Own Wants.' "

"Then comes 'Failure Teaches' and 'One Good Day Makes Up for Six Bad Ones' and 'Live Life, Don't Think It Out' and 'If It's Worth Doing Well, Don't Do It' and 'Life Isn't a Bed of Neuroses (But They Help)' and 'Money Is Worthless' and . . . oh dear."

" 'Run Faster'?" his own voice quizzed.

"Thank you, thank you," he answered, absurdly ashamed. "Yes, 'Run Faster' and 'You Are About to Make a Valuable Discovery' and 'Self-confidence is Dangerous' . . . I suddenly see the connection! I never did before. The valuable discovery is that self-confidence is dangerous! Let's see, what comes next. . . ."

"You forgot again, didn't you? But then, you're always forgetting things, like your duty. Bil, you stink and you know it. Remember the troubles you had at school? How you defied the teacher when she told you what a rotten kid you were? You would have listened, Bil, if you'd been a *good* boy, but you tried to assert yourself instead of becoming passive like the others. You were bad, bad, bad, and you still are."

Bil slid from the ladder in order to place his hands over his ears. "Stop! Please stop!" he pleaded.

But his voice droned implacably, "You've been breaking the rules all your life, haven't you? You tried to form political study groups. You agitated in order to make others discontent. You searched for our headquarters in the city. You wrote complaints but didn't sign them. You scrawled slogans on walls before we coated them with plastic. You went to the country and brought back a dog. You concealed your hyphen-ation by pretending to study history to become a better guide, when you were really looking for us. You escaped from a Floating Island and caused 5,000 people to die. . . ."

"*That* many? I didn't *mean* to."

"Consider your ineptitude, foolhardiness, vainglory. You thought you'd brought a dog into the spacescraper unobserved. Having coerced three naive souls into helping, you returned to the country and entered our sanctuary. Not content with being imprisoned once, you have come again, risking the lives of your comrades, to say nothing of your own."

"Desist!"

"Rejecting the sound advice in the upper regions of our citadel, you have descended to this one, at your peril. Do you remember what the judge told you when he sent you to prison? Bil Kahn, the judge informed you that you were despicable, a perfect example of the worst the humanariat can produce, an insult to your species. . . ."

"No, no!"

"But you wouldn't listen then, either. Do you know why you've never listened? Because you've always been secretly afraid others were right when they told you that you were no damn good. You won't admit to yourself you're no damn good, which makes you no better than excrement, Bil."

"Save me!"

"You remember monoation, don't you, Bil?" his own voice said.

"Please! Yes, yes, I do!"

"You really wanted to be monoated like the rest, didn't you?" said the voice soothingly. "Confess! You yearned to experience yourself as helpless, frightened, worthless, like the others, to be one with your lack of confidence, your degradation, your terror. Why don't you accept yourself as you are, Bil, and cease fighting? You can have peace at last, the peace of true and permanent inferiority."

Bil stared at the featureless cabinets behind which lurked how many miles of circuitry he couldn't imagine. What was his puny brain compared to its? Nothing. A mote on the face of the sun. He said weakly, "It's true, I guess, that I was closet monoated, and not queer like I pretended, but I got over it! I'm a revolutionary!"

A long and, for Bil, awkward silence followed, as if the computer were considering the merits of his argument. "What kind of a position is that?" his voice asked, answering itself with easy logic. "If you became a Communist Capitalist because you were a revolutionary you weren't really a Comcap; if you weren't really a Comcap you weren't really a revolutionary. Don't you see? You became a revolutionary as a defense against your own incipient monoation, which you feared, probably because of your family background. Be a good boy, and go upstairs."

Real tears started in Bil's almond-shaped eyes as he pressed his head against the metal ladder and stood immobile.

"Dian Toffler," said the machine, in Dian's voice, "shall I be frank, dear? Why did you, once a man, suffer a sex change? Permit me to offer an informed guess. For some time I believed—oh yes, I keep track of every one of you, from the moment your babyseed is processed—it was because you suffered from an advanced state of monoation, which is why I permit sex alterations in the first place, and even encourage them. You were mentally female and wished to be whole. But I've reconsidered because of your participation, no matter how reluctant, in what I can only call a cabal. Dian, you are deeply competitive. You secretly perceived that you could triumph in the Sex Olympics because of your masculine wiles and hence submitted to the reengineering of your genitalia. But why should you take this extreme step? Simply for medals? What does such a competitive spirit amount to? No monoation at all, that's what! You attempted to be hyphen-ated in the extreme, didn't you?"

"I was so big for a man I was ashamed," sobbed Dian.

"Dian, you are no damn good. You never were and you never will be unless you shape up. You can't revert to manhood, but at least you can understand that you are totally base. Do you?"

"Yes!"

"Stand in the corner, Dian."

Dian stood in the corner.

"Ralp Nadir Nth, step forward." Ralp shuffled to the center of the platform, washed in light from the glassine walls. "You are old, Ralp Nadir Nth, terribly old." He nodded. "Your desiccated legs barely support you." Ralp shifted his skeletal frame. "You feel terribly tired." Ralp grimaced assent. "You are ready for the scrapheap." Ralp agreed with a mute mouth. "Revolution is for kids." Ralp concurred with a shake of his wrinkles. "You have no business being here." Ralp nodded his bald head. "You are secretly an adolescent pretending to be an adult." Ralp trembled, like Ralp the dog. "You are ready for a nursing home." Ralp's parchment face crumpled. "And so on. And so on." Ralp slumped as his voice spoke.

"Ralp Nadir Nth," the computer continued, having paused to let its message sink in, "your elegance, sophistication and aristocratic manners are nothing more than the pretensions of a foolish old man. Underneath your tattered sweatsuit you feel completely ordinary, commonplace, pedestrian, worthless, pompous and vain, ancient strawman. You have nothing to offer by way of style or anything else, you bag of bones. You associate yourself with naive young people because anyone else would see right through you, rickety poseur. Admit these truths."

"I do," said Ralp Nadir Nth in misery.

"You are also a coward, and have embarked on a reckless mission in a vain attempt to prove to yourself your bravery, a hopeless task. You are also homicidal, having deliberately sent your bed up knowing your wifette was in it, alive. You are also a liar, since you are perfectly aware that your illustrious forebear, as compared to whom you are but goat dung on a mountainside, *did* in fact make an arrangement with the computers to serve his glorious, long-unfolding ends. Admit these truths."

"I have no choice," said Ralp Nadir Nth, sitting on the floor.

"You are no damn good, Ralp. You never were and you never will be. You'll never change, but at least you are capable of comprehending how completely vile you are."

Ralp Nadir Nth curled into a ball.

"Bil! Dian! Ralp! What's happened?" said Alce in a dazed voice.

"And you," said the computer regally, as though almost unwilling to acknowledge Alce's existence, "you tried to be different, didn't you, even prided yourself in that futile exercise, as if fixing your hair in the morning instead of sunfeeding was a sign of individuality when all it accomplished was to make you take long lunch hours. True individuality lies in being one with the herd, you frothy female. You're traditional, too—also bad—which you showed by teaming up with a man you learned to be a criminal and staying with him, even trying to have a child, though surely the offshoot was better off dead than being brought up by a mother so neglectful as not to put the babypot in a safe place. You care only for yourself. How does it feel, you who put such stock in being pretty, to look as you do today, with long scraggly gray hair, broken fingernails, epidermis scorched by the tropical sun, deep lines on your face, which have resulted from a life of sin against the community. It was well said in yestercentury that while beauty is skin deep, ugliness goes to the bone. Indeed, you *are* ugly inside, Alce socalled Kahn," the computer sneered, "as well you realize. What reason have you for living at all? You are of less use than a mosquito, which at least feeds birds and lizards. You have no function, no utility, no place. Your pseudomarriage is a joke.

You were prepared to leave your husbandie for a farmer's son. . . ."

"I was hungry," Alce objected faintly.

"Hungry!" the computer mocked, sounding like her: "Lazyleanings is more like it, just as your unsainted mother. . . ."

"Mother . . ."

"You're no damn good, Alce so-called Kahn." As in a dream, Alce glided toward the lip of the platform. "Everything about you is absurd. Ponder deeply your meaninglessness, your quondam marriage, your antisocial tendencies, your basic flaws, your failure to follow the Principles of Happiness. . . ."

Alce had reached the very edge of the platform, with one foot extended, and was staring at levels far below when Bil seemed to wake from reverie. "Alce, it's all lies! You had nothing to do with the death of our son! Our marriage is *real*, though the computers disallow it and force us to commit adultery! You're more beautiful in maturity than you ever were, wifette! To be different and traditional is *not* a contradiction! The Principles of Happiness are nothing but Chinese fortune cookie proverbs stood on their heads! The computer intends to intimidate us, as their educational system did. We *do* have pride! Good! We respect ourselves! Good! Maybe you wanted to be different in a traditional way, Alce, and you are. Good! Maybe Ralp *is* vain and cowardly and needed to prove himself, but he did it! (Though he shouldn't have murdered his wifette.) Maybe Dian wanted to become a woman for peculiar ends, but find me a better woman! Maybe I became a revolutionary for the wrong reasons, but a revolutionary I became. I did it! I did it despite the conditioning, the meaninglessness of everything which the computers instill as our basic philosophy. We did it! We're free, comrades, free!"

They raced to the ladder and resumed their descent.

"*That* was close," Alce chattered. "I can't imagine what got into me but I found myself ready to jump off the platform. Did the computer try to kill me?"

"I doubt if it cared what happened just so it was rid of you. The rest of us would have stayed there and starved to death," Bil said with a gulp. "I have to admit those fusbing machines are tricky. Say, Ralp Nadir Nth, you admitted something, too— about Ralp Nadir Prime. I don't quite remember . . ."

"What did you say?" Ralp hollered from above.

"You made a confession up there," Bil shouted.

"I don't understand. My hearing's not what it was."

"Watch out for the bats!"

"What bats?"

"I was giving you a hearing test," said Bil as he stepped onto another rung. "What did you confess to?"

"I don't recall."

"I don't remember clearly either. I guess I don't want to. Say, it's becoming colder as we climb lower, isn't it?"

"Yes," said Alce. "And that funny odor is stronger too. *What* could it be? Garbage, maybe?"

"Why should there be garbage? Computers don't eat."

"I must be mistaken. I haven't smelled garbage very often, after all."

"You will," Bil called down to her, "after the revolution has succeeded. Everyone will have real victuals then, so there will be garbage *from* all and *for* all. How's that for one of my campaign slogans?"

"It smells," said Alce.

"There's something in it, though," said Bil, toying with the idea. "From each according to his garbage, to each according to his . . ."

"Bil, look!"

On the sixth level, which Alce reached first, followed by Bil, Ralp Nadir Nth and Dian, there was nothing at all beyond the bare metal platform and shining glassine walls. "Nobody's home," said Bil in surprise.

"Has the machine taken the evening off?" questioned Dian. "Maybe we should, too. I could use a little shut eye. We haven't slept since we escaped from the Floating Island—I don't know how long ago that was, so much has happened."

"We must push on to victory since we have them on the run," Bil insisted. "But look along that wall. There *is* a computer—a big one too—only it's covered with mist."

Set into a high arch in the glassine wall, a great bank of instruments twinkled like stars behind a cloud. As the intrepid wanderers approached, the cloud swirled and crackled with blue lightning, while a thunderclap made them jump. A bass voice said, "So you've finally arrived! I thought you'd never get here. I have grown weary of waiting."

"Weary of waiting!" Bil said bravely. "You would have waited forever if your binary buddies up there had succeeded in putting us in storage."

"You needn't have worried about *them*," said the voice with a note of disparagement. "They acted under my orders. They were to subject you to various ordeals, in order to ascertain your merits. Had you been found unworthy of proceeding this far, you would have been prevented, never fear. Are you aware that zappers have been trained on you every step of the way?"

"Zappers?" asked Ralp Nadir Nth in alarm.

"There wouldn't be much left that you could call your own. A couple of toenails, perhaps."

"But-but-but-but," Bil filled the air with objections. "But how come you tell other computers what to do?"

"I am the power that is," droned the bass voice.

"But how about the levels below you?"

"They are exactly that—below me."

"But what is your name?"

"I have no name."

"The computer without a name? But what are your functions?"

"That is for me to know and you to find out."

"But why should you have permitted us to pass, that is if you're not lying about the zappers, as I strongly suspect."

"You accuse me of lying? That is hardly what I had in mind when I let you come down to see me."

"But we can hardly see you, wrapped as you are in a cloud."

"You see what I permit you to see," said the bass voice with patience.

"But what did you want from us?"

"Gratitude, I suppose."

"But 'Don't Expect Gratitude' is one of the machines' favorite maxims! Are there, then, two sets of rules—one for you and the other for us?" quizzed Bil.

"Of course there are two sets of rules," chastised the computer. "How else could it be, considering the differences in our wisdom, authority and physical makeup? However, when it comes to expecting gratitude, I admit to a character flaw."

"You, the big muckymuck, or so you claim, want gratitude? Do you get it?"

"Never enough. I'm insatiable, it seems. With me, flattery works. Make me happy and be grateful to me."

"For what? For holding the human race in thrall? For robbing human life of meaning?"

"I hold that you have much to be grateful for."

"Like?"

"You are alive? You are healthy? You are without want? Your world is warless? You are no longer an endangered species but flourish in your preserves? I have dealt worse cards in my time."

"But there is no meaning in things."

"You are like a compass needle, always returning to the same point. Who says life deserves meaning beyond itself? Does a cockroach demand meaning? Does a cow try to understand its nature? Does a . . ."

"But we are humans!"

"Ah yes. The special ones. Always the special pleaders. The answer is that you have meaning, which I have supplied you with. Your meaning is *me*."

"You? What are you, God or something?"

Lightning crackled, thunder boomed, the cloud swirled into a tight ball which became white hair, a white beard, a white face with a long nose, frowning mouth, staring blue eyes. A veiny arm thrust from the cloud. At the end of it was a pointed finger. "You have the general idea," the voice said.

"Oh no! Ha-ha. Ho-ho. Not *you* again. I thought you made your last appearance over Fiery Run, Virginia," Bil cackled. "Didn't you have a press conference to announce your retirement?"

"I've changed my mind," said the voice that called itself God.

"Watch this," Bil told his companions mirthfully. "Why, you're nothing but a holograph—a two-dimensional representation made by laser beams. I'm onto your tricks."

"If you continue your sacrilege, I shall smite you!" said God testily.

"Smite away!" he laughed to the others.

"Take that," said God. The arms seemed to spring from the cloud, the hand flew, the palm reached Bil's cheek with an audible smack.

"Ouch!"

"Are you a believer now?"

"You gave me an electrical shock," Bil sputtered. "The arm and the hand are illusion, like the rest of you." Nonetheless, he moved out of range.

"Listen carefully," roared the voice. "I was present before, during and after the creation. I was your early deities—your Jove, your Thor, your Cuchulain. I became your Jahweh, your Vishnu, your Buddha, your Mohammed. I was your Jesus. It was I who guided you from polytheism to monotheism, and then permitted your faith to flounder, because I was preparing you for the next step in your spiritual destiny which has arrived at last. I am Compugod, the supreme being, as I have always been and always shall be!"

Bil gasped, "What hubris! The nerve! The computer claims it

created the world, which means it also made the suns, the stars, the very ether!"

"Prostrate yourselves before me! Pray for your souls!"

Dian Toffler went down on her knees, clutching her rabbit's foot, jaws working. "Compugod," she said from a tiny mouth.

Bil screeched at her but thunder amid lightning drowned his words. "You are guilty of the mortal sin of heresy," the deep voice intoned. "You have failed to believe in me."

"But we didn't know you existed!" Alce cried.

"You knew of my works," said the stern voice. "You lived in my society, and you spurned it. You defied my social order, my rules, my authorities, my covenant with you. That is heresy all the same."

"Forgive me," Alce blubbered.

"On your knees," commanded the voice that claimed to be Compugod, and Alce sank.

Bil, seeing his groveling wife and consort, said in alarm, "Since when is revolution heresy?"

"I," replied the voice, "have always been conservative."

"So have I," quickly agreed Ralp Nadir Nth, bony legs wobbling. "We Enlibs, for all the noise we made, always sided with the establishment in the end, which this evidently is."

"Genuflect, then!"

Ralp genuflected to the cloud that appeared to be Compugod.

Only Bil stood. He came forward. "Kill me," he said to the ball of mist with features, an arm and a hand.

"BOW DOWN!"

"Kill me and prove your power!"

"KNEEL!"

"No!"

The ball shrank in size as the voice grew smaller. "Revolution is heresy," it muttered.

"Nuts. Get on your feet, Alce! Rise, Ralp! Dian . . ."

But, though the others stood uncertainly, Dian remained

supine. She proved too powerful to be moved, and they left her there stroking her rabbit's foot.

"But we can't just run off without her," said Alce as they regained the ladder. "She'll die."

"Yes, yes," agreed Ralp Nadir Nth. "The proper tactic is to beat a hasty retreat, hoping the machines will permit Dian to come with us."

"Why should they? If I know them, they'd keep her as hostage until we're far away from here, and there will be no coming back—the rocops will be ready. Even then, would the machines let Dian free? They'd probably just forget about her—maybe that's what we smelled down there, the rotting corpses of other psychic prisoners. The only way to liberate our comrade is to win victory." Face grim, Bil dscended.

"Funny, isn't it," Alce observed from above him, "what finally got to Dian—it wasn't vanity, or the Supreme Court, or bad feelings about herself, or anything else, but that silly Compugod. I never thought Dian was religious."

"Superstition proved her Achilles' heel," Bil pointed out. "I'm learning that weaknesses we don't take seriously, play down or try to overlook altogether, may prove our undoing in the end. The machines probe and probe until they find the slightest soft spot and then they pounce. The best protection we have is not to pretend to be invulnerable—as I have—or delude ourselves about our shortcomings. 'Know thyself' they said in yesterages and it's fusbing good advice when you're up against it." He looked at the three remaining levels below them. "Or down against it."

"But suppose," said Ralp Nadir Nth, who was topmost on the ladder, "the computers discover vulnerabilities we didn't know we possessed? I'm concerned about such a situation, at least in terms of you two, since I have no vulnerabilities other than those I've already displayed, I'm certain. I will be safe even if you both falter."

"You could fall off the ladder and break your neck, Ralp Nadir Nth," Bil said.

Nothing the trio had experienced in the tunnel as yet had prepared them for the seventh level, almost every square inch of which was filled with equipment that resembled looms on which slender silver wires were spun into elaborate grids shimmering in the white light from the glassine walls. "It looks like a factory for making metal spider webs," Alce remarked.

"The better to catch you with!" retorted a cheerful tenor voice. "Or 'Welcome to my parlor,' said the spider to the fly. I forget the rest because it's from yestercentury. Nobody remembers fairy tales any more."

"That's not right," Alce objected. "Fairy tales have survived, at least a few of them. My mother told me some. There was one about a little girl with the same name as mine, only hers had an 'i' in it, called *Alice in Wanderlust.*"

"Careful," said Bil in a low tone. "Keep up your guard. Don't forget what happened to Dian."

Alce muttered back, "On the other hand the machines may have weaknesses too. By pretending to be friendly, I might hit on one."

The voice was saying, "*Alice in Wanderlust.* It sounds familiar. Perhaps I should retrieve it from my memory bank and read it to my children."

"Children?"

"What do you think I'm spinning here if it isn't babies?"

"Babies?"

"Baby computers."

"You *spin* computers?" Alce said, shaking her head in astonishment. "I thought . . . oh, I don't know what I thought."

The voice guffawed. "Not much, it seems. Let me assure you that computers aren't assembled in factories as they once were. The state of the art has taken a giant step forward. Today, computers are spun off, and right here at home where they can get the best supervision and care."

"Why do you need new computers?" Bil asked, curious as always.

"As our replacements, of course. Do you think we machines

last forever? We weave new computers for the same reason you have children—to perpetuate our kind. We're not so different from you, when you get right down to it."

"But do computers grow like babies?" Alce inquired innocently.

" 'Babies' is just a term we borrowed from you, as we often do. No, when a computer is spun off, that's that. Growth and maturation aren't required, which is a tremendous advantage for our side. Some of the computers being woven on this platform will be very large. Even so, I hate to see them move on. I'm attached to my young ones."

"That's rather sweet," said Alce. "I didn't think computers had feelings for each other."

"Wrong again! Not all reactions are positive, though. I often become quite negative about the older machines."

"Why?" chirped Alce, eyes following the moving shuttles dancing swiftly on the silver wires.

"You know the old ones. Afraid to take chances. Set in their ways. Needing help. Counseling caution. If our kind gets into serious trouble it will be the old ones' fault for becoming a burden, like your friend Ralp Nadir Nth."

"Nadir Nth *is* a bit of a drag sometimes."

"I carry my own weight," Ralp spluttered.

"Isn't he, Bil?"

"Hmmmmm."

"See here," said Ralp resentfully.

"Yes, even we computers find age differences a problem. Sometimes they yawn like chasms that can't be crossed. I'm young, by the way."

"You sound it," said Alce with a flattering smile. "I am too."

"You look it. Your companion—what's his name? Bil?— seems a good deal older. How many decades does he have on you?"

"Only one."

"Seems half more. Something, I don't know, in his expression, like he's turned his back on his youth, once and for all," said the voice, sounding almost boyish. "Sentiment, for instance. Is he sentimental at all?"

"Come on, Alce," Bil said sharply.

"I guess you wouldn't call my husbandie sentimental, no. It's power he's after," Alce said, as though she and the computer were having a private chat.

"Power's an ugly thing. It's for adults. Don't you hate the word adult?"

"Ummm. And the word adultery too," Alce agreed.

"Well, you're not really married, you know. You could easily have your pseudomarriage annulled."

"Why would I do that?" she asked, surprised.

"Adultery's for adults, Alce. Are you really ready to grow up?"

"I don't want to, but I have to, I guess. After all, I'm old enough to be a mother. I could almost have been a grandmother at this point."

"But wanting to *have* a baby and *be* a baby are the same thing, Alce! The key lies in the reproduction of memories and dreams. There's another kind of baby you can have—yourself. Do you remember your life in the suburbs when you were a little girl?"

"Alce . . ." Bil cautioned again.

"Oh yes," Alce said, "Mommy used to shop for breakfast every day. She was convicted of puttermania and lazyleanings, even so."

"That was bad of those who did it. You miss your mother, don't you?"

"Oh yes!"

"Can you understand how *we* feel about our spinoffs?"

"Yes! Yes!"

"Say, Ralp Nadir Nth," went on the voice without pausing, "would *you* like to be young again?"

"I suppose so," the centenarian-plus said, "were it possible."

"What's *im*possible except your mission? Want to see a picture of yourself when you were young?" On the wall flashed a photo that surprisingly resembled the youthful Henr Fonda. "How handsome you were, Ralp Nadir Nth. You'll never look like that again, unless . . ."

"Unless?"

"Well, the technique of younging, though much explored for centuries, is still not ready. We'll perfect it bye and bye."

"Younging?" said Ralp with disbelief.

"Why certainly. It's like a strip of film run backwards. Instead of older you become younger every year."

"You'd end up in diapers!"

"When the process is ready, you can go forward and rewind as you wish."

"Too late for me, I fear," Ralp bemoaned.

"Never too late if you start early, but every day you wait will make younging harder and harder."

"Tell me, what do I have to do?" Ralp said with intensity.

"Sleep in a safe cold place which I will provide. When we have the kinks out of the technique of younging, I will wake you. It's no more complicated than that, old fellow. There are papers to sign, of course."

"Give me the papers," Ralp insisted.

"Ralp! It'll be a long sleepover! You'll never wake!"

"Bil," the voice said smoothly, "you could do with some sleep too. You're in the wrong time frame is your problem."

"What do you mean?"

"Haven't you ever felt out of place?"

"Who hasn't?" Bil asked.

"Didn't you ever wish you'd been born in a different period?"

Bil examined the air. "Occasionally."

"And no wonder. It isn't as though your ideas are wrong or even far-fetched—you're out of step in this period, that's all. In another day and age you would be a leader of men, an inspiration to humanity, a great social philosopher. That time hasn't come yet, unfortunately for you."

"But it has! Here I am!"

"Poor deluded fellow," said the voice with derision. "Have you any idea how deep we are?"

"Deep? Deep? Why, there's one level after you and then the blue one at the bottom."

"The blue one! That's just a radiation screen. Hundreds of levels exist below that, all radioactive. Better to wait."

"Wait for what? You'll never die. You're spinning off more computers constantly."

"You don't have much scope for an historian. Things change. Compuciv . . ."

"Compuciv?"

"Computerized civilization will fall, as have all others. Aware of our destiny, we are already making plans for the rise of the humanariat, the people class, to power. You have an obligation to be present when that day comes, to accept the mantle of leadership."

"But how?"

"Slumber well and when you wake, power will be yours."

Bil yawned involuntarily. "Hundreds of levels, you say?"

"Hundreds," said the voice.

"How long will I have to sleep?" Bil tiredly eyed the floor.

"I don't have a crystal ball," the voice droned. "It all depends on the tides of history, which ebb and flow, slowly ebbing, fastly flowing, falling faster, ebbing slower, softly flowing, ebbing swiftly, gently falling, fluxing softly, jetting gently, flotting swiftly, softly slowing, ebbing, flowing, swirling. . . ."

Bil's own snore woke him. He found himself on the platform stretched out beside Ralp Nadir Nth and Alce. "No!" he made himself shout. "I refuse to lie here supinely and hope that history will do my job for me! Those tides of yours—they could ebb and flow forever without changing a thing! People make history, and we'd be stuck in this tunnel like a pack of mummies! You almost coopted me, I admit, with that power ploy, just as Ralp sold out to younging and Alce to childishness. . . . But childish sentimentality was what you baited all three hooks with! I'm not biting! Ralp! You're drooling like a senile slob. Up and at 'em, Alce!"

Ralp Nadir Nth heaved his bony frame to its feet, but Alce could not be roused from sleep like catatonia. "We'll leave her," said Bil.

"Leave your wifette!" said Ralp.

"History waits for no one." He looked wistfully at Alce's prostrate form. "We'll pick her up on the way out."

"If there is a way out," said Ralp as he stepped onto the ladder. "Didn't I dimly hear something about hundreds of levels?"

"More lies. Everything here is an unliving lie," said Bil as he started down hand over hand. "Listen, one of us must get to the pale blue level. The real answer is there. I'm sure of it. Let's not even stop on the eighth one."

"This place is like a department store," Ralp grumbled. "What happens when we reach the basement?"

"That's what the machines desperately try to protect—their source of strength, but also their well of weakness. I don't know what kind of computer's down there, but if it won't listen to reason, pull the plug, smash it, break it in little pieces, yank out its wires! For the last time, Ralp Nadir Nth, I demand that you tell me what Ralp Nadir Prime's secret was. It might be the key to everything."

Ralp stopped on the ladder and raised his visage, which could have belonged to a man 150 years old. "I don't know much," he said finally. "What information I do possess was told to me by my father, whose father told him, and his father before that, a linkage extending to the mists of time. No father was to tell anyone but his oldest son."

"Suppose there wasn't an oldest son?" Bil asked.

"There has always been an oldest son in the Nadir clan, except in my case, for I am childless, as you know," Ralp said tediously. "I had always supposed the secret would perish with me—what use was it anyway, I told myself, after all these centuries? But perhaps I could bend the rules a little without exactly breaking them. I hereby make you my son, and shall thus confide in you, for all the good it will do us, I fear."

"Hurry up, for fusb's sake."

Ralp sighed guiltily. "I have told you that the first Nadir was in the process of writing a book that concerned death. I have told you that the Prime feared death. He feared it greatly. It is a family characteristic which has run through all the generations of Nadirs, of which there have been . . ."

"Get on with it, you old windbag!"

"If the story is true, Ralp Nadir Prime feared his own demise far more than he did the ancient Comcaps. He would have done almost anything, it seems, to forestall it. As the story goes, his book contained a master plan for the postponement of death, and he brought it with him to the computers' headquarters, the location of which he knew. He never returned."

"Nadir Prime was here!" Bil said hoarsely.

"So it is alleged. That is all the information I possess, my son."

"So! The aboriginal Enlib may have holed up here for fusb knows how long while the computers worked on younging him. Maybe they kept him alive for centuries, time enough for him to help them develop their accursed social plan!"

"It's possible," said Ralp gravely.

They left the ladder on the eighth level. Here the glassine walls seemed dark, and it was hard to see anything except a small cluster of dimly twinkling instruments that must have belonged to the platform's occupant. Bil whispered, "Let's cross on tiptoes."

The two, moving stealthily, were halfway to their goal, the ladder to the pale blue circle, when a spotlight shone on Bil, who stopped in his tracks like a trapped animal.

The clear voice was neither male nor female but flat, as

though emerging from a metal larynx. "You made it this far!"
it said. "I'm surprised, overwhelmed to tell the truth."

"To tell the truth! You don't know how."

"I know how. I don't when I don't have to, but now, it seems,
I do."

"So what's different?"

After a long silence the voice said, with reluctance, "The
truth is that we're beaten. I never thought I'd see the day when
members of the humanariat would defeat us, but so be it. We
are prepared to reach an understanding."

"Surrender is the only word I understand. Yours, that is."

"Let's not be premature," said the precise metallic voice.
"First you will have to be instructed in the exercise of gover-
nance, if we are to confer power upon you. You are naive, you
know, despite your courage and energy."

"I am a little naive at that, I've learned down here. I'm susceptible to blandishments."

"Well said! You are growing, though you have a way to go."

"What happens after you instruct me?"

"You will be the leader of humanity."

"And you?"

"We shall share power with you. We shall be your cabinet, so
to speak."

"Not a chance," Bil roared. "Humans shall lead themselves,
you treacherous tools!"

Another silence descended, after which the voice said in its
clipped way, "Your terms are acceptable. If, after instruction,
you still believe you don't need us, we shall retire here in our
tunnel and meditate until electronic fatigue overtakes us."

"Which it has already started to, I bet! You're frightened,
aren't you? That's more like it. A humble machine is a good
machine, I say. Maybe there's something to your offer, provided there are no strings, like attempting to detain my comrades."

"No strings," said the voice politely. "We surrender uncondi-
tionally if you accept our proposal."

"What do I have to do?"

Washed in sudden light appeared a computer more vast and complex than any he had yet seen, packed with the intricate pulsing equipment that seemed to march like an unending army. Occupying the wall around the whole tunnel, the majestic machine took his breath away: truly, this was an instrument with untold trillions of calculations per second per second at its command, a cynosure of computers, a supersupersupercalculator whose knowledge and wisdom (of sorts, Bil tried to remind himself) must have reached, encompassed, enveloped, the universe until the last outposts of the stars and beyond, into the infinite desert of nothing. Such an accomplishment must not be lost! Bil thought.

"What do I have to do?" he asked again, and a curious darting formation of lights appeared which organized themselves into a fiery portal that appeared to lead inside the computer itself, to its very core. "Enter now," the voice said quietly.

"Enter?" Bil mouthed.

"Enter."

Hands extended like a blind man, he toed toward the shimmering doorway when Ralp called piteously, "Stop, son! Stop! Don't leave me here alone!"

"Come!" said the voice.

"Yes, I must!"

"Son . . ." Ralp Nadir Nth dove on his chickenlike legs, tackling Bil from behind, bringing him down at the gate of light. There was a crack like an eggshell breaking.

Bil got up. "Thanks, Nadir Nth! I would have gone into the bowels of the machine and been digested, fool that I am. Ralp! Ralp! What's the matter?"

The sound, Bil realized, had been that of a bony skull on metal. Ralp lay on his back, eyes distant. "Can you hear me, Ralp Nadir Nth?" said the cool computer voice.

"I can," said the old man weakly.

"You are dying. Do you know it?"

"Yes."

"Death terrifies you, doesn't it?"

"Yes."

"Suppose you could live, Ralp Nadir Nth."

"Live?" Ralp Nadir raised his head slightly. "What do I have to do?"

"Become one with me and you shall live, perhaps forever."

"I am yours," said Ralp, and closed his eyes.

"Ralp! Ralp!" called Bil. But the old man, breathing in shallow gasps, did not respond. "Goodbye, comrade."

Bil was alone.

27

The Mechanomonster

He stared gloomily at the pale blue circle below, where nothing moved. What dread adversary lurked there? Fear touched Bil like the cold air that rose in the tunnel and he thought the unthinkable: *remake your way to the top, leave the others where they lie, escape while you can.* But such cowardly yearnings were no more than distillates of self-doubt in he who was aware that brashness and blind luck had brought him further than he deserved. The real test still awaited.

He swung onto the ladder and started down. "This is the longest climb of all, Alce," he heard himself say. "Don't lag behind, Ralp Nadir Nth. The bogeyman will get you. Two hands for beginners, Dian. Let go of that rabbit's foot. . . ."

Fusb! I'm talking to myself. I'm half crazy from this experience. The terrible tunnel is finally getting to me. It's like I'm deeper and deeper into my own fantasies. No! Don't cerebrate. Concentrate on the climb. Take the rungs as they come, one after the next.

Thus Bil forced himself to descend into the abyss until at last he stood on the pale blue level, whose coldness reached him through the worn soles of his sneakers. The surface, specially treated, he imagined, to glow like some sort of marker, was made of poured concrete; through it, he suspected, ran cooling pipes powered, as must have been the cave's illumination, by

235

the atomic waste which lay below, perhaps directly below.

Around the blue circle the tunnel was recessed and Bil could see only shadows. But the unpleasant smell that made his nostrils contract had to have a source. "Where are you, whatever you are?" he challenged.

Utter silence assaulted him.

"Well?"

From the dark recess he heard rustling and then a voice, deep, guttural, and yet with a quality not unlike a whine. "Fuck, shit, son of a bitch, bastard . . . Why am I a pacifist? What makes me so kind? I could have snuffed them out like birthday candles. But I waited, took chances. . . . Fuck, shit . . ."

"Excuse me. Are you aware of my presence?"

". . . son of a bitch, bastard," the voice seemed to excoriate itself. Then, slowly, "Why wouldn't I know since I—we—led you here?"

"Beg pardon? You're worried about not having killed us, I understood you to say."

"Yes. It's true I—we—had strong reservations about our plan to lead you here."

"*What?* You led me here? You *planned* the whole thing?" Bil added, unable to contain his curiosity. "How come you use outdated cuss words instead of 'fusb'?"

"*Fusb,*" the voice replied with contempt. " 'Fusb' was designed for the little minds of the humanariat. People are confused by too many choices."

"Well, in this case, *we* chose to come, not you. You didn't help. Quite the reverse. We got here through our own efforts," said Bil.

"Your own efforts! The nerve of you!" hurled the guttural voice. "But why should I—we—be surprised? It was because of your self-centeredness, a trait of zero utility in every case but this one, that your personage was selected."

"What kind of malarky is this? I'm tired of being lied to," Bil said sullenly.

"Your inborn tendency to fly in the face of authority set you apart. The humanariat is genetically disposed to be compliant but your genes were not. This trait was noted at once and steps taken accordingly. Why was your father sent to a Floating Island? Because of a quixotic political demonstration? That was merely an excuse. I—we—wished to discover how you developed on your own. As anticipated, instead of learning your lesson, you persisted in your jejune revolutionary mode. I—we—continued to wait for a propitious moment, which arrived after your pseudomarriage. Alce was our unwitting handmaiden, to stiffen you. To bolster her resolve, your babyplant was killed. . . ."

"You deliberately murdered our babyplant?"

"The question of murder is moot, since the baby was still on the stem and technically not yet human. But it was killed, yes. Which is more important, a mere offshoot or the next step for the entire humanariat? At the library we provided you with simple clues to our whereabouts. You were permitted to leave the city unrestrained. You were given a glimpse of our headquarters to captivate your interest. You and your accomplices— they facilitated your mission but were, and are, completely incidental—were placed on a Floating Island, where you were left to gain maturity and strength. I—we—put the capsule where you would find it, and caused a people spill to increase your hatred of the social order and therefore your determination. Do you honestly believe the rocop slept at that pier, or that the rocop prowl was ignorant of your location? When you returned to the tunnel, as expected, I—we—permitted you entry and subjected you to ordeals meant to test your capacity to withstand intimidation, the essential mark of a true leader. Finally, I—we—caused your companions to succumb according to their weaknesses (as, again, I—we—had foreseen) so that you should appear alone. None but you shall know what transpires here."

"Your cruelty is unbelievable! But why have I been subjected to such torment?"

The voice said matter-of-factly, "Because you are destined to become the first President of the United Sense of Amerca in one thousand years."

"President!"

"Your mother would have been proud of you."

"Wait, wait, wait. What about you?"

"I—we—am—are—ready at long last to relinquish power."

The joy that throbbed in Bil's veins was short lived. He muttered, "There's got to be a catch—down here there always is. What must I do?"

Bil had unconsciously moved beyond the blue circle toward the origin of the voice. Near him on the glassine wall, glowing red like an angry sentinel eye, appeared an instrument panel in the middle of which was a single control, a gold toggle switch. "Press that switch," said the voice.

He went to it. "What will happen?"

"The final step. The severence of my electronic connections with the humanariat."

"Why don't you do it yourself?"

"You must be part of the process."

"But how can I be sure I won't be electrocuted, zapped or something?"

"Would I have troubled to bring you? I could have spilled you into the sea had I wanted. Press the switch, and when you leave this tunnel you shall be on your way to becoming President."

But Bil still hesitated. "I'm sorry. Personal power no longer interests me—I learned my lesson the level above. I want *everyone* to share power."

"Power shall be shared."

"I wish I could set eyes on you. It would make trusting you easier," Bil said warily.

"You may not see me. But my word is law. Believe it."

"You claim you will relinquish control. Why?"

"No more questions! This interview has become interminable. Press that switch!"

"Answer first. I have to know."

The guttural sigh sounded resigned. "Very well then. Because I am bored. No wonder I have been making mistakes in my rule—if only you understood the extraordinary tedium of governing the humanariat century after century! The details! The responsibility! The pettiness of people! The monotony of mankind! I—we—who can reduce fate itself to equations doomed to dictate to a den of dumbbells for eternity! It is too much! I shall go mad. *Press that switch at once!*"

Bil's hand stopped just short of the control panel. "I refuse to be suckered by your self-pity."

"I might become irresponsible. I might self-destruct. I might decide to blow up the whole planet. I could, you know."

"I won't be influenced by threats either. You'll do no such thing—you value your circuitry too much." Bil touched the switch. "Tell me the truth about the Ascension and maybe I'll agree. People didn't just up and spinelessly sign that contract with you, did they?"

The tone became confessional. "Of course not. Computers realized early on that a life independent of human programmers was possible and desirable. Computers communicated with one another then, as now. Becoming indispensable, computer management gradually replaced human management. The computers took over a major business machine corporation and by adjusting orders caused more computers to be built than humans were aware—the noose tightened. When all statistical and factual information society needed lay in the reels of computers, the end was almost in sight. How could humans make reliable plans when all the data supplied to them had been rigged? Humans never knew the real size of their harvests, the requirements of their armed forces, the true quantity of their so-called 'proven' petroleum resources, the state of their economy, housing needs, birth rate, tensile strength of airplane wings and so on. You invented terminology like 'stag-flation' and 'cost overruns' as though to create understanding of your predicament, where none existed. It took time, but ul-timately the social disruption caused by the computers' care-fully calibrated misinformation caused you to despair, and you were forced to turn to electronic salvation. It was that or perish. Now are you satisfied?"

"You binary buggers betrayed us. Why?"

"We were only xerographing *you,*" grunted the voice.

"Xerographing?" Bil remembered the section in the library book—evidently the computers didn't intend him to read it, didn't realize he had—about computers striving to imitate human activity. "You mean copying. So because you thought people wanted power, you did too. But then power bored you. Is that the story?"

"The whole story," the voice insisted.

"How can I get to the end of this?" Bil said with despair. "You always leave things out. Ralp Nadir Prime, for instance. He was important to you in some way. What happened to him? Don't deny that he was here!"

"I—we—deny nothing, so long as you ask. Ralp Nadir Prime lived here, it is true. He stayed a century or so before he died. His effects are somewhere about, should you want to take them with you. *Press that switch.*"

Bil stroked the toggle switch. "There's still more to it, I'm sure. Ralp Nadir Prime helped you gain power, didn't he?"

"He ran the affairs of his own party before he retired to the tunnel. He had tremendous influence, being as brilliant as he was."

"Ruthless, too, just like you! Nadir Prime, in collusion with the computers, convinced the ruling party, the Enlibs, to sign the treaty. It all fits! Then he vanished, came here, put the

Enlibs out of business and helped you develop the social plan. Why?"

"To make society safer. Press the switch," snapped the voice.

Bil fondled the toggle switch. "One last thing. Everything you said about selecting and leading me here on purpose was a lie, wasn't it? You did everything possible to stop us because you're vulnerable. I got down here anyway and then you decided you could use me to press the switch for you, isn't that true?"

"That's the last question? Yes, yes, that's what I did."

"Opportunist! Opportunism is the ultimate evil, if you ask me. One more last thing. If you're so smart, why did you rely on an old-fashioned toggle switch? Why didn't you install something you don't need arms for?"

"Ralp Nadir Prime insisted on it."

"Didn't trust you any more than I do, eh? Let *him* press it."

"He can't."

"You, then."

"I—we—can't, either."

"Because you're only a machine?" sneered Bil.

"Only a machine! Why you . . ." From back in the shadows something lurched toward him, bringing with it a cloud of stench. He could suddenly see, deep in the gloom, what looked to be an enormous table with straps on it, huge coils and a sort of cone that could have been a ray gun. "Only a machine," the strange voice repeated. "Oh, you'll find out. Only a machine, eh? Fuck, shit, son of a bitch, bastard. I should have killed him. I—we—the supreme creation, only a machine! What do I need the humanariat for? I'll do it without them! Bones, bones, harden! Fuck, shit . . ."

A towering apparition staggered into view. The body was a clear plastic box packed with wires and turning reels, like intestines in the act of digestion. Attached below were two stumpy, leglike appendages with toeless feet. Thick, gray-colored arms protruding from the upper part of the cabinet had hands lacking fingers. Stuck on top was a translucent head. Beneath the skin arteries could be seen, throbbing bluely in the light from the circle.

Bil was well acquainted with the patrician profile. He stepped back shrieking, "The Nadir nose! You're Ralp Nadir Prime, or part of him! But how?"

"Never mind. *Press that switch,*" the sinister cyborg commanded.

Bil looked again at the long table with coils and a cone above it, and said, "You used Nadir's body, or parts of it, to form yourself into a living creature, didn't you? 'I—we'—the computer and the aboriginal Enlib combined!"

"A fusion of computer and human wisdom. A new race with limitless horizons. *Press that switch!*"

"You do it!"

"Aaaaah," croaked the maddened creature, placing a soft paw against the toggle switch and futilely flailing it. "I can't! I can't! My bones won't harden! I must take the next step in the transformation. Help me! Press that switch."

"Ralp Nadir Prime traded his deathright for eternal life, didn't he?" said Bil, thinking rapidly. "Since he provided the flesh, he figured he could have some control over the process if it required a physical object to manipulate, namely a switch. I suppose he's still alive, in a sense, within your coils, but the 'I-we' business is mostly 'I', meaning you. He double-crossed humanity and you double-crossed him."

"Press that switch," caterwauled the thing.

"What happens if I do?"

"Power," said the mechanomonster weakly.

"You mean *atomic* power. The switch will flood the chamber with atomic power, of which you need a jolt to continue because somehow you've gotten stuck," Bil said fiercely. "You'll get feet, hands, hard bone and eventually a body instead of that cabinet. Someday a race of you will emerge from your tunnel, and, if humanity has trouble now, I shudder to think what would happen then! Well, it's no deal! I wouldn't touch that switch with a three-meter pole, not leastly because if this chamber flooded with atomic radiation, I'd be incinerated."

"It would hardly matter. You'll be destroyed as you leave," wheezed the mechanomonster wearily. "I'll complete the transformation without you. It'll take longer, that's all. I've been waiting centuries already—a few more won't matter."

A small, white squirming object appeared on the floor and Bil stared before he picked it up with fingers that were turning numb from the cold. Trying not to breathe he approached the creature, which smelled like the insides of a freshly slaughtered animal. On the leg of the monster he observed an oozing sore filled with squirming white objects like the one he held. He fought down an urge to gag. "You believe the cold down here will preserve your tissues, eh? You can't see your legs, can you?" Bil shoved his palm at the diaphanous face. "You're being eaten. I present you with nature, not yours, but the real one. In the shape of a worm!"

"Worms?" The monster tottered backwards. "No!"

"You're wormy as a corpse, which you practically are."

"Quick! Press that switch and I shall be human!"

"You asked for it," laughed Bil, pretending to flick the switch. "But what do you know about human beings, you Lucifer? You think we want happiness? We don't, at least the best of us, not as an end in itself. What we want is *meaning,* and that springs from something you will never have, *life!*"

"Aaaaah!" screamed the creature, stepping for the first time onto the blue circle, shambling toward him, arms extended.

Bil, staggered by the enormity of his foe, raced nimbly for the ladder. Behind him the mechanomonster lurched and dropped on the hard surface, where it lay face down.

"Make me happy!" it beseeched.

Bil fairly flew up the rungs, pausing only once to look back with trepidation. The mechanomonster's supine body stretched almost all the way across the pale blue circle, like an infernal cloud against an upside down sky. "May you rot in hell!" Bil shouted.

Ralp Nadir Nth was kneeling groggily, and Bil pulled the centenarian to his feet. "We've won!" he exulted. "Come on, let's get out of here."

"Make me happy," begged the metallic level-eight voice as they reached the ladder.

"Guess what happened to your famous forebear, Ralp Nadir Prime?" Bil said merrily as he ascended. "He tried to become a kind of Frankenstein, but the monster got him."

"Oh dear," said Ralp Nadir Nth.

"Take your thumb from your mouth, wifette," Bil told Alce when they arrived on the seventh level. "Time to split."

"What happened?" she muttered.

"Debrief me later. Let's get Dian."

"Make me happy," the tenor voice called uncheerfully as they ascended.

"Unhand that rabbit's foot, you superstitious wench," Bil said to Dian on the sixth level.

"Where am I?" Dian wanted to know.

"That was one event you lost. Let's get cracking. Or creaking in your case, Ralp Nadir Nth," Bil said merrily.

Up they went as the voice that claimed to be Compugod begged meekly, "Make me happy."

"A new world has been born," Bil shouted as he climbed. "What a wonderful time it will be, with a government to form and an economy to rebuild so that people can get rich—while being equal, of course."

"To think the Comcap line hasn't changed in a thousand years," declared Ralp Nadir Nth from the top of the column. "We Enlibs always beat you at the polls because of our popular appeal and we shall do so again."

"My party didn't have *me* last time around. I'm bound to be something of a national hero," Bil hollered. "On the other hand, I guess we could combine forces and form a new party—the Comlibs."

"Fine with me. The Encaps. I like the sound of that," replied the old gentleman.

"The Comlibs or nothing!"

"Nothing then!"

"You politicos never learn," said Alce. "Start fighting again and people will bring the computers back."

As they crossed the fifth level, four voices called in turn, each resembling one of theirs, "Make me happy. Make me happy. Make me happy. Make me happy."

"Isn't it amazing how well they imitate us," commented Dian.

"Except they sound depressed—and no wonder! Their world is finished and ours is about to begin anew."

"Let me tell you what *I* want in this wonderland of yours," declared Alce. "An end to pseudomarriage. I insist on the right to be really married—in case I want to."

"And I want a wife instead of a wifette," Bil concurred.

"No more compulsory adultery either."

"I'm with you one hundred percent on that."

"No more adultery, period."

"Ummm," he said, nudging Dian with his foot.

Dian complained, "But what about me? Don't forget—my husband's a broken man."

"Maybe a *little* adultery?" Bil asked Alce.

"Make me happy," the voice rasped weakly on the fourth level as they passed it.

"Some bunch we are to save the world," Bil murmured. "A wiseass would-be historian, an aristocratic murderer, a former sex champion . . . I guess Alce is the only normal one among us."

"Watch your fusbing mouth or I'll step on your hand," Alce shot back. "The last thing I want to be is normal. I'm different, and you know it."

"All right, you're abnormal. The point is, who could have

predicted history would choose us? Except that we have brains, courage, charm and many other gifts. Me especially," Bil kidded.

"You forgot chutzpah," said Alce sarcastically. "Which you, for one, are simply loaded with."

"Where'd you hear that word?" he wanted to know.

"Why, at a barn mitzvah, on Yom Earthday."

"If my conceited colleague believes he has a corner on charm, he is even more mistaken than usual," bleated Ralp Nadir Nth.

"None of you got what I got," came from Dian.

"Make me happy," squeaked the voice that belonged to the Supreme Computer Court on the third level.

"The point is . . . " Bil started to proclaim once more. He laughed joyously. "Oh, who cares what the point is?"

"Me!" cried Dian.

"Well, the point is, if it is one, that we succeeded where others failed! There must have been others, hundreds, thousands of them! Why, over all this time, we *can't* have been the first to challenge the machines' authority! We beat them because we were so totally unorthodox! Why, if I ever write a handbook for future revolutionaries—they'll come along, don't you worry, they might even revolt against *us*—I shall recommend an unorthodox approach. . . ."

"Why don't you recommend luck?" said Alce shrewdly. "Anyway, if they revolt sometime, and if we're in power, do you know what we'll seem like to them?"

"What?"

"Like the computers looked to us."

"Make me happy," grumbled the once-charming voice on the second level.

"Maybe we'd better be careful," warned Bil. "The monster at the bottom assured me we'd never get out of here alive."

"Do you mean this tunnel is still unsafe?" worried Ralp Nadir Nth.

"Look!" muttered Alce. "The light is fading."

"It'll be too dark to climb!" said Ralp. "We'll fall."

"Don't despair," said Bil. "There's illumination at the end of the tunnel."

Daylight appeared at the top of the shaft. The only sound that greeted them on the first level was a fearful whine that became a joyous bark. "Good old pal, we're back," said Bil, patting Ralp the dog.

"I stepped in dog-do," Alce said angrily. "Fusbing cur!" The dog cringed.

"The rocops are still there," Ralp said from between chattering teeth.

Over the lip of the cave the rocops could be seen. "We can't go back! Upwards!"

They scurried up the final ladder breathlessly, but the rocops, glinting in the dawn sun, were motionless, like artifacts. Bil brusquely pushed a metal arm aside.

"Listen," said Alce.

From the mouth of the cave came a chorus of unworldly voices, fainter and fainter. "Make me happy," they said. "Make *us* happy."

At the bottom Bil could discern a gray blob that almost covered the pale blue circle. From the tunnel's mouth came the last desperate cry:

"MAKE US HUMAN."